Long before we~~~~ were passé, Gra~~~~ and grease. "Ho~~~~ want to singe th~~~~ was a family thing.

Beautiful brown ladies moaning hymns in church; white-gloved hands clutching funeral parlor fans advertising such and such. Look out! Miss Sadie's been hit by the spirit! Dance, Miss Sadie!

Mama's baking sweet potato pies for the family reunion. Uncle Bob's coming, Aunt Jean and cousin Grady from Chicago. Susie's expecting twins. Sadly, Great-Granddaddy has taken his long journey home. It's a family thing.

Little Janie's all grown up. Graduated with honors from Howard University, says she's going to be an attorney. Susie's twins come into the world bawling, eyes already open and checking things out. They've just begun their journey.

Families come in all shapes and sizes. Mother, father, children: two. Mother, no father? That's a family, too. No matter how you look at it, home is where you go and they have to take you in. It's a family thing!

The Book of Counted Joys

Janice Sims

That SUMMER at AMERICAN BEACH

ARABESQUE®

THAT SUMMER AT AMERICAN BEACH

An Arabesque novel

ISBN 1-58314-627-X

www.kimanipress.com

Printed in U.S.A.

ACKNOWLEDGMENTS

Thanks to my editor, Evette Porter, for asking me to write a story for Arabesque's stellar Sizzling Sands series. With authors such as Deirdre Savoy, Sandra Kitt, Gwynne Forster and Donna Hill contributing to the series, I was honored to have been included.

Thanks also to Marsha Dean Phelts, author of *An American Beach for African Americans* published by University Press of Florida. Marsha is a freelance writer for the *Florida Star,* an African-American newspaper in Jacksonville. Marsha was kind enough to allow me to interview her about her hometown, American Beach. Thanks to her, I was able to create a more realistic setting for the novel. Please visit American Beach if you ever get the chance. It's a beautiful place!

I would be remiss if I didn't mention my uncles and aunts, Jerry and Vivian Simpson and William and Yvonne Sims, who in their own way, inspired this story.

Finally, to Amelia J. Brown, my friend since the second grade, who was thrilled that I was writing a story about American Beach and who sent me wonderful information on the place and its people.

Chapter 1

A scintilla of panic seized Rayne Walker. Was that really Diane Reese, the most together woman she'd ever met, hurrying toward her in the lobby of the Waldorf Astoria with tissues wadded up in her palm and a torrent of tears flowing down her lovely face?

Diane and her husband of twenty-five years, the Honorable Judge Jeremiah Reese, were not expected at their party for at least two hours. Diane's untimely appearance certainly didn't bode well. What if something had gone terribly wrong? Like the judge had had a heart attack?

Rayne went and clasped Diane by the shoulders. Five-eight to Diane's five-four, and thirty pounds heavier, Rayne held her firmly. "What's wrong, Diane? Is it the judge? Has something happened to him?"

She directed Diane to a nearby alcove where two plush armchairs had been placed for the comfort of the hotel's guests. Pushing Diane down into one, she placed her bottom in the other and pulled the chair closer to Diane's.

Her sable-brown eyes met Diane's hazel ones. "Now tell me what's going on."

Diane dabbed her face with the tissues, which were beginning to fall apart from overuse. She sniffed, and Rayne could tell all that crying had stopped up her nose.

"That son of a bitch is cheating on me," she said softly, fiercely, as if the words were a powerful curse and, with each word uttered, her husband was that much closer to being damned to hell simply by the severity of her invectives.

Her hands trembled as she reached into her purse and retrieved a Polaroid picture. She sneered as she briefly glanced at it before handing it to Rayne.

Rayne calmly took the snapshot and lowered her gaze. In it, a young woman was standing provocatively in front of a chest of drawers in a bedroom with not a stitch on.

Rayne turned the photo facedown on her lap and met Diane's gaze. "Do you know the woman?"

"She's a lawyer. Very ambitious."

"Obviously," Rayne said dryly.

Diane laughed shortly. "Yes, well, I don't think she's the first and she probably won't be the last. I don't know why I planned this party. What do I have to celebrate? A husband who can't keep his fly zipped?"

"You're a brilliant, accomplished woman, Diane," Rayne told her, countering her negative comments. "You're an attorney other attorneys seek out when *they* get in trouble."

Diane's eyes were downcast, and her lips quivered as she said, "But all of my accomplishments mean nothing without him. I still love the bastard."

"Mmm," Rayne said, considering what her sorority sister and friend had just said.

Both of them had gone to Howard University and pledged Delta Gamma Sorority.

Diane was a good twenty years older than Rayne, but that meant little in the sisterhood.

Once they'd met and learned they were sorority sisters, a bond had developed.

She looked up to Diane, and Diane considered herself Rayne's mentor even though Rayne wasn't a lawyer. She'd been a business major at Howard, and was now a successful event planner.

Rayne sighed and looked Diane straight in the eyes. "If you still love him, then you've got to fight for your marriage."

"How?" Diane asked plaintively. Usually a woman whose mind was quick, and for whom decisions came rapidly, she was now at a loss for a reasonable course of action. "I mean, I've suspected Jeremiah of cheating in the past, but I never had proof." She reached over and retrieved the photo from Rayne's grasp and put it back in her purse. "I found this in his underwear drawer, of all places! The idiot couldn't find a better hiding place."

"At the risk of sounding like I'm defending him," Rayne said, "may I point out that he isn't in the photo with her in a compromising position? What if she gave him the photo to tempt him? And he was too flattered by her audacity to refuse to accept it? He *is* a man, after all."

"So, you're saying she could be fishing for him, but he hasn't taken the bait yet?"

Rayne nodded. "It's a possibility."

Diane sat back, deep in concentration for a few moments. Her lips were pursed, and her emotions were reflected in her ever-changing facial expressions, from frowns to looks of utter bewilderment. "I always said that if Jeremiah ever cheated on me, and I found out about it, I'd divorce him in a heartbeat, taking him for everything he was worth. It was all talk. I feel so helpless. Weak and ineffectual, two words that I'd never use to describe myself!"

She regarded Rayne with dry eyes. "Should I cancel the party tonight, or pretend everything is perfectly all right? I don't know what to do, Rayne."

Rayne wanted to plead with her not to cancel the party. It wasn't her fee she was concerned about, because she'd donated her services. However, there were others who were depending on this payday, the caterer and the wait staff to name a few. The hotel had already been paid, and there was no getting a refund at this late date.

But the little people who did not have million-dollar contracts to fall back on would be very disappointed if Diane canceled the party.

"Diane," Rayne began quietly, "if you feel as if going through with the party would be too much for you to handle, I'll understand. But we're going to be pushing it, trying to contact all of the guests. It's only a little more than two hours before the party's supposed to begin. Some of the guests are coming from out of town, and may still be en route. It's going to be next to impossible to contact them."

Diane tilted her head back as the tears began to flow anew. "She's on the guest list. If I'd known about this, she would never have been, but I asked Jeremiah for a list of the people he wanted to attend, and her name was on it."

Rayne went into her purse and got a small pad and a pen. "What's her name? I'll personally phone her and tell her not to come. And if she shows up anyway, she'll be turned away at the door. But, believe me, she won't get into the ballroom."

Diane hesitated. "Maybe I should phone her myself."

"No, Diane. You need to talk to Jeremiah first. Get his explanation. Don't give her the satisfaction of having created drama within your marriage. If you want to go ahead with the party, do it. But you need your mind clear in order to put on a good face for your friends and family. Deal with her when you're stronger. Never give her the upper hand."

Diane sat back in her chair and took a calming breath. Meeting Rayne's eyes, she said, "You're right. I'll go home and get dressed, and when Jeremiah gets home, I'll tell him what I found when I was laying out his clothes for tonight. If his explanation doesn't please me, I'll kill him, and then I won't have the party to worry about, anyway, because I'll be in jail." Her voice sounded perfectly reasonable. Rayne knew then why Diane Reese could sway a jury like no other attorney: even when speaking of murdering her husband, she sounded completely sane and trustworthy.

She felt almost sympathetic for Judge Reese. Almost. And a lot scared for his physical well-being once Diane confronted him.

Diane gave her the woman's name, and the two friends briefly embraced.

"Remember," Rayne said, "stay in control. You're a tiny, pretty woman. You don't want to go to prison for murder."

Diane laughed as she turned to walk away. "Some big momma would think it was her lucky day when she saw me coming, huh?"

"Precisely," Rayne said with an encouraging smile. "Now go. Don't worry about anything on this end, I'll take care of everything."

They then each turned and walked in opposite directions, Diane heading for the exit, and Rayne to the ballroom where the tables were being set up for the Reeses' twenty-fifth anniversary party.

Rayne always arrived on the scene of a party at least two hours early in order to oversee the setup. She wasn't particularly worried that the crew wouldn't do their jobs satisfactorily without having someone looking over their shoulders. She was simply a stickler for details.

Her specialty was "the details." Clients would describe to her their idea of the perfect celebration, and Rayne would make it come to life.

The Reeses had wanted an elegant evening for forty guests, with a jazz singer and pianist, a cellist and a violinist to provide the entertainment. They wanted a combination of jazz tunes and standards played throughout the evening, and they wanted a dance floor so that their guests could dance to every number, if they wished.

The food was to be simple fare reminiscent of both their southern upbringings. Diane was born in South Carolina, so there were low-country dishes on the menu. Jeremiah was born and raised in New Orleans, so some of the rich, spicy delicacies from that region would also be included. Rayne had employed the culinary talents of Miss Sadie Newhope, one of the most sought-after soul food chefs in the city, to do the honors.

Rayne sat down at one of the tables that hadn't yet been covered by a white, linen tablecloth, placed her briefcase on it and opened it. Riffling through the papers within, she found the guest list, and quickly went down it, looking for the name that Diane had given her a few minutes ago.

There it was: Natalie Doggett. Her contact number was right beside her name.

Rayne got her cell phone from the compartment inside her purse and dialed Natalie Doggett's number.

She was surprised when a woman answered after three rings. She'd expected that she would have to leave a message.

"Hello, Natalie Doggett, attorney at law," the woman said enthusiastically.

"Ms. Doggett, my name is Rayne Walker. I'm the Reeses'

event planner. I've been informed that your presence at their anniversary party tonight is no longer desired. I'm calling you ahead of time in hopes that any embarrassment can be avoided."

"I see," Natalie said coldly. "I suppose that request came from Mrs. Reese?"

"I'm afraid I'm not privy to that information, Ms. Doggett."

"And if I should show up anyway?" Natalie Doggett had the temerity to ask.

Rayne sat back on her chair, a wide smile on her face. "Then it would give me great pleasure to watch four burly bodyguards toss you out on your can."

She promptly hung up.

Rayne rolled her eyes and put the cell phone away. Some people. You couldn't be nice to them. You had to speak to them in their own rude language in order for them to fully understand you.

That night, Rayne circulated among the guests, some of whom were acquaintances, making sure that everyone was enjoying themselves. She prided herself on being so unobtrusive that it didn't occur to anyone that the event was an orchestrated affair.

It was a lovely, relaxed evening with the participants experiencing real pleasure at helping their friends celebrate twenty-five years of marriage. Quite an accomplishment in this day and age.

The food was eaten with relish. The champagne flowed. The music was a saucy addition to which many of the couples got up and danced with gusto, if not rhythm.

Rayne was asked to dance several times herself. She accepted only two invitations: One from the judge so that she could get a better look at that bruise beneath his right eye. And one from Diane's father, a retired doctor from Charleston, who kept trying to pinch her bottom. He was eighty years old, if a day, so she chalked it up to too much champagne. Besides, he looked really cute in his tuxedo, all five feet five of him.

Rayne was nearly six feet in her Manolos, and towered over him. It felt as if she were dancing with a little boy.

Toward the end of the festivities, toasts were offered up for the loving couple. Everyone was seated at their respective tables, the lights dimmed. The cake was rolled out on its trolley, the candles aglow.

"Make a wish, make a wish!" someone shouted in good cheer.

"Twenty-five more years!" someone else suggested, to which everyone laughed.

Rayne's heartbeat accelerated when Diane stood up and pulled Jeremiah up with her. Rayne was afraid Diane was preparing to say something scathing. Something that would embarrass the judge, and betray the state of mind she must have been in all evening, trying to hide her heartache.

Instead, Diane took her husband's hand and, smiling up at him, said, "It hasn't all been wine and roses. The best years were when we were making babies, and trying to go to law school at the same time. Three children later, we called it quits and concentrated on getting him the judgeship, while I stood in the background and raised the kids. When I told him I was going back to law school he wasn't very supportive. He was selfish in that respect, and I never forgave him for it. My mother, God rest her soul, told me that a woman always gives more in a marriage. That's just how things are. In some ways, she was telling the truth. But I fought to get my degree, and I'm proud of that. I hope I've been a positive role model for my two girls."

"You have been, Mom!" shouted her daughter Caroline.

"Amen!" agreed her elder daughter, Salina.

"But through all of it," Diane continued, "I never once stopped loving you, Jeremiah. Or respecting you, or wanting our marriage to remain sacred, a thing of beauty. I wouldn't be who I am today without you in my life. So, I can't say that I've had any regrets. And I'd do it all over again."

The guests cheered and whooped. The men called for Jeremiah to hold forth.

Jeremiah, looking a bit uncomfortable, so unlike the confident judge on his bench, cleared his throat, and said, "Most of you know I'm no saint. When Diane and I were dating, I told her how ambitious I was. I told her not to marry me, but she didn't listen, thank God!"

More laughter.

"I've been single-minded in my career. I neglected Diane and the kids more than I should have, and they continued to support me throughout the neglect. If not for them, I wouldn't be on the bench. When I was young, I thought that a wife and a family only dragged a man down, made his ascent to the top impossible, but I'm here to say, tonight, that a loving family raises a man up, it doesn't pull him down."

He peered into his wife's eyes. "I love you more than I did on the day we were married. So much more! *Please don't leave me.*"

The guests, all except Rayne, were puzzled by his last sentence, his begging Diane not to leave him, but they rose out of their seats and applauded loudly, anyway.

Rayne turned away, tears burning her eyes, and walked into the nearby kitchen where the wait staff was gathered, awaiting the time when the guests would depart and they could begin clearing away the debris left behind.

She counted this a successful party.

Chapter 2

That night, Rayne lay in bed going over the next day in her mind. Sometimes, she was unable to fall asleep, worrying about the next day. Tomorrow, Saturday, wouldn't even be a workday. There were no weddings planned, no engagement parties, no bar mitzvahs or bat mitzvahs for that matter. The problem was her mother. She'd promised to go see her tomorrow and spend some time with her fifteen-year-old sister, Shannon.

Spending time with Shannon would be a job in itself. It wasn't that Shannon was a bad kid. It was just that with eleven years between them, they had little in common. Take their attitudes, for example. Shannon talked back to their mother. Rayne was twenty-six, and she couldn't remember ever disrespecting their mom. Her mother, too, took Shannon's smart-mouth remarks in stride. Whereas, if Rayne had ever tried talking that way to her, she would have gotten a swat on the behind.

The phone rang in the middle of her musings. She glanced

at the clock on the nightstand. It was nearly 2:00 a.m. Rolling over to peer at the caller ID's display, she saw that it was her aunt Shirley calling from Florida. She immediately picked up. Aunt Shirley wouldn't be calling at this hour unless it was a serious family matter.

"Hello?" Rayne said anxiously.

"I couldn't sleep, so I figured there was no reason to let you sleep when I couldn't," said Shirley Walker-Lewis.

Rayne sat up farther in bed and laughed into the receiver. "For you, that makes perfect sense, Auntie. What's up?"

"What's up is your father is lying on his deathbed, and you're so busy you can't even take the time to call him!"

This time, Rayne could hear the indignation in her aunt's voice. In the beginning, she'd thought her aunt had been her usual joking self. But, no, she was highly upset. And what was that business about her father being on his deathbed?

"I talk to Daddy every Sunday, and he hasn't once mentioned having a cold, let alone dying," she told her aunt, her voice calm and self-assured.

"I specifically told your mother—" Shirley began.

"Wait a minute. You told my *mother?*" Rayne nearly shouted. "Mom hasn't been here in three weeks."

"It was about that long ago that I phoned, and she said you were gone to the video store."

Rayne remembered that day. It had been Shannon's birthday, and they'd had cake at her place. Shannon wanted to see a movie, and Rayne had volunteered to walk down to the neighborhood video store to rent it for her. When she'd returned, her mother had not told her that her aunt Shirley had phoned.

"Maybe she forgot," Rayne said in defense of her mother, whom she knew Aunt Shirley didn't particularly care for. Julianne had left her brother, after all. Left him and took his only child all the way to New York City just because she wanted to be an actress. An actress! To a woman as practical as her aunt Shirley, being an actress was as big a pipe dream as wanting to be abducted by aliens. It would never happen!

"Forgot, my *behind*," said Aunt Shirley.

Which is a considerable behind, and no one would ever forget it once they saw it. Rayne smiled at her thoughts, and asked, "What was it she forgot to tell me, Auntie?"

"Ray has prostate cancer, and the stubborn fool is talking about not having the operation even though his doctor has told him that, with it, he has a good chance of a complete recovery!"

Rayne's mind had gone into panic mode at the mention of the words *prostate cancer.* She hadn't even heard the rest of her aunt's sentence. "Oh, my God. You're not *joking!*" The realization seized her heart with sudden, intense fear. She burst into tears. "Why Daddy? He's too *young* to die. Isn't there anything that can be done? Colin Powell had it, and *he* survived!"

Shirley spoke firmly. "Pull yourself together, baby, didn't you hear me? I said Ray's doctor says he will make a full recovery if he has the operation. Ray's the problem. He says there's no point in living if he's, well, out of commission."

Rayne didn't know what her aunt was talking about. "Out of commission?"

"Unable to perform," Shirley said in a whisper.

"You mean have sex?" Rayne asked.

Shirley shushed her. "Don't say that too loudly, your uncle Buddy's asleep next to me, and he might wake up, hear that word, and get ideas."

Rayne chuckled. "What word? *Sex?*" She took a deep breath and calmed herself. Her emotions were running the gamut from panic to near-hysteria. The thought of her father dying had that effect on her. She cleared her throat. "Okay, so Daddy can beat this thing if he has the operation. But he doesn't want to have the operation because there's a chance he'll become impotent."

"Exactly," said Shirley. "Sometimes black men wait too long to have the surgery and end up dying because they're afraid they're going to lose their manhood. Lord, child, it doesn't have to be like that. I had a long talk with his doctor, and he says that he would use the nerve-sparing procedure on your father which would still allow him to perform, you know…"

"Sexually," Rayne said, providing the word for her.

"Yes. Your father stands a good chance of being totally normal again after the surgery, but Ray's so damned bull-headed, he says he doesn't want to take the risk of becoming a eunuch. That's the way he put it, a castrated man."

Rayne laughed. "Yeah, that sounds like something Raymond Walker would say. Listen, Auntie, don't you worry. I'll talk him into it."

"Over the phone?" Shirley said, sounding skeptical. "Ray will lie to you just so you won't worry about him. Then, months from now, we'll all be at his funeral, saying 'if only he'd had the operation!'"

Rayne sat frowning for a few silent moments. She had a big wedding to oversee next weekend, but like she'd done every year since she'd started her business four years ago, she had not scheduled anything for the summer months. The summer months from late June to late August belonged to her father. He'd started the tradition when she'd had to move away with her mother at the tender age of eight. Every year after that, he'd sent for her, and she'd spent the summer months in American Beach where her father had been born and raised. Her mother, Julianne, was a transplant from Brooklyn. She'd never been truly happy in the tiny seaside town that was founded in 1935 as a resort for African-Americans.

Her father, though, who had worked for a time as a construc-tion worker but who was at heart an artist, enjoyed the lazy pace of beach life. He quit construction work twenty years ago and began painting full-time. Today, his paintings drew interest from art lovers around the world. They sold for thousands of dollars, and even though he could live anywhere he chose, American Beach was where he was at peace. Often, he would roll out of bed and go for a swim before his morning coffee.

Rayne understood her father's stance on the operation. To a man who was grasping at life, who felt he had not lived long enough, more time on earth was desirable. But to a man like her father, a man who always lived life to the fullest, doing without something that added zest to living, something as vital as making love to a desirable woman, was a despicable notion. She knew it was going to be difficult to change his mind, but she loved him and she had to try.

"Honey, I can hear you breathing," Shirley said after a long pause.

Rayne sighed deeply. "I'll just have to come home early this year, that's all."

"How early?" Shirley asked, sounding excited by the prospect. She loved her niece, and didn't see her often enough. There was also the rest of the family to inform. Get-togethers to be planned. Crab boils, a fish-fry on the beach, endless dinners to share on the patio while the citronella candles glowed and talk flowed.

"In two weeks," Rayne promised. "I'll see you in two weeks, Auntie."

"All right, sweetie," said her aunt, complacent now that she'd accomplished what she'd set out to do. "Tell your Momma I don't appreciate her forgetting to give you my message. That's another one for the scorecard."

Rayne knew her aunt was keeping track of her mother's many transgressions, and one day she meant to make her pay for all of them.

"I'm sure there was no malicious intent," Rayne said. She didn't really know that for certain. Her mother and father had a strange relationship. They never bad-mouthed each other to her, but they never talked about their marriage, either. Rayne didn't know what had happened to break them up. Except that her mother wanted to try her hand at acting, and she couldn't very well do that in tiny American Beach. Perhaps it was just that their goals in life had differed so much, they couldn't manage to get around that hurdle.

"You and Mom should kiss and make up," she told her aunt Shirley. "It's been eighteen years since they divorced."

"I have a long memory," Shirley said, stifling a yawn. "Look, all I know is, your daddy treated that woman like a queen and she left him for no good reason. I was there to pick up the pieces, so I know how much she hurt him."

"She was hurt, too," Rayne said. She remembered hearing her mother crying in the night shortly after they'd moved back to Brooklyn to stay with her mother's mother, Grandma Layla. Grandma Layla was gone now. Her mother had inherited the brownstone in Brooklyn that had been in the family for three generations. She still lived there. "Believe it or not, she cried herself to sleep lots of nights afterward."

Shirley yawned. "We're never going to agree on this. I know things you don't. That's all I'm going to say. Maybe your mother will enlighten you one of these days. In the meantime, sweetie, I love you. Have a safe trip, you hear?"

Rayne was glad for the reprieve. In truth, she was tired of defending her mother. Her heart wasn't in it. There were too many unresolved issues between her mother and herself for her to feel passionate about defending her. The biggest issue sat between them as if it were an ape the size of King Kong sitting on her couch. He was smelling up the place, but she didn't have the courage to ask him to leave.

She was sure that if her mother would just confess the truth, it would clear the air, and draw them closer together as mother and daughter.

Each year, especially around her birthday, Rayne expected her mother to come clean about the issue. However, it had been hanging over them since her birth and Julianne appeared content to let sleeping dogs lie.

"Thank you, Auntie," she said. "Now you go to sleep. Unless you want to wake Uncle Buddy for some late-night loving."

"You've definitely got your daddy's sense of humor," Shirley said, giggling softly. "He'd better stay asleep if he knows what's good for him. It isn't Saturday night."

"One more night, and he's all yours!" Rayne couldn't help joking. It wouldn't be so much fun ribbing her aunt if she didn't pretend that talking about sex embarrassed her. She had given birth to five children. She knew plenty. And obviously enjoyed it.

Shirley tee-heed again. "Well, tonight the bank is closed. G'night, sweetie."

"G'night," Rayne said softly, smiling.

After hanging up, she switched off the lamp on the nightstand and snuggled under the covers. Her father had cancer. She felt so helpless. Even the thought of his dying terrified her. Realistically, she knew it was going to happen one day, but she'd imagined it would be far in the future when she was married, with children. Grown children.

She would be a gray-haired granny, and her father would be in his nineties and die peacefully in his sleep. Everybody would say it was time for him to take his leave. Everybody would comment on what a rich, full life he'd led. Hundreds of people would crowd the church, and many of them would get up and testify about how he'd touched their lives in some special way.

Fifty-four is too young to die.

She fell asleep with those words reverberating through her mind.

In Brooklyn, Julianne Morrison abruptly awoke from another nightmare. Knowing that she wouldn't get back to sleep for some time, she sat up in bed and moved to the edge of the mattress, preparing to rise. She sat there for a few minutes with her feet on the floor. She was perspiring in spite of the sixty-five-degree temperature in the house, and her mouth was dry.

She picked up the glass of water on her nightstand, took a swallow and put it back down. Why was she dreaming about being chased on the beach? She recognized the beach as American Beach. There was no mistaking "Nana," the huge dune on American Beach that beachcombers climbed atop to see all the way down the shore.

Who was pursuing her in the dream? The person's form was that of a very large male, but he was so shrouded in darkness that she couldn't make out any of his facial features. The dream was very real. She could feel the warm sand on the soles of her feet as she ran, and the exertion on her lungs as she fought for air. She could even hear her pursuer's labored breathing. But he never said anything. Five dreams in the past three months, and he'd never said a word, just chased her, his big hand outstretched, reaching for her in the darkness as she stayed just out of his grasp.

Superstitious people who had recurring dreams of falling from great heights believed that if they ever hit the ground in a dream, they'd die in their sleep. She fleetingly wondered what would happen to her if he ever caught her.

Reasonably, she knew that it was just her subconscious trying to work out a problem. As soon as she solved the problem in her waking hours, she'd stop having the dream. She could pinpoint the exact date she'd started having them. It was after her conversation with Ray in early March. He'd phoned and told her about his illness, and said that it was time that they tied up loose ends. "Past time," was the way he'd put it. "And let's do it right. You're welcome to come down when Rayne comes for the summer. Could be the last time I see you. I don't plan on fighting this thing that's eating me alive. Life has been good to me."

"How can you say that?" she'd asked as she'd choked back tears. Ray knew that she loved him, would always love him. "I made your life a living hell."

"You were the best part," he'd said, his voice husky.

She'd really started bawling then. "Ray, fight it. Fight it for me!"

Ray laughed. "If I thought there was a chance for us, I'd fight like hell. But I wouldn't dream of asking you for hope, Julie. I don't want your pity. Like I told you when you left, I don't want you back unless you can love me completely, not as if I'm some martyr who married you because I felt sorry for you. There was always something in your brain preventing you from believing. I trusted in time to bring you around, but you never gave me any indication that you'd changed. Not even those times you came back to my bed. But then, we never had a problem there, did we? It was out of the bedroom that everything fell apart."

He sighed tiredly. "Do this one last thing for me. Come to American Beach this summer. She'll need both of us when we tell her."

"I'll try," Julianne said reluctantly. She hated herself for saying that. He deserved more than a maybe from her. Her voice trembled when she added, "Okay, Ray."

"Good. I knew I could count on you," he said.

She heard the smile in his deep baritone. She had still been trembling when she hung up the phone.

She glanced at the clock now. It was nearly four o'clock in the morning. She lay back down and pulled the covers up to her chin. She had to try to get some sleep. Rayne was going to be there at nine, and she planned to give her the news then.

Rayne walked swiftly down the sidewalk, heading to her mother's house. The early-June air was still chilly in the mornings, and she wore a caramel-colored leather jacket over her beige, short-sleeved cable-knit sweater and Levi's. A comfortable pair of brown ankle boots, and a well-worn brown leather shoulder bag completed her outfit.

The wind tousled her shoulder-length curly black hair as she stood on the stoop feeling inside the zippered compartment of her purse for the key to the brownstone's front door. Her mother had insisted on her keeping a key when she'd moved to the Upper West Side with her best friend, Dottie Trueblood. Julianne, always thinking of emergencies, told her that she would need a key in case something happened to her or Shannon.

Key in hand, Rayne shoved it in the lock and turned. She rang the bell simultaneously to let her mother and Shannon know she was there. Of course, her efforts would have been for nothing if her mother had not come down this morning and undone all the dead bolts she had on the front door. Julianne had never forgotten to do that when Rayne was expected.

Once inside, Rayne went straight to the alarm pad just inside the foyer. She had less than ten seconds now to enter the code or, within thirty seconds, they would have the security company phoning to make sure everything was all right.

She keyed in the code, and by the time she turned around, her mother was there, smiling at her. Julianne, three inches shorter than her eldest daughter, tiptoed and planted a kiss on her cheek. "Good morning, I hope you're hungry. I'm making your grandma's pancakes."

Rayne returned her smile, and her kiss. "Starved." She looked around. "Is Shannon up yet?"

"No, she's still sleeping. Probably because she didn't get in until after one this morning."

"How'd she manage that?" Rayne asked as she removed her jacket and hung it in the hall closet. While she was in the closet she placed her purse by its strap on a hook in there. Once in the kitchen, she sat down on a stool at the center island and regarded her mother with concern.

Julianne, dressed in her nightgown and robe, both pale blue and in a delicate cotton fabric, smiled. "Don't worry, she was with someone I trust. She and two other girls went to the Nelly concert, and out to eat afterward. A parent took them."

"Oh, good," Rayne said, relieved that her fifteen-year-old sister hadn't started sneaking out with boys yet. "How was your week?"

Her mother didn't have a normal job where she went to work from nine till five. She was lucky enough to be an actress who got work on a regular basis. Sometimes that meant shooting a commercial, having a part in an off-Broadway play, or doing voice-overs. Being versatile kept food on the table and the lights on. Some years were lean, and some years were very, very good.

"I got the laxative commercial," her mother told her as she flipped a pancake. "That means I'll be doing at least four commercials for them each year. With residuals, that's going to really build up the old savings. And I read for a part in a Suzan-Lori Parks play." She smiled. "You'll never guess what part."

"The mother?" Rayne asked. Her mother complained that the only part she was ever offered was the part of the aging mother, or the aging aunt. She was an attractive, vivacious forty-five-year-old who was still in such good shape, physically, that she could execute a split from a standing position. Twenty years of modern dance had done her body good.

Up until a year ago, when she'd pulled a muscle in her groin, Rayne, too, had attended modern dance classes every Wednesday night. Now she stayed in shape by doing Pilates and walking as much as possible.

"What else?" Julianne confirmed. "But this is a choice part, and the play will probably go to Broadway. At least that's what Mort says."

Morton Selig was her agent. She'd been with him from the beginning, and even when parts for black actresses were scarce, as they usually were, Mort was able to scrape up work for her. She wouldn't dream of leaving him.

Rayne sat watching her mother, how her warm brown skin looked so fresh-scrubbed without makeup. There were laughlines at the corners of her dark brown eyes, but those were the only lines on her square-shaped face. Her short, mahogany brown, naturally wavy hair had golden highlights in it that Rayne knew she'd put there herself. Out of necessity, her mother had become somewhat of a hair and makeup expert over the years. Having three females in the household kind of stretched the beauty salon budget out of shape.

"And how is Mort these days?" Rayne asked. "Still the worst hypochondriac that ever lived?"

Julianne laughed. "You should have seen him last week. He had a sore throat, and he swore he had the mumps! He was lamenting his lost fertility. You know grown men can become sterile if they get the mumps. The doctor told him it was just allergies.

"And why'd he have to tell him that!" Julianne continued. "Now he thinks he's allergic to *everything*. He's been drinking milk all his life, but last week he, all of a sudden, developed stomach cramps. Ah, Mort…"

"He'll live to be a hundred," Rayne said.

"Who'll live to be a hundred?" Shannon asked as she walked into the room, scratching her butt. She was a child of few inhibitions, especially around her mother and her sister.

"Oh, that's lovely," scolded Julianne lightly. "I hope you don't do that in public."

"Only if it itches in public," returned Shannon with a saucy grin.

She went to Rayne and playfully elbowed her in greeting. Rayne grabbed her and hugged her tightly. Shannon wiggled out of her embrace and gave her a miffed look.

"I ain't no baby. You should treat me like I'm your girl, you know. Not like I'm a kid who needs a hug. I ain't with that!"

Rayne took a step back. "Since you've gotten me mixed up with one of "your girls," allow me to explain—*I'm your sister*. I'm not your buddy, your pal or anything as common as that. You and I have the same blood flowing through our veins, and if I want to hug you after not seeing you for three weeks, I'll do it!"

"That's telling her," Julianne said with a wide grin. "And where's my sugar?"

Shannon stomped her foot. "You two are so twentieth century, I swear. You're *so* behind the times!"

"No kiss, no pancakes," said Julianne.

Shannon went and gave her mother a quick smack on the cheek. Rayne went and hugged them both while she was doing it, resulting in a group hug.

"Ugh," fumed Shannon. "I can't wait to go to college and get out of this syrupy sweet family!" She fairly bristled with anger, her braids seeming to stand on end, when she said it. Her mother and sister laughed at her all the more.

Her mother took her face between her hands, and touched her nose to hers. "Aren't you the cutest thing when you're angry!"

She let her go after that, and slapped her on the behind. "Now go set the table."

After Shannon had gone to get the dishes from the cabinet, Julianne said in a low voice, "I need to talk with you about something important. It's about your daddy."

Rayne looked her in the eyes. "You mean about his illness?"

Julianne frowned, then smiled slowly. "Who told you? I know *he* didn't. He wanted to tell you face-to-face, not over the phone." She pursed her full lips, thinking. "Shirley, right?"

"Last night," Rayne said softly. "She wanted to know why you hadn't told me. I told her you must have forgotten."

"I didn't forget," Julianne said, exasperated now. "Your father asked me not to tell you. Shirley means well, I'm sure, but sometimes she's a big, fat blabbermouth!"

"She's concerned about him because he's thinking of not having the operation that could save his life," Rayne told her.

Julianne suddenly felt weak in the knees, and went to sit down at the kitchen table. Rayne sat across from her. Shannon set the table around the two of them, listening to their conversation but offering no comments. She loved Ray, too, and while the news of his illness shocked her and made her feel slightly ill herself, she was more interested in hearing why a dying man would opt to forgo an operation that could save his life.

"Yeah," Julianne said, eyes lowered. "I'm worried about that, too. I tried to talk him into having it, and he wouldn't budge."

Rayne rapped the tabletop in a fit of frustration, stood, and started pacing. "It's not right that he should make this big a decision without taking into account the people who're going to miss him when he's gone. He has no right!"

"It's his life, baby," Julianne said reasonably. "It's his to do with as he wishes."

"Don't you *care?*" Rayne cried, turning to glare at her mother. "You can't hate him so much that you'd be glad he was dead!"

Julianne laughed. "Hate him? I don't hate your father. I love him. That's why I left him."

Shannon had been putting the juice glasses on the table. She plopped down on the nearest chair. "Okay, I've got to sit down for this one. Go on, Mom, tell us how you loved Ray so much you had to leave him."

Julianne looked at Rayne. "Sit down. I suppose it *is* time I told you girls what really happened between me and Ray."

Rayne reclaimed her seat at the table, and Julianne started talking. "Honey, I was already pregnant with you when Ray and I got married."

"Ooh, Momma," Shannon said in awe, as if it was wonderful finding out her mother was human, and made mistakes, too.

Julianne spoke firmly to her. "Learn by my example, don't follow it. Having a baby is serious business, as you'll find out when you're getting up in the middle of the night to change it, feed it and listen to it wail like a banshee. 'Cuz I'm not the one who'll be taking care of any babies you might bring into this world."

"I'm not gonna have babies," Shannon announced loudly. "Not even if I ever get married. Marriage and babies? Not for me!"

"You're too young to make that kind of decision right now," Julianne told her from experience. "Now be quiet and listen." She turned to meet Rayne's eyes. "I always thought that Ray only married me because I was pregnant. I could never shake that feeling. So, even though I loved him, I decided that I couldn't live with a man whose love I didn't feel secure about. Besides, with me gone, he could meet someone else and fall in love."

"Which he never did," Rayne said, suddenly sad for all the lost years her parents could never get back, all due to a terrible misconception. She knew her father loved her mother. What she *didn't* know was why her mother felt the way that she did. Rayne was willing to wager that most women would have been perfectly happy to be married to their child's father, whether he married her while under duress or not.

So, she spoke her mind. "I don't understand why you can't see that Daddy loved you. Nobody tells Ray Walker what to do. If he can stand up to Aunt Shirley who, probably, warned him *not* to marry you, then he can stand up to anybody. He married you because he loved you!" She lowered her voice. "I always thought you left Daddy because you hated living in a small town, and he couldn't live in the city. That you two were incompatible. But you're telling me that the only reason you packed us both up and moved back to Brooklyn was that you didn't think Daddy *loved* you? Mom, that's insane, and a total lie!"

Julianne sat with her mouth agape. "What did you say?"

Rayne did not lower her gaze, but looked steadily at her mother. "I said you're lying. That's not the only reason you left Daddy. It must have been the guilt that got to you."

"What guilt?" Julianne had to tell herself to calm down. She wasn't on the stage, emoting, she was having a civilized conversation with her daughter. But the emotions her daughter was bringing out of her were sending her blood pressure spiraling. She was awash in something akin to panic.

Rayne rose. "Hold on," she said, and turned to leave the kitchen.

When she returned a minute later, she was carrying what looked like a letter in a business-size envelope. "Here," she said, handing it to her mother. "Read this."

Julianne's heart raced as she glanced at the handwriting on the envelope. Her mother's handwriting. She swallowed the lump in her throat as she opened the unsealed letter, unfolded the plain white sheet of typing paper, and began to read:

Dear Rayne:

I gave this letter to your aunt Reba, my youngest sister, and instructed her not to give it to you until you turn twenty-one. Knowing Reba, she'll probably send you a nice birthday present with this letter inside. I hope what I'm about to reveal will not come as a surprise to you, and that Julianne will have already disclosed what I'm about to tell you. I'm not one to beat around the bush, never have been, as you know. Ray Walker is not your biological father. He's a good man, and I love him, but you need to know the truth. Your father's name is Benjamin Jefferson. His family owns a construction company in Fernandina Beach, Florida. That's right down the road from American Beach, where your mother was living when you were conceived. I'm telling you this not to cause problems in your life, but to head them off. What if you have a child who is born with some kind of disease, and he needs a life-saving transplant, or something of that nature? I'm not doing this to be meddlesome. Though, God knows, Julianne will probably think that I am. I begged her to tell you on your sixteenth birthday, but she couldn't. I begged her again on your eighteenth birthday, and she couldn't. I don't have the strength to wait around for your twenty-first. I love you, child. Grandma Layla.

Julianne looked up at Rayne when she'd finished reading.

"I've been carrying that letter around with me for five years," Rayne said quietly, standing with her arms akimbo. "Do you know how big a burden it's been?"

Julianne sat and cried silently.

Shannon, still mostly in the dark because she had no idea what was in the letter since her mother had not read it aloud, simply looked from her mother to her sister, hoping one of them would explain what was going on.

"I kept waiting for you to tell me something," Rayne continued. "Each time I had a birthday, I thought, 'She's going to tell me today. Today, I'm going to hear the words straight from her mouth.' But you never said anything, Mom. Not a word!"

Surprisingly, Rayne did not feel any acrimony toward her mother. She'd imagined she would be fiery mad when this day finally came, but she was strangely serene.

"If you tell me that everything in that letter is a lie, I'll believe you," she said calmly.

More silence from her mother, except for an audible sob.

Shannon got up to get her mother a paper towel.

Julianne gratefully accepted it, dabbed at her eyes and cheeks, and then loudly blew her nose. Looking at Rayne, she sniffed, and said, "It's all true. It's true what you said about the guilt, too. I couldn't live with the guilt of having married Ray while carrying another man's child."

Shannon almost fell off her chair. She righted the chair and stared at her mother with wide eyes. "Ooh, Momma!"

"Be quiet, Shannon," Julianne said much too sharply.

"Don't snap at her!" Rayne said. "It isn't her fault that our mother is a liar. At least she knows who her father is. Neil *is* her father, isn't he?"

"Yes, Neil is her father!" Julianne shouted.

"Good," said Rayne. "She won't have to wait until she's twenty-six to learn the truth." She smiled at Shannon. "You're a lucky girl. Cherish the knowledge that you have. Of course, you won't have Grandma Layla send *you* a letter from the grave on *your* twenty-first birthday!"

"Rayne, be fair!" Julianne implored her. "I did the best I could. When given the choice between Ray and Ben Jefferson, I thought Ray would be the better father. We both agreed on it. As a matter of fact, Ray and I were going to tell you together this summer in American Beach."

"Well, you can call him and tell him that that's one less thing he has to do before he dies!" Rayne cried angrily. Her mother's assertion that she and her father, or the man she'd *thought* was her father until her twenty-first birthday, had planned on telling her the truth the summer prior to his death incensed her. It was a little too late for explanations now that she was losing him. Didn't they see that? Some part of her would have preferred continuing to pretend she didn't know.

Even though she'd forced her mother into a confession, the thought that they were going to tell her only because her father was dying made her want to lash out at them.

What was she supposed to do? Transfer all the love she had for him to some faceless man who was, as far as she was concerned, a sperm donor?

She snatched the letter from the tabletop, spun on her heel, and fled before she said something she would surely regret.

Julianne sprang to her feet. "Rayne, wait!"

By the time she reached the living room, Rayne had gotten her jacket and purse, and left the front door open in her wake.

Julianne slumped against the doorjamb. The day she had dreaded for years had come, and she'd handled it poorly.

Wiping fresh tears with the back of her hand, she turned and went back inside. She would have to call Ray now and tell him what had happened.

Chapter 3

Going to work for his father fresh out of college had seemed like a good idea at the time, but it was beginning to feel like his worst decision yet. More and more, these days, those words crept into Wade Jefferson's thoughts.

Like right now, for example.

His father, Benjamin Wade Jefferson (Wade was a junior, but dared anyone to call him that), had summoned him to his office to tell him, "I want you to go to American Beach next week and make another offer to Ray Walker. I hear he's terminally ill and it might be the right time to strike."

The offices of Jefferson Construction and Development were in a high-rise in Atlanta, Georgia. They owned the building, and rented the remaining office space. They owned property all over the Southeast, including a nightclub in Wade's father's hometown of Fernandina Beach, Florida. In Wade's memory, that was the only time his father could be said to be looking out for "his folks." Locals staffed the club. Otherwise, there were very few examples of altruism in Ben Jefferson's business portfolio. He'd quit his job at his father's construction company in Fernandina Beach nearly thirty years ago, gone to Atlanta to seek his fortune and never looked back.

Therefore, his rather altruistic motives of wanting Ray Walker's property, in order to open a supper club in American Beach and revive the community, was highly suspect to Wade. In its heyday, American Beach was a vacation destination for blacks from all over the South and beyond. On the southern end of Amelia Island, American Beach stretched for half a mile along the Atlantic Ocean. It had once been a resort that hosted such musicians as Ray Charles in its area clubs. Today, its former 200 acres were reduced to a mere 100 because of development. The locals claimed Amelia Island was swallowing them whole. Developers built condominiums in gated communities, and put up 18-hole golf courses that drew the well-to-do. Consequently, the American Beach residents who remained were staunchly loyal. Like Ray Walker, who was dug in, and would never sell his property to a developer.

Wade walked over to the window and gazed at Atlanta's skyline. "A supper club."

"Yes," his father said, nodding. "A supper club, and then more businesses. Back in the day, American Beach had lots of businesses that catered to the tourist. Black folks need some place to eat, some place to sleep, some place to dance when the mood strikes them. It could rise like a phoenix from the flames, but we've got to start somewhere!"

"With Ray Walker's property," Wade said skeptically.

"It's the largest piece of beachfront property in American Beach. It's easily accessible from A1A, and, this is the tricky part, it's already zoned for businesses because Walker is an artist, and he has a studio in his home."

"You looked that up, did you?" Wade said, smiling. His back was turned, so his father could not see his face.

"I do my research," Ben said proudly.

"Did you also find out what Walker's Achilles' heel is, by any chance? Because the man is as stubborn as a mule! The last time I made an offer—a very generous offer, I might add—he told me that Satan would be able to make snow angels in *hell* before he sold anything to you."

He turned around and faced his father. At six-three and just over two hundred pounds, Wade was a big man. In top physical form, he made an imposing figure in his tailored business suits. Women wanted to possess him, and men wanted to be him. It wasn't a realization that made him conceited and a boor, but which humbled him. He'd been blessed, and he knew it. He also knew where his loyalties lay. Hence, his next words were tempered by respect for the man who'd raised him.

"Tell me why Ray Walker doesn't like you, Dad."

Ben Jefferson sat behind his polished mahogany desk, formed a steeple of his thick fingers, and smiled thoughtfully. He was twenty-two years older than his son, but time had been kind to him. He'd never had Wade's height. He'd topped off at five-eleven, but what he lacked in height, he made up for in sheer presence. The knowledge that what he did mattered in the great scheme of things, that the world would feel his absence when he was gone.

The smile deepened, and crinkles appeared in the dark chocolate skin around his hazel eyes. "He doesn't like me because, years ago, I tried to steal his girl. It's as simple as that." He gave a short cough of a laugh. "One would think time and maturity would make him forgive and forget a grudge of that sort."

"You old dudes have long memories," Wade joked.

"I'm not headed to the boneyard at fifty-six," Ben told him. "Don't start adding up your inheritance this early in the game."

Wade wasn't counting his father out any time soon. He knew Ben Jefferson wasn't going anywhere until he figured out how to take his money with him.

He sat on the chair in front of the desk and met his father's eyes. "How far above market value are you willing to go this time? He's a shrewd businessman. He knows what his property is worth down to the penny."

"You can go twenty-five percent higher than market value," Ben told him, frowning. "I predict that once he sells, some of his neighbors will cave in, too, and then I'll have investors coming out of the woodwork, looking for opportunities to cash in. American Beach is one of the most beautiful, pristine beaches along the Atlantic Ocean. And a lot of black folks are nostalgic about its appeal. Some of their best times were spent on it."

His expression grew wistful. "I took my prom date to Evans's Rendezvous, it was a glorified juke joint back then with a beautiful view from an oceanfront porch. I'm not the romantic type, but Sadie sure did think it was romantic, and she was very grateful." He gave his son a knowing look.

"I assume that was way before you met Mom," Wade said. He smirked at his old man, who was sitting there with a self-satisfied expression on his mug.

"Of course," said Ben. He snapped out of his reverie and regarded Wade with serious eyes. "You want an Achilles' heel? Tell him how rich he can leave his precious daughter after he's gone."

"He's got a grown daughter?"

"Yes, the private investigator says she went with Julianne when she divorced him. She should have been mine."

"Oh, so the woman you tried to take from Walker married him and had his child?"

"That's right."

Wade counted the years in reverse. He was thirty-four years old. That made the young woman his dad was talking about older than he was, right? Then, she wasn't exactly a girl anymore. Yet, his father spoke of her as if she were some sweet young thing. Or maybe...

"What year was this, Dad?"

"It was 1979," his father answered quickly and confidently, as though it were a date so significant to him he'd never forget it.

Wade's dark brown eyes could have been made of obsidian, the expression in them had grown so hard and cold. "Did you cheat on Mom, you old fart, when she was lying sick in bed?"

Ben coolly met his son's gaze. "Wade, you're a man now, you know that people make mistakes in life. Yes, it was the year your mother found out about the cancer. And, yes, it was the year I lost my mind and fell in love with a young woman on vacation. I wined her and dined her until she fell in love with me, too. But I never told her I was married. It's all on me. She wouldn't have given me the time of day if she'd known. She was that type of woman."

"So, what happened? She found out you were married, and married Walker on the rebound?"

"She found out I was married, yes, but whether she married Walker as a result of a broken heart, I don't know. All I know is, several months after I saw her for the last time, I read a birth announcement in the local paper, and it said Mr. and Mrs. Raymond Walker welcomed a newborn daughter, Rayne, to the family. That's all. I'll never forget that. They named her after *him*."

Wade, ever the perceptive one, said, "But you suspect that Rayne Walker might really be yours, am I right?"

Ben sighed. "I suspect, but I have no proof."

Wade rose with a grunt and looked down at his father, his eyes steely. "What you're really trying to do is insinuate yourself back into their lives so you can find out, once and for all, if Rayne Walker is your child."

His father slowly nodded in the affirmative.

Wade shook his head in astonishment. "Tangled web, and all that," he said. "Why didn't you tell me everything from the jump?"

"I didn't want you to know, Wade. You're a do-right man. Aretha would have loved you. Well, the right thing would be to go straight to Ray Walker and ask him for the truth. But I believe that would be a surefire way of getting him to clam up. I would never find out anything then. He hates me, remember?"

"Exactly why does he hate you? And don't give me that 'you tried to steal his girl' spiel." Wade looked at him impatiently.

"No, he hates me more for the way I treated your mother. You see, Ray Walker and Deirdre grew up in the same neighborhood. Their families were the best of friends. When he found out about my affair with Julianne, he jumped me one night when I was leaving a local watering hole and beat me to within an inch of my life. I, of course, pressed charges, and he spent six months in jail for it. By the time he got out and married Julianne, she was obviously pregnant. I watched them leaving the church from a distance. She had to be at least eight months pregnant."

"That doesn't prove the child was yours," Wade pointed out.

"Yeah, but it could have been mine," Ben countered. "I won't rest until I find out for certain."

"Why, to get back at Ray Walker for marrying the woman you wanted?" Wade asked. "I hope Mom didn't know anything about this. You didn't feel the need to unburden yourself before she died, did you?"

Ben looked hurt by the question. "What kind of man do you think I am? No, son, your mother died peacefully."

"You're a hard man," Wade said in answer to his question. "You're cutthroat where business is concerned, and you'll do anything to win. Does that also mean that you would ruin a young woman's life just to satisfy your curiosity?"

Ben's brows arched, denoting that he wanted further elucidation.

Wade was more than glad to give it to him. His father's committing adultery while his mother was dying did not sit well with him. Mistakes were one thing, but for a man to cheat on his wife while she was struggling to stay alive seemed to call for a special kind of selfishness and detachment. He knew what his father would say if he pressed him for an explanation of his behavior: his mother's long illness had left him vulnerable and needy, and he'd found comfort in the arms of a beautiful woman. Could anyone blame him? Yes, Wade could blame him. And did.

"My concern is, if Rayne Walker doesn't want anything to do with you, what will you do? Are you prepared to walk away and never be a part of her life, if that's what she wants? If you're not, you're not thinking straight, Dad, and I won't help you do this."

Ben pushed himself up from behind his desk and glared at his son. "Whatever happened to blood is thicker than water? You're my son. Why wouldn't you help me find out whether you have a sister in this world or not?"

Wade met his father's eyes without flinching. "Don't try to bluster your way out of this. Answer my question. What do you plan to do if you find out she's yours but she doesn't want anything to do with you?"

Ben sighed, and all the wind seemed to go out of him. He sank back in his chair and lowered his gaze. "I guess I'll just have to back off," he said softly.

"Do I have your word on that?" Wade asked.

Ben sighed even deeper. He knew his son had him over a barrel. But then, no one else on earth knew him as well as his son did. How ruthless he could be when he wanted something, and to what lengths he would go to get it.

He raised his gaze to his son's. "You have my word."

Wade went and offered him his hand. His dad believed in the old way, when a man's word was as good as an ironclad contract, and a man's handshake sealed the deal. They shook hands, and Wade smiled. "It might be fun to do a little detective work on my weekends off."

Chapter 4

It took Rayne only a few minutes to realize how selfish she was being. By the time she'd taken the subway uptown, with a stop by a coffee shop to pick up a bagel and a large cup of hot chocolate, her anger had dissipated and, more than anything else, she wanted to prevent her mother from phoning her dad with the news that she already knew he wasn't her biological father.

She dialed her mother's number while she was walking down the street, heading to her building. Shannon answered the phone. "Hey, Rayne, how you doin'?" Shannon's voice sounded so sympathetic that Rayne knew what had transpired had really disturbed her baby sister. *Another thing to regret.* Rayne smiled, though, to think that her normally disaffected sister was feeling sympathy for her. "I'm okay, kiddo. I, ah, I just wanted to try to catch Mom before she called Dad. I don't want him stressed out over this."

"Don't worry, Mom's been in her bedroom crying since

you left. I don't think she's able to talk to anybody. I offered to stay with her, but she told me she needed to be alone."

"Okay, well, would you tell her I need to speak with her?"

"Sure, hold on."

A minute or so later, her mother picked up. "Rayne, thank God. I'm so sorry for everything. I didn't mean for you to find out the way that you did. There were so many times I was going to tell you, but decided to leave well enough alone. Ray loved being your father, and he was a *good* father!"

"Listen, Mom," Rayne said, as she walked up the front steps of her building. "I know you did what you thought was best for me. I understand that. That's not my main concern right now."

"Hello, Miss Walker!" Bill Gamble, an African-American in his late sixties with an ever-present smile on his pecan tan face, called to her as she walked past his desk in the lobby. The shift had changed since she'd left the building that morning.

"Hello, Mr. Gamble, working on the weekend again, huh?" Rayne returned with a smile. She knew her mother could hear her, and was aware that she was walking through the lobby to the elevators.

"Gotta eat," said Bill. "You have a good one!"

"You, too!"

Rayne continued to the elevators. She pressed the Up button. "I'm back," she told her mother. "As I was saying, I'm okay now. I wouldn't have even gotten angry if you hadn't said that you and Dad were planning on telling me together sometime this summer. That made his death more imminent to me, Mom. More real, somehow. So, I think it was fear that made me get angry, not anything you did when I was born. Besides, I had five years to get used to the idea. What I needed from you was confirmation. Some part of me was hoping that Grandma didn't know what she was talking about in that letter. But, deep down, I knew it was true."

"That's why it took you so long to confront me?" her mother asked softly, her voice slightly hoarse from her extended crying jag.

"Yes, it was. I figured what I didn't know for sure couldn't hurt me."

"Then why did you show me the letter today?"

The elevator arrived, and Rayne stood aside as a couple alighted from it. Alone inside, she pressed the seventh-floor button. After the doors had closed, she said, "When you said you had something important to tell me about Dad, I foolishly assumed that you were going to blurt it out after all these years, so I trumped you. I pulled my card before you could pull yours. I guess I wanted to hurt you, Mom. I'm sorry for that. But after carrying around the truth for five years, I guess I built up a little resentment."

"That's to be expected," her mother told her calmly. She sighed tiredly. "I knew you were going to resent me. I probably postponed telling you for so long because I was afraid of how you would react."

"Well, it's done now," Rayne said, leaning against the elevator wall. "But as I said earlier, that's not my main concern. Dad is. It occurred to me somewhere between here and Brooklyn that I could use this knowledge to my advantage." She paused a beat or two. "Is Shannon right? You haven't told Dad about it yet?"

"No, I wanted to be calm when I spoke with him."

"Good, because I have an idea."

"An idea?"

"Yeah. You said that you two were planning on telling me the truth sometime this summer?"

"That's right."

"When?"

"Your dad didn't say when. Just that he wants me to come to American Beach, and then we'd tell you together."

"When can you go?" Rayne asked.

"I don't have another job until mid-July," Julianne said.

"Then we can all go together week after next," Rayne said, relieved. The sooner they got down South, the better. They didn't have time to lose. While her father was dragging his feet, the cancer could be getting worse. She was still stunned by his bullheadedness.

Julianne immediately brightened. "Let's drive down, baby. I haven't taken the Explorer on the open road yet. It'll be good to open her up. Let's do it so we can talk on the way. Shouldn't take us more than a couple days. We can spend the night in a nice hotel, a hotel with a pool."

Rayne liked the idea. Besides, Shannon swam like a fish. She'd really get a kick out of the first swim of the season in a swanky hotel pool. "Sounds good," she told her mother. "Do you want to plan the itinerary, or should I?"

"I'll handle everything," Julianne said happily. "I know you have the Bennett-Slater wedding to do next Saturday. Those hincty folks are going to drive you to distraction, I'm sure."

Rayne laughed. "You've got that right! I haven't gotten inside my place yet, but I'm sure there are plenty of messages on my machine from either the bride or the bride's mother. They're both in the running for the Most Obnoxious Client of the Year."

Julianne laughed delightedly. She felt as if a huge weight had been lifted from her shoulders. "You know if you need me to come in and run interference for you, I'd be glad to do it."

Her mother had a talent for appeasing people. No doubt due to her acting ability, she was able to manipulate people's emotions with just the right words, coupled with just the right intonation to her voice. With a mere smile she could entice, gently reprimand, or coax someone into doing her bidding. Men adored her. Women trusted her. And children were drawn to her.

Rayne had inherited a little of her mother's charm, but more often than not, she didn't have the patience to coddle people. She did her job well and expected to be treated with respect in return. She made sure there would be no misunderstandings. Clients knew what to expect for their dollar. In the beginning, she had bent over backward trying to please the client, but soon learned that bending over backward left her in a very vulnerable position. Oftentimes, her profits weren't what they should have been because she would cave in whenever someone complained about the price. Now she simply told them from the get-go: quality came at a premium. If they wanted below-market prices they should take their business elsewhere.

"I'll be fine," she assured her mother now. "I've got their number."

She was standing before her apartment door. She heard the faint thump of the bass turned up on the stereo, and knew that Dottie was up. When she'd left that morning, her roommate, best friend and sorority sister was snoring loudly.

"All right," said Julianne reluctantly. "See you later, baby."

"Bye, Mom. Love you," said Rayne.

"Love you!" Julianne returned.

After they hung up, Rayne unlocked the apartment door and strode in. She hung her jacket in the hall closet and walked into the living room where her ears were assaulted by the sound of *Accidentally in Love* by Counting Crows.

Dottie was in front of the flat-screen TV dancing to the closing credits of *Shrek 2*. Dottie, who was twenty-eight and a respected news anchor at a local station, was like a two-year-old child where *Shrek* and *Shrek 2* were concerned. She'd seen both films more than a dozen times. She told Rayne that watching them instantly lifted her mood.

The volume was up so loud, and she was so engrossed in her weird gyrations, that she hadn't heard Rayne come in.

"What's wrong?" Rayne asked, knowing something had happened to depress Dottie.

Startled, Dottie gasped, then recovered as soon as she saw Rayne. She laughed.

"Oh, it's you. What happened? Aren't you supposed to be doing the sister thing with Shannon today?" She went and turned down the volume.

"Change of plans," Rayne told her. She dropped her purse onto the couch and placed her hot chocolate and bagel, still in their paper bag, on the coffee table. She and Dottie worked much different hours and rarely saw each other during daylight hours unless they both had the weekend off. Like this weekend.

"I broke up with Steven last night," Dottie said in answer to her question. She gave a pretty good impression of a hound dog with her big, sorrowful brown eyes.

Rayne got right back up and went to hug Dottie. "I knew you'd been unhappy, but I didn't see this coming. How'd he take it?" She released her and stepped back.

"Oh, he said he knew I'd drop him before long, anyway," Dottie said with a grimace.

Steven had always had a problem with the fact that Dottie earned more money than he did, and she was somewhat of a celebrity in New York City. Dottie tried to explain to him that the amount of money each of them earned shouldn't make a difference. Not if they truly loved each other and wanted to build a life together. She regretted telling him what she earned, but he'd caught her at an unguarded moment. Ever since then, she'd told Rayne, Steven had been turning away from her.

"Now I know that the reason he started pulling away from me was that he always thought I'd leave him and move on to better prospects," she said sadly. "After a year, I got tired of his negative attitude and, finally, last night, I gave him what he'd been expecting."

"But you love him!"

"Yes, I do. I love him with all my heart. But I realized he was never going to stop harping on the fact that I make more money than he does. What was I supposed to do? Ask for a reduction in pay?"

Five-six and slender, Dottie had flawless medium brown skin with reddish undertones and black hair, which she wore in a short, tapered cut that complemented her pretty, heart-shaped face. "I grew up in a walk-up in Hell's Kitchen. I won't apologize for being successful at what I do. The fact is I'm not as successful as I'm going to be. I haven't even gone national yet. I need a man who is going to be supportive of my career. Hell, I'll even take a man who's competitive with me. But I can't live with a guy who is always bemoaning the fact that I rake in more Benjamins than he does. If he was so concerned about it, he could have worked harder and earned more than I do."

"Your momma sure did a head job on you, didn't she?" Rayne said.

Dottie stared at her, half in shock, half in anger. "So, you think because my mother drummed into me the importance of making money that I've grown cold and heartless?"

Rayne shook her head in the negative. "You're my best friend. I could never think of you as cold or heartless. What I think is that you're scared. You're not sure you did the right thing by breaking up with Steven. But, as an outsider looking in, I think breaking up with him might make him realize how much his obsession with earnings was coming between you. Maybe you should just wait a few days and see what happens."

This time, Dottie regarded Rayne with admiration. "You could *have* something there!"

Feeling much better now, Dottie eyed Rayne's food bag. "What do you have in there? I'm starved."

Rayne picked up the bag and gave it to her. "A plain bagel and a hot chocolate. You can have it. I'm going to make scrambled eggs and sausages. Want some?"

"Yeah!" Dottie said, following Rayne into the small kitchen. Dottie couldn't cook to save her life. She had her favorite restaurants on speed-dial. "I'm really going to miss Steven."

"Yeah, he's a chef," Rayne quipped, as she took foodstuffs from the refrigerator.

Dottie sighed. "True, very true! That man made the best collard greens I ever laid my greasy lips on!"

"Mmm-hmm," said Rayne. "And now he's gonna be cooking greens for somebody else."

Across town, Julianne was vacuuming the living room carpet, her mind on something Rayne had said, or *hadn't* said. When Rayne had phoned her to see if she'd already told Ray about their fight or not, she'd said that allowing her and Ray to go ahead and tell her about her parentage together in American Beach, as they'd planned, would be to her advantage. What had she meant by that? How could that possibly be advantageous to her? Julianne couldn't imagine what she'd meant.

American Beach was about 350 miles southeast of Atlanta. Wade had to make a stop in Fernandina Beach first, though, before going on to the company's Amelia Island condo. His grandma Geneva would make his life a living hell if he didn't stop by and show his respects the moment he got in the area.

Geneva Emerson, his mother's mom, had outlived her husband, her daughter and most of her brothers and sisters. At eighty-five, she still lived alone, drove a car and was involved in more outside activities than *he* was! Often, he would phone her to check up on her and she would put him on hold while she answered another, more important, call. Blast call-waiting! It irritated him to be put on hold by his eighty-five-year-old grandmother. That is, until he realized that staying busy quite possibly helped keep her alive. She was in good health for an octogenarian, as spry as ever. And her mind was sharp. In fact, she remembered things from his childhood that even *he* couldn't recall as vividly.

Pulling onto the immaculate driveway (no nasty oil spots for his granny, who forced her great-grandsons to wash it every three months), he alighted from his late-model white SUV and walked up onto the front stoop. He rang the bell, and waited. He'd been trying to get her to hire a maid, but Geneva laughed at the notion. The day she couldn't clean her own house would be the day they nailed her coffin lid shut.

It took her a good four minutes to get to the door. When she opened it, he saw why. She had a towel wrapped around her silver curls, and her tiny five-foot-one body was clothed in a white terry cloth robe. Her feet were bare.

"Child, what you doin' here so early for?" she said, looking up, and up, at him, her tone accusatory. Her glasses were slightly foggy from her shower.

Wade laughed softly as he bent and kissed her cheek. "I'm glad to see you, too. May I come in, or do you want the whole neighborhood to see you half naked?"

Geneva pursed her lips and stepped back. "Come on in here before I catch my death of cold!"

Wade crossed the threshold and, as always, the first thing that struck him about his grandmother's house was the overwhelming smell of cinnamon. Geneva loved to bake. And, in spite of her tiny frame, she had a formidable sweet tooth. He guessed she'd made her homemade cinnamon cookies. He could overdose on those bad boys, they were so good.

His mind was so much on the tasty treat that awaited him in the kitchen that he hadn't noticed his grandmother rising on tiptoe and reaching for his ear. If he had, he would have avoided a lot of pain.

Geneva's bony fingers clamped on his ear and twisted. "What was May seventeenth?" she asked ominously, as she twisted his ear farther.

"Mom's birthday!" he answered without hesitation.

Geneva let up a little on his ear. "You didn't have flowers put on her grave."

"I did that on Mother's Day. The dates weren't that far apart. I drove down especially for Mother's Day. Give me a break, Grandma."

Geneva twisted his ear painfully before letting go of him. "You didn't even phone me on her birthday so we could reminisce about her like you used to." She turned away from him, and showed him her back as though he'd wounded her deeply with his forgetfulness.

Wade gingerly rubbed his ear. That little old lady had nearly brought tears to his eyes, and *she* was hurt? He really didn't know which was worse, though: incurring her wrath, and suffering the indignity of an ear-pull, or seeing the disappointment in her eyes.

"I'm sorry!" he cried, trying to console her. "I'll put flowers on her grave this visit. I promise. And I'll make sure the grave site is neatly manicured, like you like it."

Geneva turned back around to face him, a small smile turning her mouth up at the corners. "I don't want you forgetting her, that's all. She loved you. You were her only child. The thing she loved *best* in this world."

"I know," Wade said, contrite. Geneva Pearl Emerson knew

how to get to the core of him better than anyone else on earth. "And I know I should do more to keep her memory alive. It wasn't intentional. I just got busy at work."

Geneva sniffed derisively and turned to head back to the kitchen. Wade followed.

"I *do* have to make a living, you know. I don't get a big, fat Social Security check every month."

Geneva looked over her shoulder at him and guffawed. He could always get a laugh out of her. He knew that she was the leader of her city's AARP group, and was very politically active. "Thank God for my pension. Otherwise, I'd be on the streets."

"Not as long as I'm alive," Wade assured her.

That elicited a wide smile from his grandmother. She continued walking. "Well, it's good to know you wouldn't allow me to be homeless. But what you really need to be concentrating on is getting me a granddaughter-in-law, and some great-grandbabies. Time's flyin', Wade Jefferson, and I'm not getting any younger."

Wade placed his arm about her shoulders. "You coulda fooled me!"

She shrugged his arm off. "Don't change the subject. That's your problem. You spend so much time charming females that you haven't been able to recognize a keeper when you see one. You young people! You're about as deep as a creek, and just as meandering."

"Meaning, we have no direction?" Wade asked, amused.

"That's what I'm saying," Geneva said.

She went to the refrigerator and got a carton of milk. Wade, in a time-honored dance, went to the cabinet above the sink to get two tall glasses.

Geneva sat at the plain, round, oak table. There were four spindly-legged chairs around it. Every time he sat at the table,

Wade wondered if they would bear his weight. Geneva waited for Wade to sit down before she filled their glasses.

"Thank you," said Wade.

Geneva met his gaze. Her eyes were honey-colored, and as clear as they'd been in her teens. However, she was quite nearsighted and needed the Coke-bottle glasses to see anything more than six feet away from her. "Thank you for coming to see an old lady." She pushed the plate of cookies closer to him.

"My pleasure," said Wade, picking up a cookie.

They ate in silence. He put away half a dozen before he slowed down. Geneva nearly kept pace with him. After a few minutes, he drank the milk, then cleared his throat. "Grandma, do you remember Ray Walker?"

"What's to remember?" Geneva asked. "It's not as if I don't see him every Sunday. He goes to my church. The whole Walker clan does. Those children know how to show respect to their mother."

Wade realized that she was referring to men and women in their fifties, when she said "those children." As far as he knew, Ray Walker had two sisters and a brother living in Fernandina Beach. Ray, himself, was the only Walker left in American Beach. His sisters and brother had all married and moved farther inland. It took a special kind of person to live on the beach year-round. They got their share of storms, and most of the permanent residents didn't bother running for cover unless at least a category-four hurricane was predicted. They closed their shuttered windows or, sometimes, nailed plywood over them and rode out the storm.

"Why're you asking about Ray Walker? Ben still interested in his property?"

"How'd you know about that? I never mentioned it to you."

"Child, some of the best gossips are in the church. I hear

things. Is that it? Ben wants to swoop in and try to steal Ray's property while the poor man is sick?"

"Then, it's true? He's seriously ill?"

Geneva looked into his eyes, trying to ascertain whether there was any pleasure in them at hearing of another man's misfortune. She had never been happy about Ben choosing to raise Wade in Atlanta, far away from the family. She'd worried about the boy's morals, his ethics. She wondered if Ben would take the time to teach him the difference between right and wrong. She wondered if Ben *knew* the difference.

She smiled, satisfied that her grandson's gaze held concern, not avarice.

"He's got prostate cancer, but I hear the prognosis is good if he goes ahead and starts treatment for it."

"That's good," Wade said. He lowered his gaze. "Yes, that's why I wanted to know more about him. Dad is still interested in buying his property. He thinks it's the ideal spot for a supper club."

Geneva grinned. "A supper club? I admit, I would love to go to a nice establishment that has good food, and good entertainment. But can't he find some place else for it? Ray's family has owned that land since 1935. I don't think he's going to sell it. He'll more than likely leave it to his daughter, Rayne."

Wade's brows arched in curiosity. His father had pronounced her name Ray-Nee, putting the emphasis on Ray. But his grandmother had pronounced it like plain old rain, as in precipitation. He tried it out. "*Rayne?* What kind of name is that?"

Geneva laughed. "You're talking? *Wade* in the water? I always loved that song."

Wade smiled slowly, his full lips curling. "Rayne, Rayne, go away, come again another day. I bet the kids had fun with *her* on the playground."

They'd certainly had a ball poking fun at his name.

Geneva, never one to stray too far from the subject, asked, "So, Ben sent you down here to spy on Ray Walker? That man needs to grow up! The old rivalry between him and Ray should have died with Deirdre."

Wade's curiosity was immediately engaged. "What do you mean by that?"

Geneva casually picked up another cookie, bit into it, chewed thoughtfully, and swallowed, leaving her grandson in suspense. She then cleared her throat and said, "Your mother and Ray were high school sweethearts. Didn't Ben tell you?"

Wade knew his father hadn't been completely honest with him. That old fox had more of an agenda than he pretended to have. Perhaps his enmity toward Ray Walker ran deeper than he'd let on. His mother had dated Ray Walker. His father had an affair with the woman who would become Ray Walker's wife and, quite possibly, was the father of her child. A child Ray Walker had raised as his own.

"No, no, he definitely did not," Wade answered, his square jaw clenched in frustration.

"I bet that's not all he hasn't told you," Geneva said sagely.

Not wanting to think about it, Wade changed the subject. "Let me take you out to dinner tonight. We can go to one of those swanky restaurants on Amelia Island."

"Sorry, dear," Geneva told him, with a shy smile. "But I have a gentleman caller coming to dinner tonight."

"Rats!" Wade cried, snapping his fingers. "I should have known I'd have to make a date with you way ahead of time."

"Let that be a lesson to you," Geneva said, wagging her finger at him.

Rayne, Julianne, and Shannon made it to Greensboro, North Carolina, their first day on the road. It was dusk when they checked into a double room at a nice hotel near the interstate.

As soon as they got to the room, Shannon began rummaging through her bags, looking for her swimsuit. "I know I packed three of them," she complained.

Julianne was looking around the room, turning the covers back, making sure the sheets had been changed recently. The room looked clean at first glance, and the carpet smelled freshly shampooed, but appearances could be deceiving.

She found the sheets cool, crisp and clean-smelling.

Satisfied, she sat on one of the beds and smiled at Shannon who had found a swimsuit and was hurrying into the bathroom to change into it. Rayne, ever the practical one, was sitting at the desk in the room, dialing her father's number to let him know where they were and approximately what time they would arrive in American Beach tomorrow.

"Hi, Dad," she heard Rayne say.

Rayne was smiling as she listened to her father. Then she said, "Greensboro, North Carolina."

She laughed at something he'd said. "It's Thelonious Monk's home state, huh? Okay, if you say so." Her father was a fount of information when it came to trivia. "Oh, Michael Jordan's and Shirley Caesar's, too? Fascinating!"

Julianne laughed when Rayne rolled her eyes at something her father had said.

"Mom," Rayne said, handing the cell phone to her mother. "Dad wants to speak with you."

Julianne accepted the phone. "Hello, Ray," she said, a note of laughter in her voice.

"What was she doing, rolling her eyes?" Ray asked.

Julianne burst into laughter. Ray certainly knew his daughter. "Of course. How are you?"

"Today was a good day," he told her. "Listen, Shirley is

planning a crab boil and a fish fry on the beach tomorrow night to welcome you all."

"You mean to welcome Rayne and Shannon," Julianne corrected. "Shirley doesn't want to see me."

"She's promised to behave herself."

"I suppose you want me to promise I'll behave myself, too?"

"Will you?"

"Not if she starts something."

"Fair enough," Ray said. Even the feud between her and Shirley couldn't dampen his spirits. "Y'all drive carefully tomorrow," he said. "Good night."

"Good night, Ray," Julianne said softly.

She closed the phone and handed it back to Rayne, who'd been watching her mother's face as she'd conversed with her dad. She had fairly glowed the entire time.

"You *do* still love him!" Rayne exclaimed in genuine awe.

"I told you I did," Julianne said with a smile.

Rayne sat on the bed beside her, her eyes meeting her mother's. "I didn't believe you." She blew air between full lips and considered their situation.

They heard the shower come on in the bathroom, and realized that Shannon was preparing to shower before going for a swim, so they knew they had time to talk in private. Fastidious to the point of compulsion, Shannon would shower again when they returned from the pool.

"You know your relationship is bizarre, don't you?" Rayne asked pointedly.

Julianne nodded serenely.

"You also realize that if you asked him to, Dad would have that operation."

"I've already broached the subject, and he doesn't believe that I truly want to give us another chance. It's funny, for years I was the one who couldn't believe he loved me. Now it's the reverse, he's the one who needs to be convinced."

"Years of rejection will do that to a man," Rayne told her flatly.

"I *have* made a royal mess of things," Julianne freely admitted.

"We can fix it," Rayne told her, an excited look in her dark eyes.

"How?"

"It occurred to me," Rayne began, "that your and Dad's upcoming confession about my real parentage will be somewhat like a divorce, and I'm the poor child who's losing a parent, namely Dad. Do you remember how I manipulated you two back then? How guilt-ridden you were when I cried about not having Dad to tuck me in at night?"

Julianne nodded. "I knew you were being a little brat but, yes, I allowed you to manipulate me because I felt guilty for breaking up the family."

"Well, get ready to feel guilty again, Mom, because when you and Dad lay the big surprise on me, I'm gonna milk it for everything I can. I'm going to get Dad to promise me he'll have the operation, in spite of his objection to it. And as for you, you're going to turn on your feminine wiles and give him something to live for." She met her mother's eyes dead-on. "Are you serious about getting back together with Dad?"

"Yes!"

"Then, do you accept the challenge?"

"Yes!"

Rayne leaned over and hugged her mother tightly. "He won't know what hit him."

They drew apart, and Julianne smiled at her daughter. "So, that's what you had planned all along."

Rayne nodded vigorously.

"You're as devious as I am," Julianne accused her.

"Like mother, like daughter," Rayne agreed.

The next night, the welcome-home party was everything Rayne remembered a Walker family get-together to be: loud, boisterous, with too much food and drink and lots of love, not to mention the strains of old school songs filling the air.

The night was cool after a warm day, and the breezes felt good coming off the Atlantic Ocean. The stars were out, and Rayne found herself gazing up at the sky, wondering where that sky was when she was in the city.

About fifty friends and relatives had shown up. Shirley had taken charge, directing various nieces and nephews about how to boil the crabs and shrimp and how to fry the sea bass: cleaned and split butterfly-style and cooked whole. And when to stop giving Uncle Thad beers. He lost all inhibitions after four.

Rayne was happy that her aunt Shirley and her mother were staying out of each other's way. She was also glad that Shannon had fallen in with her teen cousins who had broken off from the group, gone a few yards down the beach, and were dancing to hip-hop music from a boom box. She could hear Shannon's laughter on the air. There had been no altercations at this Walker family bash, only lots of warm embraces, misty eyes, and reminiscing.

Rayne stayed close to her dad most of the time. She continually wanted to touch his arm, or just inhale his masculine cologne. She tried not to treat him differently due to his illness. She knew he wouldn't like that. But the fact was, he had lost quite a few pounds, and his face was drawn. His normally healthy copper-brown skin was sallow, and she could tell his energy level was lower than usual.

Her aunt Shirley caught her observing her father, as she

was standing next to one of the tables they'd set up on the beach, and playfully elbowed her in the side. "Quit that!" she said for her ears only.

Rayne looked up at her aunt, who was a tall, full-figured woman. She had coppery brown skin like her brother, and the same dark brown hair with red highlights.

Shirley smiled at her. "I know it's hard to see him like this, but he'll be okay. We've got to trust in the Lord that he'll be fine."

Rayne couldn't help it. Tears slid down her cheeks.

"Go get some air," suggested Aunt Shirley. "Take a walk on the beach."

She knew that Rayne thought the beach was a sacred place, especially at sundown when everything took on an ethereal appearance. It was like walking on another planet.

She smiled at her aunt and turned to leave, walking south, away from the party and the teen cousins, who were now engaged in an energetic "Soul Train" line. She saw that Shannon was teaching the southern cousins the latest New York City moves.

Lost in her thoughts, she simply walked, not paying attention to how far she'd gone. When she came to herself again, she was at the border of American Beach and an Amelia Island resort. She grimaced at the condominiums. That used to be American Beach property.

Turning her back to the Amelia Island side, she sighed heavily.

"Yeah, that's how I feel about it, too," said a deep masculine voice from behind her.

Rayne spun in the sand. The lights from the resort lent enough illumination to see that he was very tall and broad-shouldered. He was wearing shorts, and the outline of his legs and thighs hinted at plenty of muscles. She suddenly realized she was alone on the beach with a man who could very well be a serial killer, and she wasn't even within shouting distance of anyone from her party.

Chapter 5

The fact that his father had not mentioned that Ray Walker and his mother had once been sweethearts refused to leave Wade's mind. The next day, after another long chat with his grandmother, he went back to the condo, showered, had a bite to eat, and went to inspect the club in Fernandina Beach. It was a Saturday night, and the place was full to capacity. They had a good management team, so he only had a short chat with the manager, had a drink at the bar and left. He hadn't been interested in the two beauties who had sidled up to him while he was at the bar and tried to get him on the dance floor. His thoughts were on a solitary track tonight. And sometimes the only thing that soothed him when he was in that kind of mood was physical exertion.

There was a time when he might have accepted the offer of one of the beauties and taken her some place private for a special sort of physical exertion, but one-night stands were far in his past. They went out when AIDS became the number-one killer of young black men. As far as he was concerned, any man who had sex indiscriminately was a fool. He wasn't a fool.

That's why he was walking on the beach tonight at the same time as this strangely compelling woman who smelled like fresh flowers. He'd noticed her first, and mentally debated whether to approach her or not. He didn't want to frighten her. They were the only two people in that particular area. But he didn't want her to spot him and panic, either. So, when she'd heaved a mournful sigh after gazing across the way at the new condominiums on the Amelia Island side of the border that separated American Beach from Summer Beach, the resort where he was staying, he'd immediately known what that sigh meant, and had responded with, "Yeah, that's how I feel about it, too."

He'd almost laughed out loud when she'd audibly gulped, spun around to stare at him, and exclaim, "Where'd *you* come from?"

He nodded in the direction of the resort. "I have a condo over there."

She hmphed, like his grandmother might have done, and this time he *did* laugh.

She stood perhaps six feet away from him with her hands on her hips. "What's so funny?"

Her body language was sassy and confident. He liked that. "Well, from what I can see of you, you're a young woman, but that sound you just made reminded me of my eighty-five-year-old grandmother."

She chuckled. "I have a grandmother, too. I probably picked it up from her. Sorry, but I was raised around people who have very strong opinions about places like that." She ended with a curt nod in the direction of the resort.

"Then you're from American Beach," he guessed.

"Visiting, actually. My dad has a house on the beach."

"You're from somewhere up North," he said. "East, I'd say. Philly?"

Rayne smiled. "Most people say I have a noticeable Brooklyn accent. And you?"

"Atlanta," Wade told her.

The wind had picked up, dark clouds were rolling in, and the waves had become choppy. Rayne recognized a storm when one was brewing.

"Look, we'd better cut this short, it's going to rain soon." She turned back in the direction she'd come. "Enjoy your, um, condo."

Wade laughed again. "Thanks, I think. You enjoy your visit."

He turned in the direction of the resort.

The next thing he heard was a cry of pain and a harshly uttered expletive. By the time he turned in the woman's direction, she was sitting on the sand, grasping her right ankle with both hands. "Damn," she cried. She picked up a stick that was about three feet long and an inch in diameter, and angrily flung it toward the water.

He was by her side in a matter of seconds. "Here," he said, picking her up by grasping her under the arms so that she wouldn't have to put her weight on the ankle. "Let me help you."

Once she was up, she balanced herself on her uninjured leg, holding on to his muscular arm for leverage. "Thanks, I'm sure I'm fine."

She tested the ankle by putting a little weight on it and was rewarded with excruciating pain. She peered up at him, seeing him a little clearer now. He was taller than she'd thought, and had very pleasant features in his square-chinned face. He smiled at her. *Dimples*, she thought. *Fine as hell, plus dimples. That means trouble.*

"I can see by that grimace that you're *not* all right," he said.

Rayne hadn't been aware that she was frowning. Sure, the pain was pretty bad, but the good, clean male scent of him, the feel of his warm skin against hers all acted as an analgesic and the pain wasn't nearly as strong as her attraction to this stranger was.

"Where do you live, maybe a quarter of a mile down the beach?" Wade asked. "I can carry you that far."

Although the thought of being carried by him was enticing, Rayne didn't know many men who could carry her weight across a room, let alone across a beach. "I weigh more than you think," she warned.

"What are you, 150 pounds?"

He was close. "I'm five-eight and I weigh 155, possibly 160 since I must have eaten five pounds of soft-shell crabs and fried sea bass at the party my family's throwing on the beach. Don't you have a cell phone? I could call my dad and he'll drive down and pick me up."

"Sorry, I left it at the condo."

"You really wanted to be alone, huh?"

"Yes."

"I feel you. I walked off from everyone else because I wanted to be alone, too, and look what it got me. A sprained ankle, and I'm imposing on a perfect stranger."

"You're not imposing on me. I offered to help, and I'm going to get you home again." He turned his back to her. "Get on."

"You're kidding me," Rayne protested, making no effort to do his bidding.

"Listen, woman, do you want to go home or not? If I can bench press 350 pounds, I should be able to carry you a quarter mile down a beach."

"Okay," Rayne relented. "But I warned you."

She was wearing shorts whose hem fell to midthigh, and when she wrapped her long, smooth legs around Wade, he experienced such a rich, warm, sensual rush that he actually blushed. Him! He couldn't remember the last time a woman had made him blush just by her proximity. He started walking, hoping that the exercise would help to dispel the disturbing feelings that were doing crazy things to his equilibrium.

With her arms loosely around his neck, and her full breasts pressed against his back, Rayne tried her best not to inhale his sexy aftershave. Nor enjoy, too much, the warmth of his skin, or the pleasure of the play of his muscles as he effortlessly walked with her on his back.

"You're not that heavy," he told her.

"I bet you say that to all the girls."

"No, this is definitely a first."

She laughed softly, and the sound sent delicious chills throughout his body.

"For me, too," she said.

"So, you grew up on this beach?" he asked.

"My parents divorced when I was eight, and my mom and I moved to Brooklyn. But I spent summers here with Dad. I love it here."

"Oh, you don't mind getting your hair wet?" he joked, alluding to the old joke that black women never want to get their hair wet, so they don't go in the water.

"I have a good swim cap. It serves two functions, keeps my hair dry and water out of my ears. I love to swim. Dad taught me when I was two. Do you like the water?"

"I grew up in Atlanta, and my first experience was in a pool, but yes, I do enjoy it."

"What do you do in Atlanta?"

"My family is in construction," he told her. He thought it best not to mention that he was a real-estate developer as well as a construction company owner.

She'd already told him how she felt about developers when

she'd had such a negative reaction to catching sight of Summer Beach: she didn't care for them.

"What do you build?"

"Family homes, mostly." That was true. They had built some of the most beautiful private homes in and around Atlanta.

"Oh, I love the thought of that. Building homes in which families will live and grow together."

"Most divorced kids think that way," he observed.

"Your parents are divorced, too?"

"No, my mom died of cancer when I was eight, but I have plenty of friends whose parents divorced, and they all feel that way, the desire for an intact family. Some of them even tried to get their parents back together, but it never worked out."

Rayne wanted to get off that subject in a hurry. She was, after all, thinking of doing the same thing, and she didn't want to hear the reasons why it wouldn't work, she wanted to hear someone say it *would* work out.

"So, you're on vacation?" she asked.

"Yes," he said.

"How long?"

"I take minivacations. The condo's always available so I'll just take off for the weekend. I'll be here for the next four or five weekends, at least. My grandmother has a birthday coming up, which I can't miss, and there're other obligations. But, mostly, I come here for the solitude."

"A man who likes to be alone," Rayne said wistfully. "I suppose that means you didn't bring the wife or the girlfriend with you?"

Wade laughed softly. "No wife, and no girlfriend."

"Boyfriend?"

He laughed again. "You just say whatever comes into your head, don't you?"

"Only if I'm riding on the back of the guy. That affords me freedom of speech."

"Oh, does it?" He paused before continuing. "I'm straight. I'm just not involved with anyone right now."

"Divorced?"

"Never been married, and you?"

"I'm twenty-six. I'm not even going to start looking until I turn thirty."

"Why is that?"

"Divorced kid syndrome? Even though I have a strong desire for a family, I'm also afraid I'll fail at marriage like my parents did. So, I don't let relationships get serious. I'm one of those women who run from commitment."

"You wouldn't run if you met the right guy."

"Maybe, and maybe not. I thought I was in love once, but he proposed and I panicked. I was twenty-three then, and just getting my business going. I'm an event planner. Anyway, the closer the date of the wedding got I found myself having panic attacks at the oddest moments. One night, I was having him over for dinner, and I went into a market to get some things for the meal. I picked up a head of lettuce in the produce aisle and suddenly I couldn't breathe, the room started spinning and I nearly blacked out. Some woman, a stranger, helped me get out of the store, and once I was outside in the air, I immediately felt better. I panicked because the act of buying groceries to make him dinner reminded me that for the rest of my life, I would be making him dinner. My mind rebelled against it. My whole body rebelled against domestic bliss. I had to call the wedding off. I haven't had a panic attack since then."

"Poor guy," Wade said.

"Poor guy?" Rayne returned, with another hmph. "He married someone else in our circle less than six months later and now they have two children. He didn't waste any time getting over me!"

"I don't believe that," Wade said. "He married her on the rebound. A lot of that goes on. If he loved you, he couldn't have gotten over you within six months. Love doesn't die that fast."

"Oh, you've been in love?"

"Many, many times," he joked.

"No, one great love?"

"Is there such a thing?"

"I think so."

"Are you telling me that there's only one person for everybody? What if your one great love dies when you're still young? Will you hang it up, and remain alone for the rest of your life? I don't think so. Everybody needs companionship."

"This, coming from Mr. Solitude?"

Wade didn't get the chance to answer, because at that moment, when they were about halfway to her father's house, the headlights of an ATV hit them dead in their faces and they wound up squinting in the glare and yelling at the driver to turn off his bright lights.

They could not see the faces of the two people in the ATV. But Rayne immediately recognized the voice of one of them.

"Sis, where have you been?" Shannon cried. "We've been looking all over for you! Mom said it looked like it was getting ready to storm, and no one knew where you were. Then Aunt Shirley said you'd taken a walk. Why's he carrying you?"

Rayne was making her way, with Wade's assistance, down from her perch on his back. When she was on the ground, she put her weight on her good leg, and held on to Wade's arm. "I hurt my ankle, and this really nice man was kind enough to bring me home."

"Hey, thanks," said Shannon, smiling at Wade.

"Yeah, man, that was real cool of you," said her cousin Rick. Rick was sixteen, already six-three and a star forward on his high school basketball team. He also had a love jones for ATVs, and never went to the beach without his baby.

"It was nothing," Wade said modestly.

He scooped Rayne into his arms and carried her the few feet to the four-wheel ATV. Shannon got off the seat next to Rick so that Rayne could have it. Once Rayne was seated, Shannon buckled her in. She buckled herself into the back-seat.

Rayne turned to Wade. "Thank you." She smiled at him. "I don't even know your name." She took his big hand in hers and held on to it.

"Oh, that's smart," Shannon joked. "All up on a man's back, and you don't even know his name!"

They all laughed, and then Wade said, "It's Wade Jefferson."

"Rayne Walker," Rayne told him.

Wade's heart nearly stopped, he was so shocked. He had to remind himself to breathe normally, to appear composed, even if he felt as if he were unraveling on the inside. Crazily, something his grandma Geneva used to say when she was encouraging him to always know his relatives came back to him. *Get to know your family, baby. Because if you don't know them, you could wind up marrying one of them.*

Those words couldn't be truer.

"It's been a pleasure, Rayne Walker," he heard himself say.

"See if you can say that tomorrow morning when your back's going to be killing you," Rayne said with a grin. "See you on the beach next weekend?"

"I'll be here," Wade said without hesitation.

"Okay, then, good night," said Rayne. She waved as Rick gunned the motor and sped away.

Wade immediately turned and began walking back to the resort. He briefly gazed up at the ever-darkening sky. He felt a raindrop and picked up his pace. It wasn't that far back to the resort, he could make it in under ten minutes. He somehow didn't care if he got caught in a downpour, though. Maybe if he got drenched, he would be able to shake the lustful feelings he had for his own sister! Half sister, he reminded himself. *She's your half sister. Half sister, whole sister, it doesn't matter, you pervert! She's got your blood flowing in her veins, and all you wanted to do was tear her clothes off and make love to her on the beach!* He suddenly wished he were Catholic so he could find a church and confess his sins.

Chapter 6

D*ad could be wrong,* Wade had decided by the time he got back to the condo. He hadn't really gotten a good look at her. She could have none of his father's features. Like that Kirk Douglas dimple in his chin. Several of the Jeffersons had inherited that particular facial anomaly. He hadn't, but most people said he looked more like his mother than his father.

Rayne was tall, but that didn't mean anything. His father was only five-eleven. Ray Walker looked like he was at least six-two. If he were comparing physical attributes in order to prove which man was her father, Ray Walker would be winning right now. He was pulling for Ray Walker.

He'd gotten caught in the rain, and sand was in his athletic shoes. He pulled them off in the foyer and bent to pick them up. After walking through the house to the kitchen, he poured the sand into the kitchen garbage, then knocked the shoes together to dislodge any wet sand that had gotten stuck in the soles.

"Ain't no way she's my sister!" he said aloud as he turned to leave the kitchen, his shoes in his hand. He was determined now to find out for certain. No matter what it took, he was going to know before long whether or not he and Rayne Walker shared the same bloodline!

In the bedroom, he quickly undressed and went into the adjoining bathroom. Maybe a long, hot shower would relax him enough for him to get a good night's sleep. His grandma Geneva had wangled a promise out of him to take her to church. Bright and early in the morning.

Rayne was grateful that Fernandina Beach, the nearest town with a hospital, wasn't a major city. They were in and out of the emergency room in under an hour. Her sprain wasn't serious. The doctor had bound it, and told her to keep it elevated for a few days. Once the pain was entirely gone, he said, she would be healed.

On the drive back to American Beach, her mom sat up front with her dad, and she had the backseat to herself. She sat with the injured leg comfortably stretched out on the seat.

"You two are pretty quiet," Rayne commented after a lull in the conversation.

Both her parents were, unbeknownst to her, in inner turmoil. Ever since she'd told them the man who'd rescued her was named Wade Jefferson, they'd been wondering how to proceed.

Ray knew from her description that Wade Jefferson was the son of Ben Jefferson. He and Wade had met at least four times in the past two years. He had stood in his house on two occasions, trying to convince him to sell his land to him. What Ray wanted to know was if Wade had planned the meeting, or if it was purely coincidental. He didn't put it past the Jeffersons to cook up some kind of convoluted scheme involving Rayne whose end result would be his signing over his property to them.

Julianne had also recognized Wade's name. She wished he could possibly be some other Wade Jefferson, but held out little hope of that.

"I'm just tired," Julianne said, sighing. "Getting into town, the get-together, then the stress of your getting hurt. I'm whipped!"

"I know," Rayne said sympathetically. "When we get home, I want you to go right to bed. You, too, Dad. I'm so sorry I wasn't watching where I was going and tripped on that branch."

"Accidents happen, honey," said her father. "I'm just glad that fellow was willing to help you when you got hurt. You could have had to sit out there on the beach until one of us found you. Never go anywhere without your cell phone from now on!"

"I won't," Rayne promised. She'd learned her lesson.

"What did you two talk about while he was carrying you back home?" Ray casually asked.

"It's funny," Rayne said. "It was so easy to talk to him. I found myself running my mouth about things I usually don't tell guys until I've known them for months. Like why I broke off my engagement."

"He asked you lots of questions, huh?"

"No, actually, I was the one asking most of the questions," Rayne said, laughing softly. "At one point he told me I obviously will say anything that comes into my head. That was after I asked him if he was gay."

"Rayne!" exclaimed her mother with a laugh. "Why would you ask a stranger something like that?"

"Because I wanted to know," their daughter said, unashamed. "Excuse *me,* but you don't meet a gorgeous man who's willing to cart your carcass across a beach every day.

If I were really bold, I would have gotten the digits, but I wasn't, especially in front of Shannon and Rick, so I asked if I'd see him next weekend, and he said he'd be on the beach."

"You mean you're going to meet him on the beach next Saturday night, and all you know about him is his *name?*" her mother cried. "And for all you know, that might not be his real name!"

"Mom, you didn't see him. Okay, I didn't really get a great look at him myself, but it was more than looks. He was kind and warm and funny. And when he picked me up, he was so gentle. I know this sounds like romantic drivel, but I have to see him again."

"Well, you won't be going anywhere on that ankle," Julianne told her. "Not by next Saturday."

"If I have to, I'll have Rick drive me in his buggy," her determined daughter replied.

Julianne turned to grimace at Ray as if to say, *Talk some sense into her!*

Ray gave it his best shot. "Sweetie, don't you think you're going a bit overboard? I mean, if he were truly interested in seeing you again, he would have given you his number. Men say a lot of things they don't mean. Some of us will tell a woman what we think she *wants* to hear. Do you understand me? Maybe he said he'd be there just to avoid hurting your feelings. After all, by your own admission, you were the one asking all the questions."

"Dad, I can tell when a man is lying to me, and he wasn't lying. He's just as interested in seeing me again as I am in seeing him."

She wasn't as confident as she sounded, though. A man who was interested *would* have given her her number. At least that's usually the way it was done. What's more, she thought she'd sensed a hesitancy on his part once they'd exchanged names. That was curious. Why would learning her name make a difference?

It was probably her overactive imagination.

"Stubborn!" her father said, exasperated. "Okay, go see him, but I'm going with you."

"Fine," Rayne said. "You can wait with Rick in the ATV."

Once they were home, Shannon helped Rayne into the house and was especially solicitous of her, even aiding her with her bath. Julianne and Ray took the opportunity to speak in private. They went into the kitchen, and Julianne put on a pot of coffee.

Ray sat on a bar stool at the breakfast nook, his face drawn. There were dark circles under his eyes. Concerned, Julianne peered at him. "Why don't you go on to bed? Coffee still doesn't keep you up, right? I'll bring you a cup after it finishes brewing. We'll talk then."

Ray solemnly shook his head. "No, this is serious. What if he suspects something and he's trying to get close to her? We should go ahead and tell her, Julie. We should tell her tonight."

"No, Ray, you should wait until you feel stronger. She's not going to take it well, believe me. Rayne is many things, levelheaded, smart, hardworking. But where you're concerned she's also very emotional. She's already having a hard time accepting your illness, and your decision not to have the operation. She might lose it! If you want to tell her soon, do it after church tomorrow. We'll go to church together, and get some spiritual strength first."

"She won't be able to go on that ankle."

"No, she'll have to stay home. But that's okay. You need the time away from her in order to think of how you want to put things. Ask God to help you, Ray."

He nodded his acquiescence. Then he pushed himself up

using the counter. "I think I *will* go to bed." He kissed her on the cheek. "I'll pass on the coffee."

"I can't come tuck you in?" Julianne joked.

"Oh, yes, come tuck me in," Ray said, his face showing some of the devilish delight it used to when he would tease her in the past. "But no coffee. Just bring your lovely self."

Wade hadn't been to church with his grandmother in a very long time. Years, in fact. It was just as he'd remembered. Geneva wore a white dress, hat and hose. Her outfit wouldn't be complete without her white pocketbook and white leather pumps.

Once they were at the church, she directed him where to sit in the multitiered edifice, and then she and several other elderly ladies in white went about the place ordering people to sit here or there, and brooking no disobedience. He actually saw one of them grab a teen boy by the collar and pull him to a seat in the back. He wondered what they would have done if the boy had become belligerent. Probably body-slam him into submission. Those were some tough little old ladies.

When the music of the processional began, his grandmother came to claim her seat beside him. She smiled angelically, opened her hymnal and started to sing, badly.

He joined her, singing loudly just like everyone else around him. What they lacked in harmony they more than made up for in enthusiasm and volume.

Several women turned around to briefly stare at him. He only smiled politely. The elderly ladies knew he was Geneva's grandson. The young women showed their interest with either a sweet smile or a discreet moistening of their plump lips.

With the latter, he would lower his gaze to his hymnal and pretend great interest in *Amazing Grace*. A couple of times, Geneva caught a cutie staring openly and nailed her with a razor-sharp glance. Blushing shamefully, she'd quickly turn around and give the pastor her full attention.

After the service, Geneva took great pleasure in introducing him to the pastor, the pastor's wife and their church pianist daughter, who was a tall, thin, plain woman with a degree in music. She was so shy she didn't once meet Wade's eyes.

Wade excused himself after a few minutes, saying he was going to the men's room.

Instead, he stepped outside for some fresh air. The church smelled like old books and perfume to him. The church grounds were neatly manicured, and palm trees dotted the lawn. Children darted back and forth, playing, laughing, releasing pent-up energy. He remembered how awful it had been having to sit for long periods when he was a child. He couldn't wait to get outside and stretch his muscles.

"Mr. Jefferson?"

He looked up and saw Ray Walker strolling toward him.

Both men wore summer suits. Ray's was charcoal gray, and Wade's was navy blue. Tall and broad-shouldered, they made striking figures, although, due to his illness, Ray's carriage wasn't quite as erect as it usually was.

"I wanted to thank you for helping my daughter last night," Ray said once he was within five feet of Wade. Wade noticed the dark circles under his eyes, how his movements were somehow measured, as if he were judging just how long his legs would hold up his body. He felt sympathy for this man whom his father considered an enemy.

"I couldn't leave her out there alone, it was getting ready to storm," he said.

"Not everybody would have done what you did," Ray insisted.

"Contrary to what you must think of me, I *am* a decent man!" Wade said. He didn't know why he was touchy all of a sudden. He hadn't sensed any ill will in Ray Walker's manner, or speech. Perhaps it was his secret knowledge that condemned him. He knew his father was out to ruin this man. If his father got his way, Ray Walker would lose his property *and* his daughter.

Wade didn't want to be a party to that.

"I apologize, I didn't mean to snap. Meeting your daughter was an accident. We just happened to be in the same part of the beach last night. After she learned who I was, it was obvious she'd never heard of me. But I recognized her name right away."

Since Wade was being forthcoming, Ray decided to lay his cards on the table, too.

"Rayne has nothing to do with what's going on between your father and me. Our animosity goes back years before Rayne was born."

"Yes, I know that. He said he stole your girl. Julianne, Rayne's mother."

"That's a lie," Ray told him matter-of-factly. "Your mother was the girl he stole from me. I went away to art school when I was nineteen, and your father swooped in and dazzled her. She was married to him when I got back in town. You were a newborn. Julianne was just somebody he amused himself with years later. I didn't even know Julianne until after she found out he was still married to your mother, and quit seeing him because she didn't want to be a kept woman. That's the truth, son. You can believe it if you want to."

It had the ring of truth. Wade was inclined to believe him. Besides, he was more prone to give Ray Walker the benefit of the doubt because now he wanted something from him in return for his faith. He wanted Ray Walker's trust.

"I believe you," he said quietly. "I believe you because I really need to distrust my father's veracity at this point." Ray looked puzzled, but Wade continued before he lost his nerve. "You see, my father told me something that I'm hoping is far from the truth."

Ray's eyes narrowed suspiciously. "Something about me?"

Wade shook his head in the negative. "Something about your daughter."

"What?"

Wade paused, thinking that his father was going to be livid because he was about to do just what his father had joked he might: he was going to ask Ray Walker, point-blank, if Rayne was really a Jefferson.

"Well, don't stop talking now!" Ray cried angrily.

"My father believes that Rayne is his daughter," Wade said.

Ray didn't say a word. An expression of sheer panic came into his eyes, and he stumbled weakly toward Wade. Wade had to catch him before he fell to the pavement. Guiding him to a nearby wooden bench on the grass, Wade said, "Forgive me, I shouldn't have put it so bluntly."

He eased the older man onto the bench and sat down beside him. "Maybe you should put your head between your knees."

Ray took a deep breath. His face was ashen, and his hands were trembling with outrage. But he insisted, "I'm all right."

He met Wade's eyes. "How long has he known?"

"I don't know for sure. He admitted it to me only a few days ago. I was as shocked as you are now. You see, I didn't believe he kept sending me to make an offer on your property simply because he wanted to own a piece of American Beach. I sensed there was more. Finally, he told me that he suspected Rayne was his daughter, and that he would not rest until he found out for certain."

Ray shook his head in disbelief. "He beat me to the punch again. Julianne and I haven't told her."

Wade frowned. "So, she doesn't know she has a brother?"

Ray looked up at him, his face tight with concern. "Yes, this changes both your lives, doesn't it? And if I know my daughter, and I do, she's not going to be happy that a man she's attracted to—"

"Oh, no!" Wade interrupted. "I was right. There was an instant attraction between us out there last night. This is like some Greek tragedy."

"Not a tragedy at all," Ray disagreed. "You learned the truth before tragic events could be set in motion."

Wade leaned forward with his elbows on his knees, and his face in the palms of his hands. He'd never burst into tears in his life, but he felt like doing it now. He told himself that the feelings he'd had for Rayne last night were because of their connection. He hadn't intellectually known she was his sister, but he'd felt drawn to her because of it. The only reason his body had reacted to hers was that he was male and she was female, and their respective hormones had kicked into gear. That was all. It was an honest reaction. Now that he knew she was his sister, the next time he saw her he would physically react to her in the manner a brother would toward a sister. And that's all there was to it. His brain would dictate to his body the proper way to respond to her.

"I'm sorry, son," Ray commiserated. "In the beginning, I left it all up to Julianne, who, I figured, should have the final say in the matter. And then, as the years passed, I grew to love Rayne so much I didn't want to lose her. I know it was selfish of me. Your father should have been told. Julianne was bitter after being lied to. She thought he didn't deserve to know he was a father. She thought that if he could deceive her the way that he did, he might not be good father material, so she chose me, and because I loved her and Rayne, I accepted the role. It wasn't fair to Rayne, or to you, or to your father."

"Life is rarely fair," Wade said, raising his head from his prostrate position to look into Ray's eyes. "If life were fair, Mom wouldn't have died so young."

"She was a wonderful woman," Ray told him. "She was the first woman I ever loved. I was going to ask her to marry me when I got back from art school. I guess I should have told her what I had in mind. Maybe she would have waited for me."

It seemed that both of them were locked in personal memories of Deirdre.

"After she had me, she found out that she couldn't have any more children," Wade said softly. "I used to feel so guilty, as if I'd done something to her insides when she'd had me. As if I'd somehow ruined her. Whenever I would tell her how sorry I was that she couldn't have any more babies, she'd take me in her arms and say, 'You're all I need, sweet boy. You're all I need.' Then she'd playfully thump me upside the head and say, 'Besides, you're a handful. God knew what He was doing when He gave me only you.'"

Ray laughed softly. "That sounds like Deirdre."

They laughed together, then sat up and looked at one another. A few minutes ago they'd been on opposites sides of the situation. Wade was nothing more than the son of his enemy. Ray was nothing more than a man Wade's father wanted to make pay for some past slight.

Now they shared a secret and much more: mutual respect.

"What's our next move?" Wade asked.

"You have the right to get to know your sister," Ray told him. "Julianne and I are going to tell Rayne the truth today. Rayne said that you told her you would meet her on the beach next Saturday night, is that right?"

Wade nodded. "Yeah, that was our plan."

"Then keep your word. Both of you will have six days to think about things. You're welcome at the house. Sound reasonable?"

Wade sighed. "I want to go to her right now."

"I know you do," Ray said. "But hopefully those confusing feelings you're having will have dissipated by Saturday." And he gave Wade such a knowing look that Wade had to lower his gaze.

"I would never have felt that way if I'd known who she was," he said in his defense. "I'm not a sexual deviant."

"I know you're not. You're just a man," Ray told him. "I've heard tell of men *marrying* their sisters before finding out the truth. Count yourself lucky."

At that moment, Wade didn't feel lucky. He felt bone weary. He did not relish going back to Atlanta. His father would be gloating in triumph, while he would be wondering if the next time he saw his sister he would desire her still.

Chapter 7

Rayne sat on the back deck at her father's house, marveling at the brilliant blue sky. After a stormy night, there was nary a cloud in the sky, and the breezes were soft and gentle. She longed to put on a swimsuit and go test the waters. If she weren't hobbled by a sprained ankle, she would be floating on her back in the Atlantic Ocean, right now, checking out God in His sky.

Everyone else had gone to church this morning. Even Shannon, who had protested that someone needed to stay with the cripple. Both her mother and her sister had nixed the idea. They knew that what she really wanted to do was feed her addiction to MTV. Today, she would be getting her "soul drug," as her mother referred to attending church.

Rayne was fine being alone. She had a tall glass of diet iced tea, the latest novel by Dean Koontz and a portable CD player tuned to her favorite local hip-hop station. Usher and Alicia Keys were singing a duet just for her.

The phone rang in the middle of the song, and she turned off the CD player and picked up the cordless phone from the patio table next to her. "Hello?"

"Rayne?"

"Daddy?"

Her caller laughed softly. "No, this is Wade Jefferson. Do I sound like your father?"

Rayne sat up in her chair. He didn't sound anything like her father now, but for a second there she could have sworn it was her dad.

"Of course not," she said, laughing softly. "I was just expecting my dad to call and check up on me, that's all."

"How are you?"

"I'm fine, really. The doctor says I should be back in fighting form in about a week."

"Good, I'm glad to hear it."

Rayne cleared her throat. "Not that I'm not pleased to hear from you, but how'd you get my number?"

"As it turns out," Wade said, "I know your father. You're going to find out before long anyway, my company tried to buy his property. We made him several offers. All of which he turned down."

"Then you're a developer," said Rayne.

"I am," Wade said with a soft sigh.

"You mean you knew who I was yesterday when we met?"

"No, not when we met. I knew after you told me your name."

"Why didn't you say anything?"

"Because I didn't think it was the right time. You were hurt, and needed to get to a doctor. It would have taken a while to explain."

"Yeah, I guess so," she said, conceding to the reasonableness of his statement.

"That would explain why you didn't ask for my number. You already had it."

"Listen, Rayne, I'm pressed for time but I wanted you to have my number in case you wanted to talk. I'm going back to Atlanta this afternoon, as soon as I take my grandma home following church services. I'm calling you from the church grounds. I just had a conversation with your father. A very *interesting* conversation."

Knowing how protective her father was, Rayne hoped he hadn't asked Wade if his intentions were honorable. "Oh, no," she cried. "He didn't interrogate you, did he?"

"We both had questions that we needed answers to," Wade told her quietly. He paused. "Do you have caller ID?"

Rayne glanced down at the display. "Yes, and your number's on it."

"Great. That's my cell's number. Use it, Rayne. I've got to go now, but I'll see you at around seven on Saturday at your father's house. No need for you to make that trek down the beach on your ankle. Is that okay with you?"

"That's fine," Rayne said, her voice husky.

"Goodbye, then." Wade's tone was tender.

"Bye." Rayne hung up the phone and placed it back on the tabletop. She couldn't help smiling. She was a little apprehensive about his having spoken with her father. And *their* conversation had left her with still more unanswered questions. Like, why hadn't her father mentioned last night that he knew Wade? But, overall, hearing from him had really brightened her day. He was thinking about her. He wanted to get it out in the open that he was a developer so that they would be starting their (dare she think it?) relationship in an honest way. She admired that.

She opened her book and began to read where she'd left off, a contented smile on her lips. She couldn't wait to tell her mother and sister that Wade had called while they were out. Her father probably wouldn't be thrilled to hear it, though.

Geneva waved Wade over. She and another elderly woman, also dressed entirely in white, were standing at the bottom of the church house's steps. Wade smiled as a vivid memory of that same lady grabbing him and giving him a big bear hug when he'd been a teen came to mind. He'd been engulfed in an ample bosom and a cloud of baby powder that wafted up out of her cleavage. She was Ray Walker's mother.

"You remember Mrs. Vivian Walker, don't you, baby?" Geneva asked.

Both his grandmother and Vivian Walker looked at him so expectantly that he would have said yes even if he hadn't remembered the tall, handsome woman. Her hair was silver like his grandmother's, but where Geneva's was short and curly, hers was long, thick and wavy. She wore it in a bun.

"Of course I do. How are you, Mrs. Walker? I just spoke with your son not ten minutes ago."

A surprised expression fleetingly crossed Vivian Walker's face. She masked it with a gorgeous smile as she stepped forward for her hug. "As handsome as ever," was her opinion of him. Wade hugged her back as generously. He was a man who appreciated a heartfelt hug when he got one.

Mrs. Walker held him at arm's length. "My, my, why hasn't some lucky girl gotten you down that aisle?"

"Unlucky in love, I guess," Wade joked.

"No, honey, you're just taking your time and waiting for the right woman. God'll send her to you when you least expect it." She looked at Geneva for confirmation.

Geneva nodded in the affirmative. "Mmm-hmm," she said. "That's how it works."

Geneva got on Wade's right side and took an arm while Vivian commandeered his left arm. "Come on, sugar," said Vivian. "The ladies have been cooking all night to get ready for today's dinner. You've got to try some of my sour cream pound cake."

"It's divine," his grandmother concurred.

He was practically kidnapped and taken to the church's adjoining dining hall where at least a dozen ladies wanted him to try their specialties.

An hour later, stuffed, and figuring if he were a camel all the food he'd eaten would hold him for at least a month, he emerged from the dining hall with his grandmother looking satisfied with his behavior. He always knew that Geneva put great store in what her friends thought of him, and therefore he was always respectful to them.

Pocketbook in hand, she led the way to the car. "Thank you, sweetheart. You made those ladies' hearts glad."

Wade put his hand over his own heart. "Then I can die happy."

Geneva laughed heartily. "Oh, a little bit of soul food ain't gonna hurt a big, strong boy like you."

She reached in her purse and retrieved something wrapped in aluminum foil. "Vivian cut you a big chunk of her sour cream pound cake to take with you. Don't you throw this out now. You eat every bit of it. Just not all at once."

Wade groaned, and Geneva broke into laughter again.

"Wash the dishes?" Shannon yelled. "But I washed the lunch dishes this afternoon!"

"And you'll wash every other dish your entire visit if you don't quit talking back to me," Julianne warned.

"But, Mom—" Shannon wailed.

"You wanna try me?" Julianne asked, then made the button-your-lip motion at her own mouth. "Not one more word."

Shannon went to say something, thought better of it, and then closed her mouth.

She got up and began clearing the dinner dishes.

Julianne turned her attention to Rayne. "Sweetie, would you join your dad and me on the back deck? We can watch the sun go down."

"Sure," Rayne said, grabbing her crutches that were leaning against an empty chair at the table. A nervous pain shot through her stomach. *This is it,* she thought.

She'd been mentally practicing how she would react to their news. Her initial reaction couldn't be over the top because then her father might get suspicious and start asking questions. On the other hand, she couldn't appear unaffected by the news, either.

Whatever she said or did after their admission, it had to be believable.

By the time she got to the deck, her mother and father were already seated: Julianne on the chaise longue, and her dad in a chair with his feet on a matching ottoman. They'd thoughtfully left her the sofa so that she could stretch her leg out on it.

Looking at the horizon that the setting sun seemed to be disappearing behind, Julianne sighed. "Beautiful," she said softly. "This is one of the things I miss most about American Beach, sitting on the porch at dusk, watching the sun go down and feeling the wind on my face."

Ray reached over and gently grasped her slender hand in his big one. "You can always move back if you miss it so much." His eyes held laughter in their depths, but Julianne knew he was serious.

"If you two want to be alone I can make myself scarce," Rayne said with a smile.

Ray released Julianne's hand and turned his gaze on his

daughter. "We, um, asked you to come out here because we have something important to tell you, sweetheart."

Rayne watched him intently. Perspiration had broken out on his forehead, and it wasn't very warm this evening, perhaps in the lower seventies. Her father normally thrived in warm weather.

She hadn't anticipated that having to tell her he wasn't her biological father would have a physical toll on him. She was having serious misgivings about going ahead with her performance if he were already in distress.

"Yes," said Julianne, picking up where Ray had left off. "We should have told you a long time ago, but it never seemed like the right time."

"It's my fault," Ray said. "After your mother and I split up, she felt so guilty for leaving me that she couldn't tell you. Then we let the years slip by, content in our separate roles. I loved you so much, I couldn't bear the thought of losing you."

"Losing me how?" Rayne asked and was surprised by the genuine emotions she was feeling at this moment, hearing the words from her father, feeling the anguish coming off him. This wasn't anything like the play she'd seen in her mind's eye.

Tears came to Ray's eyes. He was so choked up he couldn't continue.

"No, it's all my fault," cried Julianne, going to hug Ray. She looked at Rayne.

"Ray would have supported me whenever I decided the time was right to tell you."

Rayne could not bear to extend this scenario any further. "Tell me what?" she snapped.

Her mother narrowed her eyes at her as if to say, "I thought we were supposed to be acting?"

"Tell me what?" Rayne repeated in a calmer, more respectful tone.

"Honey, Ray is your father in every way that counts. He has done for you what any good father would have done. Cherished you from the day you were born, raised you with love and devotion. Please don't blame him for my mistake."

Rayne was suddenly frightened. What if she couldn't pull this off, and her father still refused to have the surgery? She steeled herself and said, "I won't. I won't blame anyone for anything. Just, please, tell me what's wrong. Why is Dad so upset?"

She'd never seen her father cry. Her heart was breaking. She inwardly chided herself for ever cooking up the idea of deceiving him. He deserved a much more virtuous daughter. But she was committed to seeing it through to the bitter end.

He needed that operation!

"Ray is not your biological father, Rayne," Julianne said at last. Tears were now rolling down her cheeks. "I was pregnant with you when I married Ray. Your father's name is Benjamin Jefferson. He was married at the time. I didn't know it until after I'd conceived you. I broke off with him, and I never told him I was expecting you."

This was Rayne's cue to act hurt and shocked by their revelation. She didn't have to summon up the hurt part. Watching her father sobbing while her mother held him was causing her a great deal of pain.

"What am I supposed to say to that?" she asked. "I don't believe a word of it."

"It's the truth, baby," Ray managed to say. "He's your father. For years we assumed he didn't know anything about you. But after yesterday we decided that we had to tell you before someone else told you."

Now Rayne was really confused. Who else had known the circumstances surrounding her birth except her grandma Layla, her mother, and her dad?

"Aunt Shirley knows?" she asked.

"Shirley suspects, but she doesn't have any proof," Ray said.

Julianne looked at him, surprised by that bit of information. "That woman hates me. Of course she'd think that."

"Mom?" Rayne said. "Can we stay on the subject? What happened yesterday to make you go ahead and tell me?"

"You met your brother," Ray said softly.

Rayne had heard him with a clarity that she'd never before known. It was a mind-blowing moment of self-realization that put everything that had happened since her confrontation with her mother in Brooklyn two weeks ago in perspective. Her mother had not told her the whole story. No, while she'd admitted that Ray Walker wasn't her biological father and a man named Benjamin Jefferson was, she'd neglected to tell her that she had a brother. Perhaps it was an honest omission on her mother's part. Julianne had been upset. She could have easily forgotten a pertinent fact or two, but this?

Rayne wanted to scream at her mother, *Why didn't you tell me I had a brother?* But she couldn't. If she did, her father would know that she'd had advance knowledge about her parentage.

"Wade Jefferson is my brother?" She didn't have to pretend to be shocked.

She turned her gaze on her father. "Is that what you and Wade talked about today?"

He nodded slowly. "He told me that his father knew about you. And that he would stop at nothing to prove that you're his daughter. After seeing how you felt about him, and seeing his reaction whenever I said your name, I thought it best to go ahead and inform him about the true nature of your relationship."

"Can't have us committing incest," Rayne said bitterly, as she reached for her crutches. She rose with some difficulty due to the state of mind she was in.

Her mother got up and went to help her. "Be careful, honey."

She glared at her mother. "I can do it!"

Julianne stopped in her tracks. "I'm sorry, Rayne."

Rayne finally got her crutches straight and began hobbling toward the door to go inside. "You're always sorry, Mom. If it's not one thing you're sorry about, it's another." She could barely see her mother for the tears in her eyes.

Ray got up with effort. "Rayne, don't put this all on your mother, I'm also responsible for keeping this a secret all these years."

Rayne carefully turned around to cut him with a glance. "And you! I know you said you're telling me this because you were afraid Wade or his dad would tell me first. But isn't it convenient that you've decided it's your time to die and *you* don't have to live with the consequences? That's the cowardly way out! If you were really sorry about this, you'd try to do everything within your power to stick around and see it through!"

She left them then. Shannon came up to her to ask if she was okay when she went through the kitchen on the way to her bedroom. But she didn't say a word when she saw her older sister's face. She simply put her arms around Rayne and helped her to her bedroom. Rayne hugged her tight, and let her.

Once in the bedroom, Rayne sat on the edge of the bed, tears still flowing freely. Shannon bent and removed her sandals, then encouraged Rayne to lie back. Shannon put a pillow below her injured leg so that the ankle would be elevated.

Throughout this, neither sister said a word.

Then Shannon asked, "Can I get you anything? A glass of water or a cup of tea? A soda?"

Rayne shook her head no. "Thanks. I just want to be alone."

"Okay," Shannon said softly. She left the room, closing the door behind her.

Rayne now knew why Wade had phoned her and given her

his cell phone number. Not because he'd had any romantic interest in her, but because he'd just found out she was his sister and figured she might need someone to talk to once the devastating news was laid on her. That's how she felt, as if some huge weight had been laid on her chest, and it was crushing her. She tried to reason that she'd just met him, and she shouldn't have put such hope in the possibility of a romantic relationship with him. She didn't normally react to men this way. Instant attraction wasn't even in her vocabulary until she'd met him yesterday. Was fate this facetious that it would send her someone she would have an instant rapport with, and then let him turn out to be her brother?

She pushed up on her elbows in bed. *Proof,* said her feverish mind. *I want proof!*

She picked up the phone that sat on her nightstand, leaned over, pressed the button on the caller ID that would display the number of the last person who'd phoned her, and dialed it. As the phone was ringing, she made a mental note to write the number in her address book later.

The display revealed that Wade had phoned her at 12:31 p.m. That was more than six hours ago. Depending on how fast he'd driven, he could be back in Atlanta by now.

Wade was, in fact, in a suburb of Atlanta. He'd gone straight to his father's house in a gated community. After being let in by a security guard at the gate, driving to his father's house and parking, he was sitting in his car, thinking.

This was madness. When his father had asked him to help him find out whether or not Rayne Walker was truly his daughter, he'd scoffed at the idea, thinking that the old man was just being nostalgic, hoping to regain some of the excitement he must have felt when he was seeing Rayne's mother, Julianne. Old men were known for living in the past. Wanting to recapture their youth. What better way did a man have of living forever than through his offspring? Yes, Ben Jefferson was going to be a happy man.

Rayne was wonderful. She was bright, funny, loyal. He knew all of that after only twenty-four hours. Any man would love to have her for a daughter. Any man would love to have her in his life, period. So, why was he sitting in his car depressed as hell? Feeling like he'd lost something special, something irreplaceable? Feeling like all hope had gone out of the world?

He put his hand on the door's handle, preparing to get out. He had to snap out of this. Even if she wasn't his sister, and she was just a woman he'd met on the beach, he shouldn't be this attached to her already. It didn't make sense that just the thought of her made him ache inside.

He got out of the car and locked it. His phone rang just as he stepped on to the walk that led to his father's front door. He glanced down at the pale green display. His heartbeat accelerated when he saw the name Raymond Walker.

Rayne, he thought with longing. He willed himself to calm down as he flipped the phone open and answered with, "Hi, how are you?"

Rayne had waited until she'd stopped crying to phone him. But now, with just the sound of his voice, more tears felt as if they were ready to fall at the slightest provocation. "I've been better," she said truthfully.

"Then your parents told you," he guessed.

"That you're my brother? Yes."

"Are you okay with it?"

"I don't know how I feel at this point. It's too new. You've apparently had a longer time to think about it. How do you feel about it?"

"Frankly, I'm pissed. There's no use lying to you, Rayne.

Last night on the beach, before you told me your name, I thought we'd made a connection. The kind of connection brothers and sisters are not supposed to make. Was I right about that?"

Rayne took a few seconds to reply. She felt they might be crossing the line, talking about what could have been if they were not brother and sister. But she also thought they needed to be honest with each other if they were going to build any kind of a lasting relationship.

"Yes, you're right. You're the first guy I've been attracted to in a long time."

"My feelings, exactly," he told her. "I work so hard my love life is nearly nonexistent. But with you I immediately felt comfortable. Excited by the prospect, if you know what I mean."

"I do," she told him. "Listen, this isn't getting us anywhere. And, anyway, if the DNA tests are negative, we will not have even needed to have this conversation."

"DNA tests?"

"I want proof that you're my brother, Wade Jefferson. I won't accept anything less."

Wade smiled broadly. She was his kind of woman. Show her, without a shadow of a doubt, that what you say is true; otherwise get out of her face. Besides, her request had given him his second wind. There was still a chance that she wasn't really his sister. Could Julianne be mistaken about Rayne's paternity? He hated to suggest it, but perhaps his father wasn't the only man Julianne was sleeping with at the time she got pregnant with Rayne. It could happen.

He didn't suggest it to Rayne, though. "I'm outside my father's house now," he told her. "I'll tell him what's happened so far, and then tell him you'd like to be tested to make sure."

She sighed. "Okay, great. Call me later to tell me how it went."

"He might want to tell you himself. Are you up to that?"

"Yes," she said without hesitation. "The sooner we get this over with the better." She must have thought her tone might have sounded insulting to his father, because she added, "I'm sure your father is a wonderful man, Wade. I'm just hoping against hope that you and I are not related by blood. You understand?"

Wade was standing outside on his father's walk, getting turned on by the sound of her voice. "Yes, I understand," he told her. "I'm going inside now. Talk with you later."

"Okay, bye," Rayne said.

Wade closed the cell phone and continued up the walk. If it turned out he *was* her brother he would have to go to a certified hypnotist in order to be hypnotized so that his body would have no reaction to her voice, her body or the very thought of her.

Chapter 8

Ray lay in bed in his darkened bedroom, staring into space. He was remembering when Dr. Kimble had given him the results of the biopsy: he had cancer, but Dr. Kimble was optimistic. Ray was only fifty-four. He was strong and healthy otherwise; plus the cancer was in the early stages of its growth.

He stood there smiling, as if he were giving Ray good news.

Ray had done his homework. He'd gone to the library and checked out every book on prostate cancer that he could find. He'd surfed the Internet, looking for alternative treatments that Dr. Kimble might have neglected to mention.

So, when Dr. Kimble said the word *surgery,* Ray was armed with questions.

"Are you talking about a radical retropubic prostatectomy?" he asked, pleased with himself for even being able to pronounce the unfamiliar words.

"No, I'm talking about a newer version of the technique

called nerve-sparing radical retropubic prostatectomy," Dr. Kimble said, still smiling like a mailman delivering a big tax return check. "This way, there is less of a chance of your becoming impotent following surgery. I'm sure that's a consideration."

"Is Florida a swamp?" said Ray.

Dr. Kimble had felt free enough to laugh out loud then, but abruptly stopped after meeting Ray's eyes and realizing that Ray was dead serious.

"No matter how careful you are, there is still the chance I'd be rendered a eunuch, am I right?" Ray asked.

"A eunuch?" Dr. Kimble laughed nervously. "Ray, I'm not going to castrate you. I'm trying to save your life!"

"I read that someone in my condition can sort of keep an eye on the growth, and have the surgery later on."

"You'd be playing Russian roulette," Dr. Kimble said. "The best thing to do is to get rid of the cancer as soon as possible and not give it a chance to spread. What are you hoping to gain, Ray? A few more years of sexual pleasure in place of good health and a longer life? Don't be a fool, man. Have the surgery now."

"I'm going to pass, Doctor," Ray told him. "I've still got some living to do."

"Ray, you're already having difficulty urinating. That pain you have is going to get worse and worse. You'll lose weight and your energy level will decrease. Do you really want to live with those symptoms when you could be cancer-free and get back to being a normal, healthy man?"

"Doctor, no man in his right mind can describe himself as a normal, healthy man if he can't get an erection. I'm just stating the plain truth."

"Promise me you'll give it more thought. Your sister cornered me in the waiting room after your biopsy and asked all kinds of questions. She told me how stubborn you were, but I didn't want to believe her. Don't you trust my skills as a surgeon? I would not tell you I could do something if I were incapable of doing it, Ray."

"I know you're a good surgeon," Ray said honestly. "But I'm still going to have to pass."

A few hours ago, his daughter had called him a coward. *Him!* The man who had hung up his tool belt and taken on the art world when those around him were telling him he should stick with the work that brought in a steady income. He'd shown them that when you did something you loved, the money followed. That took bravery, didn't it?

And his choosing to forgo the surgery and, instead, live his life to the fullest *right now* had taken courage. Why was he allowing Rayne's words to get to him? It was his damned life to do with as he wished!

She was hurt, that's why she'd lashed out at him. Hurt and confused. He'd expected her to be angry at him and Julianne. He had not seen that coward comment coming though. Rayne had always thought he was the bravest man who ever lived. She adored him and told him so on numerous occasions. Perhaps that was why her comment was riding him, making him think too much about his decision not to have the surgery. Was she right? Was he taking the easy way out? The way Shirley saw it, if he didn't have the surgery he'd be dead inside of a year. Dr. Kimble said he couldn't predict how long he'd last without the surgery. He personally thought he could live well for years to come without it, but it was true that the painful urination and the lack of energy bothered him. He used to enjoy perfect health. Would roll out of bed and go jogging at five in the morning. Now, most days, all he wanted to do was lie in bed an extra hour or two, and then drag himself to his studio to paint while the light was good.

If he were being honest with himself, he would admit it was a half-assed existence.

He sat up, swung his long legs off the bed and stood. Wearing only his pajama bottoms, he went and stood in front of the full-length mirror attached to the back of the closet door. His musculature was still taut due to his former exercise regimen of jogging and weight lifting. His belly was flat because he was not a man who did anything excessively, drinking alcohol or overeating.

He stared intently into his face. How had cancer invaded his body when he thought he'd been doing everything right? He'd quit smoking when he was in his twenties, seeing no sense in it. He drank socially, especially with his buddies on poker night or down at the club where he and his old friends met to catch up with each others' lives and toss back a few while they were laughing at how old they were getting and how the women in their lives were either making them crazy or giving them such good loving that they really didn't care about the other hassles. Lots of lies got told. Lots of lies got refuted.

He had to admit, drinking alcohol had never done anyone in his family any good. Perhaps the Walkers were cursed with weakened immune systems when it came to alcohol. He didn't really know if the alcohol had anything to do with his condition. Researchers didn't know exactly what caused prostate cancer. They did, however, agree that African-American males had a higher incidence of the disease and should start being tested for it as early as forty-five.

Ray couldn't change the fact that he was a black male, but he could stop drinking, which might be exacerbating his condition. He hadn't had a drink since the biopsy came back positive.

Grabbing his pajama top from the hook on the back of the closet door, he slipped it on and left the bedroom, padding softly down the hall until he arrived at the door of Julianne's room. It was nearly four in the morning and he knew she was sound asleep.

He knocked as quietly as possible and waited. After a few moments, she came to the door and cracked it. He breathed in the scent of her warm skin and the body wash she'd used in her shower.

Her short hair was sticking up on her head, and her brown eyes were dreamy with sleep. "Ray," she said, her tone so sexy that Ray's body reacted immediately and urgently.

She pulled the door open farther and he saw that she was wearing one of those short, nearly sheer gowns she loved so much. Sleeveless and scoop-necked, it was made of the thinnest cotton fabric he'd ever seen. She had a dancer's legs, trim yet muscular, the muscles elongated and elegantly formed.

"Come in," she said, and took a step backward.

Ray went in and shut and locked the door. His back was against it as he looked into her upturned face. "I've decided to have the operation. But I need to know what it's like to hold you again before I do. Would you mind if I slept in here with you tonight?" He was suddenly nervous. "Just to hold you."

Julianne reached up and silenced him with a finger pressed to his lips. "Shh, honey. I'm glad you're here. I was feeling kind of lost in that big bed."

She tiptoed and met his mouth in a tender kiss. Some things never changed. Ray Walker was still the best kisser she'd ever had the good fortune to lock lips with.

The next morning, Rayne got up before the rest of the household and went ahead and started preparing breakfast. She'd mastered the crutches by now, and could get around with just one of them.

She was getting a carton of eggs from the refrigerator when her dad came into the kitchen, barefooted and wearing a robe over his pajamas. Rayne had earlier opened the curtains at the bay window that offered a great view of the beach, and when she glanced up at him the sunlight gave his curly brown hair red highlights.

"Good morning," he said cautiously.

Rayne laughed shortly, set the carton on the counter and reached above the sink for a bowl to whip the eggs in. "Don't worry, I'm not still angry at you. I realize that you and Mom were doing what you thought was best for me."

Ray was busy pouring himself a glass of orange juice. "It's good to know that you got some of your mother's acting talent." He gave her an enigmatic smile.

Rayne set the bowl on the counter next to the carton of eggs and turned to look her dad in the eyes. He drank the orange juice as the crinkles around his eyes became more marked. He was definitely enjoying this moment.

Rayne's brows drew together in a deep frown. He was laughing at her! "Somebody's been spilling her guts!" She realized her mother had told him *everything*.

Ray put the empty orange juice glass in the sink. "Don't get bent out of shape, sweetie. Your mother only told me after I'd agreed to have the operation, so you got your point across. I've been a selfish horse's ass."

Rayne forgot her anger in an instant, and fell into her father's open arms. It was an awkward hug, with her leaning on a crutch, but it was a satisfying one. "I'm so relieved! If I could, I'd dance around this kitchen, you've made me so happy!"

She beamed up at him. "When are you going to schedule the operation?"

"There's no time like the present," he said, smiling.

Rayne was ecstatic. It was Monday morning. His doctor's office would be open.

"You can phone now!"

"After breakfast," Ray said. "Promise."

Rayne's head was on his chest. She sighed contentedly. "All right. I'm going to stop being pushy from now on. After breakfast is just fine."

Ray laughed and planted a kiss on the top of her head. "You? Stop being pushy? I won't live to see the day!"

Rayne straightened to peer into his eyes. "But you *will* live to see me walk down the aisle with some hunk. And you *will* live to see your first, second and third grandchild. That's what counts."

"You're gonna make me a grandpa three times over, huh? All I've got to say is I hope they take after their father, whoever he'll be, and not their mother, who was the hardheadedest—"

"I don't even think that's a word," Rayne interrupted.

"—little daredevil this neighborhood ever saw!" Ray finished with relish.

"No," said Rayne. "They're going to be just like me, and I'm going to send them to stay with you every summer!" She kissed his cheek. "Now sit down while I get breakfast on. I've got some things to tell you."

Ray obeyed, releasing her and going over to the breakfast nook to sit on one of the stools. "Go ahead, I'm all ears."

Rayne talked as she got the link sausages from the refrigerator and put several in a cast-iron skillet to cook on low. "I told you that Wade phoned yesterday to give me his number in case I needed to get in touch with him."

"Yes." Ray appeared anxious for her to continue.

"Well, I phoned him last night and told him I wanted a DNA test done on me and his father. He was at his father's house when he got my call, so he told me he'd give him the news and call me back. A few minutes later, his dad phoned and I spoke with him." She poured grits into a pot, added twice as much water, swirled the contents around, poured off the debris that came out of the grits, replaced the water then added a little salt and margarine.

Looking up at her father, she went on. "He cried."

Ray could tell she'd been disturbed by Ben Jefferson's display of emotions. "Honey, of course he cried. Any parent would upon hearing the voice of his child for the first time." Why was he defending his enemy? All he knew was, after more than thirty years it was time to put aside animosities for the good of Rayne. Rayne was what mattered here, not his opinion of Ben Jefferson.

"I felt peculiar standing there with the phone to my ear, listening to a stranger weep, when I felt nothing except curiosity." Having put the sausages and the grits on to cook, she began cracking eggs into the glass bowl for scrambled eggs. "Is something wrong with me, Dad? Because I didn't feel love or even hate for him."

Her eyes pleaded with him for reassurance.

"Baby, first of all, this was thrust upon you. Your mother told me about the letter from your grandma Layla. How you held on to it for five years before confronting her with it. You did that because you didn't want to face this. Or, if you had to face it, you wanted to face it on your own terms. You did that when you gave your mother the letter to read. But this is different. You didn't have five years to get used to the idea that you might have a brother out there somewhere. Plus the fact that you and Wade are obviously attracted to each other…"

"Dad, I don't want to talk about that. I'm trying to forget it."

Ray shook his head. "There's no forgetting it. He's your brother, and you're going to have to either face it or see him as little as you possibly can. I'm afraid that those are your options, Rayne. A DNA test would be a waste of time because, if I'm not mistaken, your mother was a virgin before she was seduced by your father. Think of the statement you'd be making if you went ahead with a DNA test. You'd be saying you don't believe your mother knows whom she's slept with. Your mother never slept around, Rayne. She's always been a one-man woman."

Rayne stopped whisking the eggs to turn to stare at her father. "You're right. In my rush to prove that Wade isn't my brother, I hadn't realized what asking for a DNA test would mean." She blew air between her lips and leaned against the counter for support instead of her crutch. She felt as if things were hopeless now, and she was fresh out of bright ideas. She couldn't insult her mother by demanding a DNA test.

After the four of them had breakfast, and Rayne had helped a grumbling Shannon with the dishes, she went to the back deck to phone Wade.

It was another beautiful day, the temperature was still in the low sixties, but the weatherman had said the high would reach the midseventies. It wasn't noon yet. There was a nice breeze coming off the Atlantic.

Rayne settled on the chaise longue, which was perfect for stretching her legs out on, and dialed Wade's number. He didn't answer, so she left a message.

"Hi, this is Rayne. About the DNA test, it's a no-go. I didn't realize that asking for a test would be like saying my mother doesn't know whom she's slept with. I can't do that to her. Your father wanted to know whether I wanted to come to Atlanta to do the test, or whether he should come here. I won't be able to travel for a few days yet, but I think I should come there to meet him. No test, just a meeting, okay? I'll make travel arrangements as soon as you get back to me with a date when your father can give me a few hours of his time. Talk with you later."

She hung up. She realized she'd referred to Ben Jefferson as "your father" the entire time she'd been speaking. She didn't know *what* to call him. "Dad" was taken by Ray Walker.

Wade was returning from a hearing at the courthouse when his cell phone beeped, denoting that he had a message. He flipped the phone open and listened to Rayne's message as he crossed the street to the parking garage. He found it more convenient to drive in the city than to take public transportation, even though parking could be a hassle.

He was not surprised that Rayne had decided against the DNA test. He knew it would be tricky. That's why he hadn't pressed the point with her last night. He wanted, more than anything, for her mother to be wrong about his father also being Rayne's father. But to suggest that Julianne didn't know whom she'd slept with would be tantamount to labeling her a loose woman, and that was no way to start a relationship with his sister.

Sister! He didn't think he'd ever get used to the idea of Rayne being his sister.

Why did fate have to throw them together like that? It made no sense. It made him think that maybe there was no great Creator up there watching over His children, gently guiding them and keeping them out of harm's way. That maybe his grandmother's faith in God was unwarranted. What kind of God would create a mess like this?

And if prayers worked, why had the sound of her voice made his heartbeat quicken and a part of his body harden? He'd been praying nearly continually the past two days. *Please, God, help me to feel absolutely nothing but brotherly feelings for her. If you see fit to answer my prayer, I promise I'll seriously seek a wife and get married and give Grandma Geneva some grandbabies like she's been bugging me to do for the past five years. Amen.*

Behind the wheel of the SUV, he started it and turned on the air. He sat for a minute or two, thinking, before he dialed his father's number. Ever since he'd told him that it appeared that Rayne was, indeed, his daughter, his father had been as high as a kite. Intoxicated on life. Wade wanted to be excited right alongside him, but although he was happy for him, he could not help being disappointed by the turn of events. He tried not to let it show when he was in his father's presence.

"Hey, son, how're you doing today?" Ben was smiling. Wade could hear it in his voice.

"I'm fine, Dad. And you?"

"I couldn't be better! She has a Web site. Did you know that? My baby girl is a businesswoman, a savvy business-woman. You know she got that from me! Ray and Julianne are both artists. Ray paints, and Julianne is an actress. She had to get her business sense from me." He was talking so fast Wade could barely follow him. "Why didn't you tell me she was so gorgeous? She looks like her mother, but that's my chin. She's got the dimple. You didn't even get the dimple," he crowed.

"Listen, Dad," Wade said evenly. "Rayne phoned a few minutes ago. She says the DNA test is off. She doesn't want to upset her mother—"

"That test would have been a waste of time anyway," Ben said. "I was Julianne's first. She told me so."

Wade felt a little uncomfortable listening to details from his father's affair. His first loyalty was to his mother. "I don't want to hear that," he said. "If you could have kept your pants zipped, we wouldn't be having this conversation. I phoned because Rayne wants to know when she can come for a visit. She wants to meet you. But it won't be for a few days because she needs time for her ankle to heal. When should I tell her she can come?"

"She can come any time she wants to. I'll cancel everything for her," his father said. "Why didn't she simply phone me directly? I gave her my number."

"She's going to need time to feel comfortable doing that," Wade said. "Give her time. I suppose you'll want her to stay with you?"

"Of course," Ben said. "Tell her she's welcome to stay as long as she wants."

"Okay, I'll tell her," said Wade. "By the way, the annexation was rejected. The vote was three-to-two not to annex the site. That means no commercial development in the West Pine area."

"You win some, you lose some," said his father.

Wade knew his father was a changed man then. Before Rayne came into his life, a lost chance to make more money was not taken in stride.

"I'm only going to stay two or three days at the most," Rayne said as she hugged her father goodbye at the airport in Jacksonville. Her father released her, and then she was enveloped in her mother's arms. "I'll be back in plenty of time for the operation," she whispered in her ear. She bent and kissed her cheek. "Take care of him."

Shannon stood on the side, back in her I-ain't-with-that mood and against public displays of affection. Rayne hugged her anyway. Then she took a step back and looked at them all, her little family. "Well," she said, "let me go and get this over with."

It was no secret she wasn't looking forward to meeting Ben Jefferson. She was even more apprehensive about seeing Wade again. It had been more than a week since he'd told her that his father would be glad to see her whenever she arrived in Atlanta. She had purposefully not phoned him since then. She was not happy that he had chosen not to phone *her,* too. But she assumed he was attempting to do what she was attempting to do: namely, to get over any romantic notions that were still floating around in their systems.

With a final wave to her family, she went and joined the moving line of passengers boarding the plane.

Wade had been relieved when his father told him that Rayne had phoned him to say that she would be arriving on Thursday and planned to stay with him until Sunday. He would pick her up at the airport. He let Wade know that he was welcome to come spend the weekend with them. Wade told him that he had plans for the weekend, but he wished them a happy visit. Whereupon, his father asked him to at least drop by the house on Saturday evening when he was having a few close friends over to introduce them to Rayne. Wade expressed concern that it might be too early to be throwing parties and perhaps that time would be better spent simply getting to know Rayne.

His father refused to listen to him.

Rayne didn't have to look around the terminal for her father. He had a chauffeur standing just outside her carrier, holding a sign with her name on it. When she walked up to the chauffeur and identified herself, a well-dressed gentleman rose from one of the seats in the waiting area and slowly walked over to her.

Rayne watched him as he walked toward her. He was a couple of inches taller than she was, trim, brown-skinned with a thick black mustache and thick, short, black curly hair. Her eyes lowered to his chin. No one in her family had that dimple except her. When she was a little girl, she'd spent many hours putting her finger in it, wishing the cursed thing would disappear. It had taken her years to come to terms with it, and accept that instead of something to despise, it made her unique.

"Welcome to Atlanta, Rayne," he said, his voice deep and warm.

"Thank you," she said. She knew she was staring, but he would just have to forgive her. He looked at the uniformed chauffeur.

"Mac, take my daughter's bags, would you?" he said.

The young brother quickly complied. Rayne was left holding only her shoulder bag.

Ben Jefferson took her elbow in his big hand and directed her toward the exit. "This way, my dear."

At his touch, Rayne suddenly found her voice. "You've got the curse, too."

Ben chuckled briefly. "You mean the hole in my chin? I didn't like it when I was a kid, either. But when I got in my teens I found out the girls thought it was cute. I haven't had a problem with it since then."

Rayne laughed softly. "It wasn't until I went to college that I stopped wishing it would go away. Boys thought it was attractive, too."

"Unfortunately, you could never be a criminal," Ben joked. "With that chin, you'd be identified by even the worst of witnesses."

Rayne relaxed. She didn't know what she had expected. Certainly not that he would have her laughing within five minutes of their meeting each other.

Soon, they were seated in the back of the limousine and cruising down the highway en route to her father's house. "I had your room redecorated. I'm afraid my tastes run to the masculine, but I had my decorator come in and make it more feminine. I hope you like it. And I have not made any plans whatsoever, except for a little soiree Saturday evening. But I'll cancel that if you'd prefer to just let this long weekend be about the two of us getting to know one another without the intrusion of anyone else."

He paused, realizing he was monopolizing the conversation.

Rayne smiled at him. "I'm still adjusting to the fact that we look alike."

"I'm sorry," he said. "I'm so used to taking charge that it didn't occur to me to ask you if you wouldn't mind meeting a few of my close friends this Saturday evening."

"No, no, I don't mind meeting your friends," Rayne told him sincerely. "The problem is, I didn't bring any evening clothing. Only casual clothes."

"That's no problem," Ben assured her, a happy light in his eyes. "It would give me great pleasure to treat you to a shopping spree, my dear."

He promptly ordered the chauffeur to take them to the most exclusive shopping mall in Atlanta.

"No, really, you don't have to do that," Rayne said. "I can afford to buy my own clothes."

"Get used to being spoiled, Rayne," Ben said with a smile. "I've got a lot of time to make up for."

Chapter 9

Rayne thought it was kind of strange that their first activity together was a shopping trip. However, Ben seemed so jazzed by the notion that she soon loosened up. He instructed Mac to pull up to the entrance to the mall and then he got out, reached for Rayne's hand and helped her out of the car.

He glanced at his watch. "Mac, it's two-fifteen now. Come back for us in two hours."

Mac gave him a curt nod and pulled away from the curb.

Ben took Rayne's left hand and put it through his arm in a courtly manner. "This is going to be fun," he said, smiling down at her. "I haven't taken a woman shopping in ages."

Their first stop was an exclusive clothing store where the saleswomen were so solicitous that Rayne didn't even have to ask for assistance, someone was always nearby and eager to help. It was a far cry from the stores where she usually shopped.

Ben, who was having a private chat with one of the saleswomen, did not follow her around as she checked out the shop's merchandise, for which she was grateful.

She spent several minutes looking at cocktail dresses, all of them too expensive for her to seriously consider buying. There were some rare beauties here, though.

She lingered so long with a little black dress by Oscar de la Renta that the salesperson who'd been in private conference with her father came over and said, "You won't know for sure until you try it on." She picked up the size ten. "Your size, yes?"

She had a good eye. Rayne smiled. "Yes, but I don't think—"

Lowering her voice so that only Rayne could hear her, the salesperson said, "Honey, if my sugar daddy wanted to treat me to anything I wanted, I'd let him."

Rayne didn't know why the woman's comment irked her so much. But it did. "Listen, you've got the wrong idea. He's not my boyfriend, he's my father."

It was the first time she'd said that. To anyone!

"Seriously?" asked the salesperson, an African-American woman in her early forties. She eyed Ben with interest. "He's very good-looking. A wonderful dresser, too."

"Yes, seriously," Rayne said.

"Please forgive me," said the woman sincerely.

"No harm done," Rayne said. She reached for the dress the woman was holding. "Point me to your dressing rooms."

"I'll do better than that, I'll take you to them," the salesperson said happily. Rayne kept trying to read her name tag, but her long auburn hair was covering it.

"You're going to love this," she said as she escorted Rayne across the room. "You've got just the curvy body to fill it out."

A few minutes later, Rayne was admiring her reflection in the mirror in the dressing room, which, she was happy to note, didn't make her look distorted like a funhouse mirror, but showed exactly how she looked. The sleeveless wrap dress fit her perfectly. It clung to her curves, but wasn't too tight, and revealed only a glimpse of cleavage. Smart, and sophisticated, it could be worn at any black-tie affair from a wedding to an intimate dinner party. She knew she'd get a lot of use out of it, a selling point she always looked for when buying clothing. She was very money-conscious. It came from being raised by parents who had rarely spent money frivolously.

She glanced down at her brown ankle boots. Her jeans had covered them. They certainly didn't go with the dress.

The salesperson who was helping her came to stand on the outside of her dressing room. "Your father wants to see you in these," she said, handing Rayne a thick bundle of dresses.

Rayne laughed shortly. "He does? Well, I'm not doing a fashion show in these boots."

The salesperson tossed her locks behind her, and Rayne could finally see that her nametag read Jenay. Jenay frowned at her boots. "No problem. What size are you, a nine? You tall gals are hard to judge sometimes." She was a neat, petite woman who was probably just above five feet tall, and a hundred pounds soaking wet.

"Nine and a half," Rayne told her. "I can't abide tight shoes."

"Oh, I hear you," said Jenay. "I have the cutest pair of black sling-backs in mind that are going to be perfect for you."

She left, and while she was gone, Rayne hung the dresses up. There were seven of them in various shades and styles. All of them in size ten. She wouldn't have put it past Ben Jefferson to tell the saleswoman, "Take her every size ten dress you have in the store." She couldn't imagine him picking out the dresses himself. Unlike her father, who used to take her shopping for school clothes, and chose several outfits for her. Over the years, he'd learned what style of clothing she enjoyed wearing, and which styles she would not put on her body.

Rayne held a white clingy knit dress against her and looked at her reflection in the mirror. She knew she wasn't being fair to Ben Jefferson, comparing him to her father. She would have to watch that. She wasn't here to find fault with him, but to get to know him.

Jenay returned smiling triumphantly, a shoe box in her hands. She handed Rayne the box and a pair of panty hose: cinnamon brown and sheer. "If you're like me," she said, "you don't like putting on dress clothing without your hose."

"Thank you," said Rayne, smiling warmly. *Talk about good service!*

"You're welcome," Jenay said, turning to leave. "Yell if you need anything."

A few minutes later, Rayne walked out of the dressing room wearing the black Oscar de la Renta dress. Ben was sitting regally on a chair, Jenay at his side. She was showing him several pairs of shoes that would match the dresses he'd sent in to Rayne.

Ben quickly got to his feet when he saw Rayne standing there, and his heart thudded in his chest. It was as if time had rewound, and he was gazing upon her mother, Julianne. Mounds of blue-black, wavy hair falling down her back, beautiful brown skin that glowed with health, those big brown eyes, that cute nose of hers and the full-lipped mouth. He and Julianne certainly had made a fine-looking child together.

He went to her, took her hand and spun her around slowly. "You look beautiful."

Rayne smiled at him. "Thank you, it's my favorite of all the rest."

"Nonsense," said Ben. "We're just getting started." He glanced back to where he'd left Jenay. "Jenay, my dear, you may be able to retire on your commission once we're through."

Jenay beamed her pleasure.

Ben turned Rayne around and pointed her in the direction of the dressing rooms. "Go try on something else, sweetheart. Put on the red one. It's just right for the Manhattan nightlife. Don't those New York fellas take you to fine restaurants and elegant nightspots?"

He had a rich southern accent that crazily reminded Rayne of Clark Gable's in *Gone With the Wind. Must be that mustache,* she thought, as she went back into the dressing room.

And so it went for the next hour. She would go change into another dress, her second father would rave about how gorgeous she looked in it, and insist on buying it for her, with accessories, of course.

Rayne had to put her foot down at dress number five.

"That's it," she cried as she stood before him in a white tank dress and matching cardigan by Tashia of London. "Thank you, you've been more than generous. But you've already convinced me to accept more than I intended to." She gave Jenay a sympathetic look. "Please ring us up, Jenay."

Jenay, who hadn't had such a good sales day since she'd started working at the shop, was more than pleased to total the bill. She knew her commission would be several hundred dollars. She, however, looked to Ben for his go-ahead.

He reluctantly nodded. "All five pairs of the shoes, too."

Jenay's smile broadened considerably.

Rayne went to protest, but Ben silenced her with a raised hand. "I agreed to end the shopping spree here, but you must allow me to end it in my own way."

Rayne closed her mouth and went to change out of the Tashia of London dress. She didn't even know who Tashia of London was!

At the register, Rayne purposely avoided looking at the

receipt. Her second father, for that's what she'd decided to call
him in her thoughts, if not to his face, folded it and shoved it
in his wallet without an expression of shock or wonder that
would give away the massive amount he'd just spent on her. It
was a given that it was a huge amount. She had seen the price
tags on the dresses, none of which was lower than five hundred
dollars.

She had no idea how much the shoes cost.

Both she and her second father were loaded down with
bags as they left the shop.

"Y'all come back, now, you hear!" called an elated Jenay.

"Girl, if I never see *you* again, it'll be too soon," Rayne
joked, to which Jenay laughed heartily.

Her second father threw back his head and bellowed
with laughter.

Rayne smiled at him. He seemed to be having a blast.

They stood outside the dress shop getting their bearings as
other shoppers walked around them in the crowded mall.
"Where to next?" asked Ben. "We have a good thirty minutes
before Mac is supposed to pick us up."

"Why don't we find some place to sit and talk?" Rayne
suggested.

They decided on a Chinese restaurant in the food court
where they went to the counter and bought cups of tea, then
sat down, either leaning the packages against their chairs or
putting them under the small, round table.

Back in her jeans, layered T-shirts—bright orange underneath and turquoise on top—Rayne felt comfortable again.
She crossed her legs and relaxed. "Mom told me that you were
married."

Their eyes met. Ben lowered his first, and took a sip of his
tea. "I *was* married when I met your mother. My wife, Deirdre,
Wade's mother, died when he was eight. Cancer killed her."

"I'm sorry."

He raised his gaze to hers. "Your mom and dad didn't tell you anything about me?"

"Just the basics," she said softly. "I think they wanted me to form my own opinion of you and not have it colored by theirs."

"That was very kind of them considering that I'm the bad guy in all of this. I was married, and relentlessly pursued your mother. I conveniently omitted the fact that I was married. She found out by accident. There was a special event at Deirdre's mother's church, and we, Deirdre, Wade and I, went as a family. A friend of Julianne's invited her to church that Sunday. Deirdre's mother proudly got up to introduce her daughter, her husband and their son, and Julianne recognized me right away. As luck would have it, I turned around and looked directly in her face when the announcement was made. I'll never forget the shocked expression on her face. And all I could do was stand there unable to do anything except smile politely when the church welcomed us with applause.

"That summer was the worst of my life. We'd found out that Deirdre was dying of ovarian cancer and I'd gone slightly crazy and started pursuing an eighteen-year-old girl. I'm not going to lie to you and tell you I didn't love my wife, because I did. I loved her with all my heart, and still I could not get Julianne out of my blood. When Deirdre died, I was mourning twice over. For Deirdre and for Julianne, who never spoke to me again. I'd lost both of them, and I've never loved another woman the way that I loved them." He stopped talking and drank his tea in silence.

Rayne had nothing to say. What he'd said had the ring of truth. Could someone love two people at the same time? Yes, of course. Should they? Probably not, someone was bound to get the short end of the stick. In their case, all three of them had lost something.

"I can't sit in judgment about what you did in the past. It happened, it's over, and no one can change that," she said. "From what Mom told me, she never told you that she was pregnant."

"No, she didn't, but I can understand why she didn't. She probably thought I'd do what most married men would have done, tell her to get an abortion, give her some hush money, and send her on her way. To Julianne, I'm sure, what I did was cold and callous. She probably especially thought that after she found out that Deirdre was dying while I was carrying on an affair with her."

Rayne leaned in closer to him. "After all these years, you've never forgiven yourself for what you did?"

Ben remembered his reaction when Wade had asked him if he'd cheated on his mom while she'd been sick in bed. He'd coolly said that everybody made mistakes in life.

That's not how he'd really felt, though. He grieved for Deirdre. And he grieved for the man he could have been if he had been able to do one thing: forgive her. But, no, he'd carried her sin in his heart. He'd pulled it out whenever he wanted to punish her. He'd let it grow to enormous proportions and kept it fed by his distance, his refusal to love her as she'd loved him. Deirdre was a good wife. She bent over backward to please him. Supported him in every endeavor. But he was too small of a man to meet her halfway.

"I'm a man of many regrets," he found himself saying to his daughter. "If you really want to know me, you have to know this about me—as hard as I am on everybody else, and I'm a real bastard to work for, I'm even harder on myself."

She stunned him with her response. "Oh, then you're not finished punishing yourself for what you did twenty-seven years ago."

"Not by a long shot," he said.

Rayne reached across the table and gently placed her hand

on his. "I couldn't stay angry at my mother for not telling me Dad wasn't my biological father, because I kept thinking of the alternative she could have chosen when she found herself pregnant at eighteen. She could have had an abortion. I didn't have to be here. And your meeting Mom and falling in love with her when you were married, that's not something anyone would condone, but again, if you two hadn't gotten together I wouldn't be here. I don't know why it happened. You have to forgive yourself in your own time. But remember, one good thing came out of all the chaos. Me." She laughed shortly. "At least I hope I'm a good thing. You might not think so after you get that bill."

Ben grasped the hand that was atop his and gratefully squeezed it. His eyes had grown misty. "You are definitely a good thing."

Rayne grinned at him, and thought it best to change the subject before things got more maudlin. "Tell me about Wade. What was he like when he was a boy?"

Ben's mood immediately brightened. He looked at her with smiling eyes. "He had a million questions and no patience with my answers. He wanted to experiment and find out for himself. He's still like that to some extent. He keeps his own counsel. In other words, once he's made his mind up about something, you can't change it. And most of all, he's an honest man. I guess you know by now that I sent him to snoop around and find out what he could about you. He couldn't do it that way. He simply came out and told your dad exactly what we were up to, and why. And he got an honest response from Ray. I, on the other hand, would have spent years trying to gather information."

"You're proud of him," Rayne said, smiling.

"I would give my life for him," Ben said sincerely.

After that, Ben asked her to tell him about her childhood

and she obliged him, telling him how she'd loved school, how she'd spent many of her formative years searching for her talent because her grandma Layla had told her that everybody was born with a talent. She took piano lessons, and could not get the hang of finger placement. Her left hand could not work independently of her right hand. Therefore she never could play two-part harmonies. She tried singing. Tone deaf. Then, finally, she took a modern dance class and found that she was a natural-born dancer. She'd discovered her talent.

They got so lost in conversation that by the time they remembered that Mac was waiting for them at the entrance to the mall, he had been there for more than thirty minutes.

The night before Rayne was supposed to arrive in Atlanta, Wade went out on a date. He usually didn't date during the week. Even though he was a young man with plenty of stamina, he still thought of dating as a weekend activity. Business came first during the week.

But he was a man on a mission. Get Rayne off his mind and out of his system. So, when Tonia Greene, a woman he'd dated a couple of times in the past when she had broken up with her longtime boyfriend, only to get back together with him later, phoned him and asked him to go to a play opening with her, he agreed to. The play had been written by a local woman who was Tonia's sorority sister, and it was performed by a theater group on the campus of a historically African-American college in town.

The play wasn't bad. It was after the play that the evening began to unravel. Tonia wanted to go back to her place for a drink. Though she was a lovely woman whom he had known socially for at least four years, Wade didn't know what to make of her invitation. Their other two dates had not gone further than a kiss at her door. Did she think that because they had known each other for four years that made them, well, more than *acquaintances?* Because that's not the way he saw it at all. Perhaps he was already on edge due to the prospect of having Rayne in town and he wasn't even planning to go see her. But he asked Tonia what she had in mind, and that she be brutally honest with him about her expectations of what was to happen once he was at her place. Tonia told him that since both of them were between "that special someone," then perhaps, as friends, they could satisfy one another sexually until "that special someone" came along.

The woman was horny, plain and simple.

Wade beat a hasty retreat, with Tonia yelling at him, "What kind of man are you? Is something wrong with you, turning *me* down?"

He could have told her that sex for sex's sake didn't interest him. But she was so upset by his rejection that she wouldn't have heard him anyway.

Now he sat in his father's study at five in the afternoon on Thursday, wondering why his father hadn't gotten back from picking Rayne up at the airport. So much for his vow to stay away. He'd canceled his afternoon appointments to be here.

Mrs. Elizabeth Knox, the housekeeper, stuck her head in the room. "Mr. Wade, your father's car is pulling up now."

Wade smiled at her. "Thank you, Mrs. Knox."

He got to his feet and calmly strolled through the big house to the foyer where Mrs. Knox was preparing to open the door for her employer and his long-lost daughter.

Wade stood to the side, knowing the protocol. Mrs. Knox would get the door. As the housekeeper, she insisted on doing things properly. She would meet Miss Walker and welcome her, and then she would leave the family alone to talk in private.

Wade could barely contain his excitement. He hoped that what he'd felt for her on the beach that night was a fluke. He hoped that once he looked her in the eyes, and got a really good look at her, he would feel nothing except a brotherly affection that was chaste and pure.

Mrs. Knox opened the door and Rayne, preceding Ben, stepped across the threshold.

She was laughing at something Ben had said, and her dark brown eyes were alight with pleasure. Her long, wavy hair fell down her back, and moved sensually with the shake of her head.

"Good afternoon, Mr. Jefferson, Miss Walker," Mrs. Knox greeted them.

Ben smiled magnanimously. "Rayne, this is Mrs. Knox, she has been ruling my house with an iron fist for a very long time. Don't cross her."

Mrs. Knox laughed. "Sir, you'll give Miss Walker the wrong impression! How do you do, Miss Walker? Welcome to Atlanta."

Rayne smiled at her. "Thank you. It's a pleasure to meet you, Mrs. Knox."

Ben noticed Wade then, and laughed. "Son, what are you doing here?" He hurried past Rayne and Mrs. Knox to briefly hug his son.

Mrs. Knox excused herself and went to help Mac with the bags.

Rayne watched as Wade and Ben hugged.

After he released Wade, Ben turned around and grabbed Rayne by the hand. "Rayne, look who's here. I had no idea he was going to come today, or I would have told you."

Wade and Rayne approached each other hesitantly. Ben wasn't aware of the war that was being waged right in front of his eyes. Rayne looked up and saw Wade across the room and immediately knew that what she had felt for him at their first encounter had been real and not imagined, as she'd hoped.

Upon seeing him, she'd had a sharp intake of breath and slowly released it. Being attracted to a man you could hardly see was one thing. But now she could see him clearly, and instead of shattering her expectations of how he would look she was forced to admit the fact that she hadn't dreamed big enough. His skin was a dark golden brown, and beautiful. She knew he was big, but her memory hadn't served her well enough. He was broad-shouldered, trim in the waist, his stomach flat, and even in his business suit, she could see how well defined his muscles were. She saw now that his hair was dark brown and natural with a slight wave to it that was more noticeable when he wore it cut close to his scalp.

He wasn't perfect by a long shot. His nose was too long. His mouth was wide and full and when he smiled she saw that while his teeth were straight and white, there was a small space between the two front ones. And there was a scar, a slash, through his right eyebrow. There was also a small scar on his square chin. No, he wasn't perfect, but he was still the most attractive man she'd ever met. And she wished she'd never met him.

Wade made the first move. He pulled her into his arms and hugged her, trying his best to avoid holding the entire length of her body against his. It was a perfunctory hug at best.

He set her away from him, he hoped not too abruptly, because his father was watching, and said, "It's great to see you again, Rayne."

Rayne instinctively knew that he was lying. She could tell he was sweating underneath his cool demeanor. For some reason, she felt more in control when she knew he was *out* of control. Perhaps she could survive his being there if she could make light of the fact that they were attracted to each other. "You call that a hug?" she asked, and put her arms around his neck and pulled him down for a closer embrace. She whispered, for his ears only, "You know, brothers and sisters married in biblical days."

He set her away from him as if she were the veritable serpent in the garden of Eden.

Rayne laughed.

Ben laughed, too, though he didn't know what they were laughing about. His son was behaving strangely, that he knew for sure. And at his earliest opportunity he was going to find out why.

"Come on," he told them, walking away. "I don't know about you two but I'm famished, and Mrs. Knox makes a delicious roast beef with new potatoes and baby carrots. But first, Wade, why don't you show Rayne to the south guest room? I'm sure she'd like to freshen up before dinner. I'd do it, but I need to make a quick business call."

Ben disappeared into his study and Wade and Rayne continued up the stairs.

"What was that about? That brothers and sisters marrying in biblical times comment?" Wade said in a harsh whisper when they were alone.

Rayne pierced him with a hard stare. "You totally stopped calling me. Don't think I don't know you're avoiding me. That was my way of paying you back!"

Wade didn't try to deny he'd been avoiding her. "I've been trying to desensitize myself to you. It's obvious it didn't work." His eyes were ablaze with anger.

"Don't get mad at me! It isn't my fault you're lusting after your baby sister."

"You're not doing anything to help the situation," Wade accused. "Look at you!"

Rayne glanced down at her jeans and T-shirts. "There is nothing improper about my clothes, thank you very much!"

"It's not the clothes, it's the body in them," Wade said, gesturing to her breasts, her hips, her long legs in the jeans.

"Well, I can't help that, now, can I?" Rayne said. She stuck her chest out. "These are mine, as is everything else, and none of it's going to be altered to suit you!"

"Will you stop yelling at me?"

"When you stop yelling at me!" Rayne said defensively.

They arrived at the bedroom door, and Wade opened it and allowed her to go ahead of him into the spacious, eclectically decorated boudoir. That's the only way he could describe it. It was as if some English countryside had been shipped, piece by piece, to this bedroom on the outskirts of Atlanta. Chintz was everywhere in pink and pale green. The canopy bed was covered in it. His father should have fired the decorator. Or perhaps this was his father's idea of femininity.

Rayne went silent when she saw the room.

They stood there looking at it for two solid minutes before either of them said another word. Then Rayne said, "Don't you say a word to your father about this atrocious room. I love it! If you have to say anything to him, you can tell him I love it."

Wade turned his gaze to her. He wanted to kiss her senseless. The urge was so strong that he knew he would grab her and do it unless he put some distance between them, and in a hurry.

He backed out of the room. "Okay, you've got it. You take all the time you want freshening up. You know how to get downstairs. See you later."

He pulled the door shut behind him.

"Chicken!" Rayne called after him.

She turned in a circle, looking around her. "Hey, I'm only going to sleep in here. My eyes will be closed most of the time."

Chapter 10

Ben quickly made his call to his lawyer, and when it was over he sat down in his favorite leather chair in the study and enjoyed the quiet all around him. Divine. That's what she was. She lifted his spirits without even trying. He realized that he was seeing her through rose-colored glasses. From the moment he'd entertained the notion that he and Julianne had made a child together, he was determined to love her and, one day, deserve her love.

Loving her was going to be the easy part. Deserving her love would be the killer. Something she had said about Ray Walker had stuck in his head. How Ray had not told her much about him because he had not wanted to sway her opinion of him. That was very decent of him. Perhaps it was time to bury the past in favor of a brighter future. In order to do that, he needed to see Ray face-to-face. What he had to tell him would be best served warm.

Wade came into the room, and Ben sat up in his chair expectantly. "Well, if it isn't the man who had other plans for the weekend." He smiled knowingly. "Couldn't stay away, could you?"

For a moment, Wade, who sat across from his father on the matching brown leather sofa, thought that his father had noticed the attraction between him and Rayne. He didn't know how to proceed without looking like an utter fool. Then his father said, "It's exciting having a sister, isn't it? I knew you wouldn't be able to stay away. She's a wonderful girl, don't you think?" His grin was infectious.

Wade smiled and shook his head in wonder at his father's euphoria. "That, she is."

Ben slapped his thigh and rose, too elated to sit still for long. "I hate to admit it, but my worst enemy managed to raise her so that she's nonjudgmental, thoughtful and sweet. I can't believe it! I couldn't have done a better job myself."

Wade was beginning to feel a bit left out. "You didn't do a bad job on me, either!"

Ben laughed happily. "You're both great kids."

"I'm thirty-four, she's twenty-six. We're hardly kids."

"You'll always be kids to your parents." Ben's eyes shone with an idea. "I wish I could find a way to bring her to Atlanta. I could set her up in business. Or better still, marry her off to a successful bachelor who lives here. Then I could see her all the time!"

"Hold up," Wade warned. He sat back on the sofa, his arms spread across the top of it. "She's been here less than a day, and you're already planning her life? You left out several adjectives about Miss Rayne Walker. She's also independent, stubborn and opinionated. You don't know her well enough yet. She can be very argumentative." He remembered their argument on the stairwell. *And pigheaded,* he silently tacked on.

Rayne walked into the study at that instant, and Wade blushed. His cheeks grew warm and the heat suffused his entire body. She'd changed into a sleeveless apple green silk sheath dress and a pair of cream colored strappy sandals. Her long, beautiful legs were bare, smooth-looking and ultrasexy. He'd never really noticed a woman's shoulders before, but hers were delectable in the scoop-neckline. He wanted to walk up to her and kiss her clavicles.

"Don't let me interrupt," she said, smiling at Ben, then at him.

The mischievous gleam in her eyes told him she didn't mind interrupting him at all.

"You look as fresh as a spring day in that frock," Ben told her as he walked over to her and grasped both her hands in his. "Doesn't she, son?"

"She's fresh, all right," said Wade, keeping his tone light.

He saw Rayne's brows arch a fraction of an inch, but that was enough to let him know she got his meaning. If she wanted to play an undercover game of zingers, he was her man.

"Shall we go in to dinner?" Ben suggested, putting Rayne's hand through his arm and escorting her from the room. Wade followed at a sedate pace. He still needed time to recover from the sight of her in that dress.

He observed her throughout the meal. She had a good appetite, and wielded her knife and fork with such delicacy that he was sure she'd been taught proper etiquette early in life by someone significant to her. Maybe her mother, or her grandmother. Of course, in her line of work, planning parties, good manners served her well.

He smiled to himself, remembering his own lessons in table manners learned at the ruler of Mrs. Crawford, the woman his father had hired to keep house after his mother died. Oftentimes, his father wouldn't be home for dinner, and Mrs. Crawford would eat dinner with him, and if he took a misstep during the meal, she would hit him on the hand with a wooden ruler, the same kind he used in math class. He was eight at the time, and missing his mother terribly. He accepted the woman's abuse without complaint. But when his father came home early one night and witnessed what was going on at the dinner table in his absence, he'd blown up at the woman and fired her on the spot.

Tonight, his father was just as fervent about finding out all he could about his daughter.

"Are you dating anyone special?" he asked, just before taking a bite of the roast beef and chewing thoughtfully.

"No," Rayne said. She drank a little of the merlot and set her glass back on the white linen tablecloth. Wade thought her lips looked as sweet as the wine. He drank some himself, quite a good swallow. Then almost laughed out loud when the thought that she was the type of woman who could drive a man to drink floated through his feverish mind.

"I haven't gotten serious about anyone since my engagement was broken off."

By you, Wade thought. *Be a good boy, and just eat your meal.* He dutifully speared a piece of beef and put it into his mouth.

"Oh, that's a shame," said her father sympathetically. Secretly pleased, he went on. "But it wasn't meant to be. If you two were really meant to be together, you would be married to him by now. You know, Atlanta has some very eligible bachelors. On one of your future visits, I'll be sure to introduce you to a few of them. Although I certainly don't want you to get married too soon. I'd like to have you to myself for a while."

"You don't have to worry about that," Rayne told him. "I've decided I'm not even going to start looking for a man who's husband material until I'm thirty."

Wade did laugh this time. He was able to contain his mirth

quite quickly, though, and looked at her with apologetic eyes. "Sorry, but it occurred to me that of all my friends who've gotten married in the past few years, none of them were actually looking for a wife. You make it sound like you can plan love like a writer plots a novel. Will you also choose how he'll behave, how he'll speak, how he'll dress, what career he'll be in when you meet him? Oh, and how, and where, he'll eventually pop the question?"

Rayne smiled slowly. And here she was thinking that he was going to sit there all evening like a bump on a log while she and her second father held a conversation by themselves. Pleased that he'd come alive, she was more than happy to elaborate.

"That's not what I meant. What I meant was that I don't have any plans to fall in love and get married any time soon. Of course, if it happens, it happens! But lately I've been working so hard that I rarely go out at all. A man has to be very persistent to get my attention."

"You're saying you're a high-maintenance woman?" asked Wade.

"If you like," Rayne replied.

She blinked, her long, thick lashes kissed her cheeks for a moment, and Wade seemed to watch it all in slow motion. It was not meant to be a seductive move, he knew, but it had been, nonetheless.

She raised her gaze to his. "I'm good to a man when I'm dating him. I expect to be treated well in return. If that means I'm a high-maintenance woman, then, yes, I am."

Her eyes seemed to dare him to challenge her. He merely smiled and said, "You deserve to be treated well. And now that we're brother and sister, anyone who doesn't treat you well will have me to answer to."

Rayne felt a rush of pleasure at his statement. She smiled sweetly at him.

"Hear, hear!" Ben cried, raising his wineglass for a toast. "Let's drink to that."

They all raised their glasses and drank to Wade being a protective brother. Rayne's smile never wavered, but she was suddenly saddened by the sense of surety that no matter how she wished it, Wade Jefferson was her brother, and there was nothing she could do about it.

The conversation lagged after that, and they finished their meal in silence. When he rose from his chair a little while later, Ben suggested to Wade, "Son, it's just dusk out. Why don't you take Rayne for a drive around the neighborhood?" He glanced down at Rayne, who was still seated. "I'm sorry, my dear, I would take you myself, but I'm not a young man any longer and, well, I'm a little tired. But you young people go ahead and have a good time."

Wade didn't know how he could refuse. He didn't want to be alone with Rayne, but if he made up some lame excuse, his father would see right through it, and then demand an explanation for his rudeness, possibly right in front of Rayne.

He and Rayne locked gazes across the table. His brows rose in a helpless expression. She shrugged slightly as if to say, *why not?* "That sounds like a good idea," he said, assuming he had her consent.

"All right, let's put everything on the table," Rayne said once they were alone.

Wade calmly pulled away from the circular drive and pointed the car in the direction of the gatehouse. "I assume you're talking about our little problem."

Rayne sighed in frustration. "Yes! You're making this harder than it has to be."

Wade briefly glanced at her. "Do you have a quicker way for us to stop being attracted to each other? Because I've tried everything I could think of. I didn't phone you because the sound of your voice does me in. I even went out on a date, but ran when she wanted to get physical."

Rayne was surprisingly relieved to hear that he hadn't gone to bed with anyone since they'd met. It almost felt as if he would have been cheating on her if he had. "This is crazy, no doubt," she said softly. "But it isn't our fault, and we don't have anything to feel guilty about unless we act on our feelings. And we're not about to do that. I don't want to have to avoid you, Wade. I want to get to know you. We're blood. And I don't want to feel as if I'm on the defensive every time we have a private conversation. I don't want to be attracted to you any more than you want to be attracted to me. So, I'm not going to take your accusing me of *tempting* you."

"You're right," Wade said. "You can't help how you look, or sound or smell."

"Smell?"

"Wonderful."

"Stop it!"

Wade laughed. "Okay, that wasn't fair." He paused as he decided where to take her. "There's a nice park near here that's safe at night. Would you like to take a stroll with me? Walk off some of that roast beef?"

"A little exercise sounds nice," Rayne agreed. "And you smell nice, too."

He smiled. In spite of all the messages his brain was sending his body—*she isn't all that* and *any woman can smell that good if she uses the same perfume*—he was unconvinced. This felt like a date to him. He instinctively knew that she was all that, and no other woman on earth would ever smell as wonderful to him as she did right now.

In the park, as Wade helped her out of the SUV, he glanced doubtfully at her sandals. "Are those going to be comfortable for walking?"

"Oh, they've got great insoles," Rayne told him.

"There's a path all the way around the pond," Wade told her. He let go of her hand once her feet were on the ground. Her touch brought back memories of that night on the beach when she'd wrapped her arms and legs around him. He pushed the thought aside and told himself those images would eventually subside.

There was a soft breeze tonight. The park had been laid out around a large pond, and a paved walkway surrounded it. Park benches sat on the grass at intervals of about thirty feet apart. A streetlamp stood near each bench, and because it was getting dark, they were on.

"How is your dad doing?" Wade asked as they began walking. "We heard that he was ill."

"He found out that he has prostate cancer a few months ago. For a while, he had planned to just let things run their natural course."

"Is it late stage? Nothing can be done?" Wade asked, concerned.

"No, that wasn't it at all. It's in the early stages, but Dad was of the mind that he'd prefer to live the rest of his life as a whole man, rather than half a man. Anyway, that's how he saw it."

"It's practically an epidemic in the black community," Wade said. "Largely because black men don't get examined early enough. So, what course of action did your dad decide to take?"

"He's going to have surgery next week," Rayne said, pleased to be able to report that considering what her family had gone through because of her dad's stubbornness.

"Good," said Wade. "I hope everything goes well for him."

"Thanks, so do I."

"Are you staying for his recovery? Or do you have to get back to New York?"

"I'm staying all summer. I work like a crazy woman for nine months out of the year so that I can afford to take the summer off. Spending the summer in American Beach has been a tradition for my dad and me since I was eight. I'm looking forward to helping him get back on his feet."

Wade smiled at her. "I'm sure his recovery will go even swifter with you by his side."

"I think he would prefer it if it were Mom there with him, but she has to report for work on an independent film on July 17th. Dad will have the surgery on Wednesday, July 5th. When the film wraps she'll come back to American Beach, so she'll leave Shannon with me while she's gone."

"How do you two get along? I've never had a sibling, but I imagine you have your ups and downs."

"Shannon's a good kid. Even though we don't always see eye to eye, when it comes down to it, we love each other, and that's what counts. We're there for each other."

"Yeah, I always imagined that's how it would be if I had grown up with a brother or a sister. Love would win over differences."

"Enough about me," said Rayne. "I want to hear about you."

"You can ask me anything," Wade said easily. A guy on a bike sped past them.

"When is your birthday?"

"May 3rd."

"Then you just turned how old?"

"Thirty-four."

"You were eight when I was born!"

"That depends on when you were born."

"July 31st. You're eight years and nearly three months older than I am. It's funny, your mother died when you were eight. I was born when you were eight. I've been spending summers in American Beach since I was eight. Do you see a pattern here?"

Wade laughed. "You're not a numerologist, are you?"

"Of course not, but they say the number eight means a new beginning. Maybe instead of what's happening to us causing confusion, it'll turn out as something very positive for both of us. I'm looking forward to having a brother, someone I can talk to about men other than my father, who, let me tell you, has never been good on that subject. He wants me to stay his little girl. I think he did a back flip when I broke up with Tony."

"What makes you think I'd be more objective?"

"Because you and I don't have a history. You can listen to me talk about a guy, and simply give me your opinion based on his attributes, not based on how you feel about me, and how much you're going to get left out of my life because I'm seriously involved with a man."

"Fathers are selfish that way. He was, after all, the first man in your life. Dad's already getting possessive about you and he hasn't known you twenty-four hours."

"He's sweet, your dad."

Wade laughed. "Sweet? Nah, Ben Jefferson is *not* sweet. You're seeing his best side, his tender side. You lucked out and got him at a time of his life when he's trying to make amends for all of his sins."

Rayne was silent, considering what he'd said. She had sensed that Ben Jefferson was at a crossroads in his life. He'd admitted to having a lot of regrets. "Maybe things are revealed to us in life when we're best equipped to handle them," she said.

"You think this thing between us is something that we're capable of handling without completely staying away from each other?" Wade asked.

"Sure," Rayne said confidently. "A little aversion therapy, and we'll be cured."

"Oh, you're going to tell me all the negative things about you, and that's supposed to turn me off?"

"Let's try it." She thought for a few seconds. "When I was a kid, I used to bite my toenails."

"Do you still do it?"

"No."

"Not a turnoff," he informed her. "Now, if you still did it, that would be nasty."

"Okay, well, tell me something gross about yourself," Rayne challenged.

"I don't do anything gross. If anything, I'm fastidious to the point of obsession. I'm so neat that my housekeeper gives *me* a Christmas bonus."

"Do you ever leave your clothing on the floor?"

"Never."

"Do you track dirt into the house?"

"I pull my shoes off in the foyer when I come in from jogging."

"Do you leave the kitchen a mess when you cook?"

"I clean as I go so that when I'm done cooking, there will be fewer pots and pans to wash."

"Wet towels on the bathroom floor?"

"Nah."

"Do you leave the toilet seat up?"

"I live alone, so yes, I do. But if you lived with me, I'm sure I'd learn to put the seat down in a hurry."

"Yeah, that'll happen," she intoned.

They laughed.

"Not coming to live with your older brother any time soon, huh?"

"No, I don't plan to get anywhere near you and a bed until I stop getting happy every time I hear your voice or see your face."

"You get happy? I get all jittery like I'm a pimply-faced teen having his first crush. I'm pathetic!"

"I went to bed the night we met spinning romantic scenarios about 'the new guy.'" Rayne laughed shortly. "Just my luck, meeting a great guy, and he's my brother!"

The cyclist was making his second trip around the pond when he passed Rayne on the left and got so close to her that she thought he was going to hit her. She leaped aside, the heel of her right sandal got stuck in the grass, she lost her balance, and would have taken a spill if Wade hadn't caught her in his arms.

"Hey, man, watch it!" he yelled at the cyclist.

"Sorry, dude, I didn't realize I was that close to your lady!" the cyclist yelled back.

Rayne had to quickly throw her arms around his neck and hold on to him. Wade held her about the waist. He pulled her to a standing position. "Are you okay?"

"I'm fine," Rayne said.

But, still, he held her. He bent his head so that their faces were mere inches apart. He breathed in the wonderful scent of her, a combination of fresh flowers and spices. The warmth of her skin undoubtedly heightened the effect. His eyes lowered to her full, sensuous mouth. Then he looked into her eyes and saw something that floored him: desire. She wanted him as much as he wanted her.

She made the first move. She tiptoed and placed her mouth on his face, right next to his mouth. He had but to turn his head and they would be kissing. He fought for control, willing himself to stop this madness. If they crossed the line, they might never find their way back. Or care, for that matter.

Rayne thought that if she could kiss him just once, it would be enough to last her a lifetime. However, deep down, she knew they couldn't afford to play with fire. Not if they were to be able to look at one another without the shame of what they'd done mirrored in their eyes.

They drew apart simultaneously. Rayne removed her arms from about his neck. Wade relinquished his hold on her waist. She stepped onto the walk, afraid that the heel of her sandal might have been damaged. It was fine.

She smiled up at him. "I'm a little tired. Would you take me home now?"

"Sure," Wade said. He went to put his arm about her shoulders as they turned to walk back to the car, thought better of it and allowed his arm to fall to his side. "Dad's probably eager to have you all to himself again."

"Then you have plans for tonight?" It was only around seven in the evening.

"Yeah, with some paperwork," he said.

"Am I going to see you again before I go home?"

"I might drop in on the dinner party Saturday night. You'll need someone to help fend off the advances of the suitors Dad has invited over to meet you."

Rayne laughed softly. "He doesn't waste time, does he?"

"Our old man?" said Wade. "Nah, he's pretty much on the ball, all the time."

Chapter 11

Rayne couldn't believe her eyes when Mac started following the signs that led to Six Flags Over Georgia, the amusement park. She stared at Ben, who was looking at her with a mischievous glint in his eyes. "Have you ever been on the Great American Scream Machine?"

It was Friday morning, and Rayne had thought he was going to show her the sights of Atlanta when he'd said he had a surprise for her. She should have known something was up when he'd advised her to wear jeans and sneakers, and not to indulge in a big breakfast. Now she knew why: he didn't want her to lose it on the Great American Scream Machine.

She regarded him with a scowl. "The roller coaster?"

Ben laughed at the expression on her face. "Yes, the roller coaster. You can't come to Atlanta without going through that rite of passage."

"Oh, yes, I can!"

He ignored her and began talking about the famous roller coaster. "It was built in 1973. It's one of the last surviving woodies, that's a coaster constructed mostly of wood, left in America. It's 105 feet tall and 3800 feet long. Its maximum speed is 57 miles per hour, and it's guaranteed to make you holler."

"And give you a heart attack," Rayne said skeptically. "Heart problems don't run on your side of the family, do they?"

"Not that I know of. Your grandparents were well into their eighties when they passed away. I was a late child for them. You have uncles and aunts in their seventies. You'll get to meet them all in time, of course."

"No instances of anyone keeling over while clutching his heart, huh?"

"None," Ben assured her.

She cocked a brow at him. "Is this rite-of-passage thing some kind of a test? You're trying to see what I'm made of?"

Ben laughed at the notion. "No, I'm just trying to share one of my favorite pastimes with you."

"Oh, I see. You're one of those people who'll go anywhere to ride a certain coaster."

Ben nodded. "I've been all over the United States. Six Flags Over Georgia is my favorite place to ride coasters. Other parks have newer rides, but none as satisfying. Come on, sweetheart, give it a try, and if you hate it I won't try to persuade you to go on any others. Ride the Scream Machine, and you'll be hooked."

"Or you might get what I had for breakfast all over you," Rayne warned him.

Mac, listening up front while he drove, laughed. "Just make sure you do it on him and not the car seats, I just had them cleaned."

"You zip it, or I'm going to make you go on it, too," said Ben.

"Zipping it," Mac returned cheerily.

An hour later, they were being securely locked into their seats. She and Ben were in the front, and Mac, who'd decided you only lived once, was behind them. Rayne's legs were shaking and her palms were moist from anxiety. Her second father grasped her hand in his. "Piece of cake!" he said confidently.

"I should have had cake for breakfast," said Mac. "This could be my last day on earth!"

"We should have left you in the car," Ben said. "Be quiet, you're making Rayne nervous."

"I was nervous before we got this far," Rayne informed him shakily.

Ben kissed her fingers. "Wait, you'll see, you're going to love it."

The coaster began to move slowly. "Here we go!" cried Mac.

Rayne gripped Ben's hand so tightly it was painful.

She squeezed her eyes shut.

"Open your eyes, baby girl, you're going to want to see this."

They were picking up speed now. They leveled off at around thirty-five miles per hour. Rayne thought, *What was I afraid of? This is no more frightening than sticking your head out of a car window.*

She opened her eyes just in time to see the first long drop they would be taking. The coaster picked up speed as it dipped and made a swift turn. Her stomach seemed to be somewhere back at the first dip. She screamed loudly, and squeezed Ben's hand even harder.

Ben was screaming and laughing at the same time. Mac was just yelling his head off. Rayne felt the coaster slowing a little. She breathed a sigh of relief, thinking maybe the ride was coming to its end. But, no, they were only slowing down because they were climbing again, and she knew what came after a climb: a severe drop. The coaster gained momentum in this drop and picked up tremendous speed. Rayne's cheeks were windblown. She imagined she looked like the astronauts during one of those stress tests in which they're put into simulators to find out how many g-forces their bodies can take. She'd forgotten to tie her hair back and it was flying everywhere, smacking Ben in the face, which he didn't seem to mind. He was having a ball.

All through this, she screamed as if some masked maniac were chasing her with an ax. There was one more dip to come. Ben told her, "Everybody raises their arms over their heads and screams all the way down on this one." He tried to disengage his fingers from her grasp. "Want to do it?"

Rayne reluctantly let go of him. She was still alive, so she supposed she would actually survive this ordeal. Might as well go all the way. She let him go and they raised their arms above their heads and yelled all the way down.

They took the dip at over 55 miles per hour, and Rayne felt like her heart was going to explode, as if her internal organs were knocking against one another. She prayed that if she was going to die, it would be a mercifully quick death.

Then, all of a sudden, the coaster began to, well, *coast* into home. They crawled to a stop, and as soon as the bars came up, so did Rayne. She was out of her seat in a split second. Her eyes had tears in them. Her nose was running. Her hair looked as if she'd stuck her finger in an electric socket or had gone to the Bride of Frankenstein's hairdresser. Ben's face was a mask of concern. He knew she was getting ready to burst into tears or, worse, cuss him out. But she laughed instead, and said, "I loved it!"

"Oh, Lord," said Mac. "She really is your daughter."

Ben grabbed her and hugged her, and then they got out of the way of the eager masses who were waiting to ride the legendary coaster.

They rode three more coasters before Rayne's appetite for thrills was satisfied.

On the ride home, exhausted, she curled up in a corner of the big limousine and fell asleep. Ben watched her, a contented smile on his face. *Another regret*, he thought. *I should have been there to watch her grow up.*

That night Wade phoned her just before she fell asleep. "I hear you inherited the old man's penchant for death wishes."

She laughed. "Translation—I like roller coasters?"

"Mmm-hmm," he said, his voice husky. "He's as happy as a cat in a barn full of milk cows. That's one of my grandma Geneva's sayings. Next, he'll want to take you to ride some of his favorite coasters around the country."

"I can't wait," Rayne said. She was lying down with her head on a couple of fluffy pillows. She was comfortable, mellow and enjoying listening to Wade's deep voice. She mentally checked herself. But then just let herself go. She was tired of always checking herself whenever she saw him or spoke with him. It was her secret that she found his voice madly arousing. She would add up all of her transgressions later and pray about the entire pile at once. "And, yes, I got a kick out of riding the coasters. I never did that when I was a kid. I don't know why. Do you share your dad's passion?"

"I would go to make him happy," Wade told her. "But those kinds of things didn't thrill me back then. I loved sports. I played high school and college football. The only thing I did as a hobby was drawing."

"Charcoals? Pencil?" Her father sketched in charcoal. Beautiful sketches of people's faces, beach scenes and other landscapes. His paintings would sometimes take weeks to complete, depending on his muse. But he sketched furiously, finishing in a matter of minutes. She had one of his sketches on her bedroom wall in her apartment in New York. It was of her when she was three years old. She'd been a child with chubby cheeks, a bow mouth, and huge eyes. *You're all eyes,* her dad used to say.

"Both," Wade told her. "I never had any formal training."

"Self-taught," Rayne said softly. "Like my dad, mostly. He went to art school for a while when he was barely out of his teens, but came back home, forgot about art for years, and worked in construction."

"He's got the build of a construction worker," said Wade.

"Yeah, so do you." She was sorry she'd said that. Her tone had been intimate. She had been imagining his body when she'd said it, and she knew he'd picked up on it.

"Um, so do you think you might know any of the guys your dad invited to the dinner party to meet me?" *Good save,* she thought, deriding herself. "Forewarned is forearmed."

"More than likely he invited Mike Curran," Wade said. "He works for us. He's kind of the third in command. Mike's a nice guy. You'll like him. Then there is Joe Jakes."

"Joe Jakes, the football player?"

"You're a fan?"

"Absolutely not, I've met the creep before, that's all. He came to a wedding I planned and persuaded the maid of honor to run off to a hotel room with him. We had to find a stand-in for her, and for him. He was the best man."

"You know, he actually told me about that incident, and I didn't believe him," Wade said with a laugh.

"Well, it's true," Rayne told him. "And the next time I saw him, I let him have it. Oh, he's going to remember me!"

"My guess might be wrong, and he *isn't* one of the men Dad has lined up for you," Wade told her.

"I hope he isn't," Rayne said. She sighed. "But if he is, I'm not going to act a fool. I'd never embarrass you or your father."

"Darlin', you wouldn't embarrass me, no matter what you did," Wade said softly.

Rayne didn't know what he'd said after he'd called her darlin'. She was certain he'd said something else, just not what it was.

She faked a yawn. "I'd better get some rest. After Six Flags today, there's no telling what your father has planned for tomorrow morning."

Wade laughed shortly. "You know, you're going to have to call him something other than 'your father.'"

"I know, but I haven't settled on anything yet. You call him Dad, right?"

"I call him different things at different times. Most of the time it's Dad. Sometimes it's Father, Pop or Old Man. Call him whatever you want to, Rayne. He'll happily answer to it. He's sold on you. You should hear how he talks about you."

"How do you feel about sharing your dad after all these years?" Rayne had to know.

"I feel fine about it," Wade said sincerely. "Don't even lose one brain cell worrying about that. I don't mind sharing my dad with you. I just don't want to share you with any dudes with romance on their minds." He paused. "Sorry, we were supposed to be good, weren't we?"

"Yes, but one slipup is forgivable," she told him. "I've thought worse during our conversation. But we'd better say good night before this gets too heated. Night, bruh."

"Good night," said Wade.

In his apartment, Wade lay on the bed wearing only boxer shorts. He sat up and placed the receiver on its cradle, then settled on his back, his right hand resting on his washboard stomach. His desire for her had not lessened one iota. He still craved the sound of her voice. He still longed to kiss her, and more. Was it a case of wanting what he knew he couldn't have? Was it as simple as that? It was a common human foible, wasn't it? That which was near to impossible to attain was considered the most desirable thing.

No, that couldn't be it. That night on the beach, he hadn't known she was taboo. All he'd known was that something inside him had connected with something inside her, and he'd felt pure joy at the prospect of getting to know her better. That's what was so hard to give up, the joy he derived from thinking about her. Hearing her voice. Touching her.

Last night they had been so close to kissing that he could almost taste her lips. He was tense with longing right now, thinking about what might have happened if both of them hadn't come to their senses. She talked about their getting over these feelings, but he didn't think he would ever stop wanting her.

A few miles away, Rayne turned off the lamp and lay curled up on her right side. Crazy, that's what this thing was. It wasn't as if she was actively concentrating on Wade. She didn't wallow in the reaction that thoughts of him raised in her body. She immediately tried to shake it off and concentrate on other things. The fact that she failed every time really irked her.

She wasn't inexperienced when it came to men. She and Tony had been lovers. And there had been one other after Tony. So she was not romanticizing her responses to the stimuli that Wade exuded. She'd known many men to whom she'd been attracted but when it turned out they were not suited for each other, she'd been able to stop fantasizing about them. Married men were a real turnoff for her. They might be charming and wonderful to look at, but the moment she found out they had wives at home, and were out flirting with her, they became untouchables. She let them have a piece of her mind, and then they were excised from her thoughts completely. The same thing for single guys who appeared to be fine catches but later manifested some habit or quirk that she couldn't live with. Like excessive possessiveness, or verbal abuse. She had an aversion to both physical abuse and verbal abuse. The physical kind could destroy your body, but the verbal kind could destroy your spirit. She stayed clear of men who routinely put women down in their speech.

She sighed and turned over in bed. Okay, she'd established that Wade was unique in that she could not get him off her mind, even though it had turned out that he was an untouchable. Incest was frowned upon in most of the modern world. She didn't want to start a trend. Therefore, she would have to find a man capable of pushing Wade completely out of her mind.

She fell asleep thinking about his hands on her body. Lifting her and wrapping her in his arms where he held her securely against his chest. In the place between waking and sleeping, she could smell his aftershave, feel his cheek against hers, and if she turned her head a little to the left they would kiss and… She awakened and sat up in bed. Turning the light on, she picked up her suspense novel and continued reading about a killer who chose his victims based on their high body weight because he planned to remove their skin and make a suit for himself. That should take her mind off Wade Jefferson.

A few minutes later, she fell asleep with the book on her stomach and dreamed she was making love to Wade in her bed in her New York City apartment. There were white rose petals strewn on the sheet, and her body and Wade's were brown and faintly glistening with perspiration. Those were the only colors in the dream, white, and the brown of their bodies.

In the morning, she awakened with a lingering feeling of guilt, as if her dream were a portent of things to come.

Rayne learned, right away, that Ben had not told the guests that they would be meeting his long-lost daughter. She was both amused and mortified by some of the comments they made as she, at Ben's insistence, and he greeted them at the door.

"Hello, darling." This to her from a woman in her early fifties. She had café au lait skin, wore a slim black dress and was dripping in diamonds. "Aren't you lovely?"

She turned her green eyes on Ben. "Isn't she too young for you, Ben? What are you doing nowadays, trolling the malls?"

"Sweetheart, meet Meredith Huston-Bates, an old, *old* friend," Ben said. His eyes swept over Meredith, an attractive black woman with short, wavy, salt-and-pepper hair, a tall, trim body and killer legs. "Meredith, this is my daughter, Rayne."

Meredith's mouth popped open in astonishment. "You old dog!" she cried, laughing suddenly. Her steely green eyes went soft when she regarded Rayne. She gently took Rayne's hand in hers and stroked it with her other one. "However you came to be in this scoundrel's family, I welcome you. It's a pleasure, my dear."

Rayne smiled sweetly. "Thank you, Ms. Huston-Bates."

"Oh, call me Mere. Everybody does," said Meredith, delighted. She screwed up her face at Ben. "As for you, I will think of a suitable punishment for your not telling me about Rayne before now." She peered behind her. "But not this minute. The Gastons have arrived." She reluctantly went on into the house where Mrs. Knox was waiting to take her evening wrap.

Aaron and Judith Gaston had not gotten to the end of the long walk, so Rayne took the opportunity to say to Ben, "Mere seems nice."

"She can be a green-eyed monster," Ben said with a smile. "But we dated for five years, and after that we remained bosom buddies. If I had ever decided to marry again, it would have been to that complicated woman."

Rayne was pleased that he'd had a social life after his wife died. As for his liking complicated women, that was a given. He had, after all, been taken by her mother, the most complicated woman she knew.

After they'd welcomed Meredith to the party, four couples arrived in quick succession. Rayne assumed Meredith had come without a date, because she was Ben's companion for the night. They were all in the great room enjoying cocktails when the doorbell rang again. "Ah," said Ben. "That must be Joe."

Rayne's stomach muscles immediately constricted painfully. Wade had been right about *one* of the bachelors he'd guessed that his father might invite. Mike Curran hadn't shown up, but Joe Jakes had.

She painted on a smile and, arm in arm with Ben, went to answer the door.

Joe Jakes, six-two, 235 pounds of gridiron magic, stood on the other side of the door, looking resplendent in a casual black suit, with an expensive white cotton crew-neck shirt underneath. He threw a fake punch at Ben's head. Ben ducked, and both men laughed uproariously while Rayne stood to the side. It was obviously their routine greeting. They clasped hands in a mighty handshake worthy of the titans that they were: Ben in business and Joe in football.

Then Joe stepped across the threshold into the foyer and got his first glimpse of Rayne. "What is this *she-devil* doing here?" He didn't try to mask his disappointment. Rayne supposed that his bad manners were forgiven so often due to his celebrity status that he'd gotten used to saying whatever occurred to him.

Instead of being insulted, however, Rayne was happy he'd remembered her. She didn't have to pretend she liked him, either. "I'm a she-devil because I think you ought to learn some manners and stop behaving like a spoiled brat?"

"What I do is none of your business, lady," Joe said, puffing up his chest. He was so muscular that Rayne was sure he was on steroids. Veins were popping out all over, and his eyes were bulging as well. He looked as if he were about to explode.

"It is when you nearly ruin a wedding that I'd put so much work into planning, you moron!" She kept her tone low so as not to attract the other guests.

"Then I guess you two know each other," Ben said haplessly. He didn't know whether to ask them to take it outside or to simply push Joe out the door and slam it shut. He did believe his daughter could take the football star, though.

Rayne was standing in a boxer's stance, looking so incongruous in her black designer dress, black strappy sandals with three-inch heels and her favorite ruby stud earrings. "I know him, all right. He and two of his buddies held me over a balcony, ten stories up, because I told him to grow up and take responsibility for his behavior."

Ben looked at Joe like the guy was crazy. "You did that to my daughter?"

"After she kicked me in the balls."

"I kicked you because you touched me inappropriately, you scum!"

"Scum?" Jaws clenched in fury, Joe took a step toward her, and Ben stepped between them. "Hold on, Joe. It's obvious that you and Rayne don't like each other. If I had known about your, um, past, I'd never have invited you. You've got to go, buddy. Come on now, get to steppin'."

Joe actually looked hurt that he was being asked to leave

his friend's house. Then he glanced at Rayne again and scowled. "You embarrassed me in front of my friends. You had them telling me I needed to go to detox or something."

"I hope you took them up on it," Rayne told him evenly.

Joe's eyes grew dark with rage and, in one swift motion, he pushed Ben to the floor and leaped at Rayne, who calmly sidestepped to the right while he ran headfirst into the wall.

He hit his head hard enough to daze himself, but not hard enough to knock himself out. He straightened, turned around to get his bearings and saw Rayne at Ben's side, helping him to his feet.

Wade was walking up the steps of the front portico at that moment and, since the door was wide open, saw the scene unfolding. His father on the floor, Rayne trying to pull him to his feet, and Joe Jakes staggering toward them with his big bear claw hands poised to throttle one of them. He didn't know which, but he assumed it was Rayne.

He ran the rest of the way into the house. "Hey!" he shouted at Joe.

Joe turned to look at him with murderous intent in his eyes. "Stay out of this, Wade. I'm not going to kill her. I just want to choke her until she passes out. I've been waiting months to get my hands on that bitch!"

Rayne had pulled Ben to his feet by now. He appeared to be fine. He pushed Rayne behind him, and tried to reason with Joe again. "Look, Joe. What did she do to you that was so bad?"

"She had my buddies thinking I have a drinking problem. She said I needed to see a psychiatrist about my anger issues. That's how she put it, *anger issues*. Then she accused me of ruining my best friend's wedding just because I took some chick to bed."

"When the wedding was supposed to be taking place!" Rayne shouted. "And you were supposed to be standing up for your best friend. If you don't think that was wrong, then something's wrong with your brain!"

She moved around Ben and faced Joe. "Listen, you probably don't want to hear this because you're the mighty Joe Jakes, but you're going to flush all that fame and fortune down the drain with your erratic behavior. I told you months ago. Obviously your friends have been telling you ever since. What is it going to take for you to listen to somebody?"

Joe growled deep in his throat. Rayne stood her ground.

His left eye started twitching in agitation. Rayne would not be moved.

He yelled in frustration, a soul-shattering cry for help, then he fell to his knees in tears. Rayne stepped back, thinking it wiser if Ben or Wade went to comfort him, if comfort was what he wanted. She was trembling inside.

Joe Jakes had threatened her life several months ago. He was a man out of control and she'd stood up to him. Her bravery had gotten her an unobstructed view of a busy New York street, upside down. To tell the truth, she'd been too frightened to go to the police about the incident, thinking that Joe was crazy enough to seek revenge if she reported what he and his friends had done.

But she swore that if she ever saw him again, she would not back down.

Ben knelt beside Joe and spoke soothingly to him. "Son, I'm going to phone your brother and ask him to come get you, all right? You don't need to be alone tonight."

Wade walked over to Rayne and pulled her into his arms. He could feel her body trembling. "You're either the craziest woman I've ever met, or the bravest," he whispered. He led her away. "Come on, Dad'll see that he gets taken care of. Let's go inside. You need time to calm down."

Rayne glanced back at Joe Jakes. He was standing now and

still crying like a baby. Ben had a hand on the big man's back, leading him inside. She sincerely hoped he got some help before he self-destructed.

But she'd kept her word, and stood up to him once. If he ever confronted her again she would do the safe thing and get out of his way.

Chapter 12

"**R**ayne!" Wade spoke sharply because it appeared that Rayne's steps had faltered somewhat after they had walked through the house to the patio. The guests were in the great room and he thought it best to take her where she could have a little peace and quiet for a few minutes before going in to dinner.

Now, as they walked through the French doors that led to the patio, she managed to stay on her feet long enough to sit down on an overstuffed chaise longue.

"I guess he upset me more than I thought," she said with a nervous smile. Wade squatted in front of her and held one of her hands in his. He smiled gently at her. "I thought you said you weren't going to make a scene," he joked.

She laughed, remembering their conversation last night. "I wouldn't have if he hadn't called me a she-devil from the jump. I know he's your friend but..."

"We grew up together," Wade said. "But Joe has become

another person lately. I've told him he needs to get help for his substance abuse problem. Everybody in his family has, but he wouldn't listen. What you did tonight, making him see himself for the first time, was a good thing. I don't want you feeling anything but good about it."

He rose and sat beside her. Putting his arm around her shoulders, he drew her close and looked into her eyes. "What did he do to you in one of his drunken rampages?"

"In retrospect," Rayne began, "I wish I had kept my nose out of his business. But this is what went down—I've already told you about his disrupting his best friend's wedding?"

Wade nodded in the affirmative.

"With less than thirty minutes before the wedding was to start, one of the bridesmaids came and told me that no one knew where the maid of honor and the best man were, and I got worried. The wedding was held in a luxury hotel in New York. I knew Joe Jakes had a room, so to be on the safe side I found out which room he was in and went up there. One of his friends, another ballplayer, opened the door and asked me if I was the hooker they were expecting. I forced my way into the room, and Joe Jakes came out of one of the bedrooms with a bottle of booze in one hand and a pair of panties in the other. I guess he was getting ready to show his trophy to his two pals who were in the suite with him. 'What the hell do you want?' he asked. He and I had already had one run-in and he'd dubbed me 'that bossy witch.' Guess he was being nice. Anyway, I politely asked him if he'd seen the maid of honor. He laughed and said, yes, he had. She was passed out in his bed. He'd screwed her senseless. That's not how he put it, but I don't want to say what he said.

"So I went in the bedroom he'd indicated with a nod of his big head and, sure enough, she was passed out in his bed. At that point, I phoned downstairs and told my assistant to immediately locate stand-ins for the maid of honor and the best man, who was stinking drunk. Joe Jakes heard me call him stinking drunk, and he wasn't too happy about it. I told him I called them as I saw them, and as I tried to walk past him, he grabbed my backside and squeezed hard. I shoved him backward and kicked him in the balls. He doubled over, yelled for his buddies and told them to hold me by my ankles over the balcony until I apologized to him. And they did. By the time they let me go, I was a nervous wreck."

"And you didn't report it to the police?" Wade asked, incredulous.

"After that? I thought I was lucky to be alive. The man has serious problems. I didn't think the police could protect me from somebody like that!"

Wade's scalp grew tight. He felt his heartbeat slow as if to a deliberate pace that he could control with his anger. He clenched his powerful fists. Heat traveled from his neck to envelop his entire face and singe his ears.

Rayne saw the expression in his eyes go from concern to steely determination. She knew what he was thinking when he got to his feet so fast he nearly toppled her from her perch on the chaise longue. She was up in an instant and clinging to his right arm.

"No! Let it go, Wade. I was unharmed."

He was so strong he pulled her right along with him as he left the patio and went back into the house. "I'm gonna smash his face in, then maybe he'll learn he can't treat women like that!"

"I reduced a two-hundred-pound man into a whimpering baby," Rayne reminded him. "Maybe you ought to protect him from me!" She leaned backward while holding on to his arm, hoping her weight would prevent him from going any farther.

Wade simply turned around and picked her up and carried her the rest of the way to his father's study. As he'd guessed, his father and Joe were in there talking quietly. Both men looked up when he and Rayne entered the room.

Ben rose, concerned. "What happened to Rayne?"

Wade looked up at her, still in his arms. "Nothing." He set her on the floor. "She was just trying to keep me from coming in here and knocking some sense into *his* head!"

Wade regarded Joe with contempt. "You could have killed her!"

His father and Joe immediately knew what he was referring to. Ben stood between his son and Joe. He'd never seen Wade so worked up before. He'd always thought of his son as a gentle giant. He'd been big for his age. But he didn't use his size to intimidate others, or gain the advantage in any way. A superb athlete, he took his aggression out on his opponents on the field. Ben couldn't recall one fistfight that his son was ever involved in. Now he looked like he was ready to tear his friend from limb to limb.

"I'm sorry for what I did," Joe said, looking at Wade with watery, red eyes. He glanced at Rayne. "I haven't always been this way. You were right, I let everything go to my head. I wouldn't let anyone tell me that my personality changed when I got drunk. I always felt like I was the one in control, but it was controlling me. I'm sorry for holding you over that balcony. I look back now and think what could have happened." He rose.

Rayne instinctively moved behind Wade.

Wade firmly grasped her hand in his. "You don't have anything to be afraid of, because Joe is going to a treatment center tomorrow. Am I right, Joe? You're going to check yourself into a facility first thing tomorrow morning. When Gerald gets here, that's what you're going to tell him."

Joe's eyes grew frightened at the mention of his older brother's name. Gerald had told him the last time he'd had to come to the jail and bail him out that he was done with his foolishness, and the next time he was calling a family conference and they were going to sign him into a treatment center whether he wanted to go or not.

Gerald was a detective with the Atlanta police. He wasn't as big as Joe, but he was tougher. Joe knew how to knock a guy on his butt on the football field, but Gerald had learned how to fight on the streets and he didn't fight fair. If an elbow to the face got the job done, that's what he would do.

"You *have* already called Gerald, haven't you, Dad?" Wade wanted to know.

"As soon as we got in here," Ben told him. "He's on the way."

"You never said it was Gerald that you phoned," Joe accused Ben. He'd assumed that they'd phoned his younger brother, Dwight, who was a doctor. Dwight was like a lapdog where his brother Joe was concerned. He jumped to do whatever he asked him to. Manipulating Dwight would have been easy. Gerald could not be tricked.

"Well, you were kind of out of it when we came in here," Ben explained.

"He's going to kick my ass!" Joe cried.

"It's either him or me," Wade said. "Which would you prefer?"

Joe sat back down when he saw the look in Wade's eyes. The man appeared as if he was hoping he'd accept his challenge and fight him. "I'll take my chances with Gerald," Joe said. "You're acting crazy, man."

"Look who's talking," Wade replied. He looked at his father. "Don't you think you ought to go tell your guests you'll be with them shortly? I'll stay here with Joe until Gerald comes."

But first Ben went to Rayne and briefly hugged her. "Honey, are you still up to dinner with my friends? Because if you aren't, I'll tell them you're not feeling well and we'll cancel."

Rayne smiled at him. She felt better after hearing Joe Jakes apologize for what he'd done to her with real sincerity. "I'm fine," she said. "Don't cancel. Just tell them it'll be delayed a few more minutes."

He kissed her forehead. "Okay, sweetie. Whatever you say." He left the room.

Wade and Rayne sat on the couch across from Joe. An uneasy silence settled over the room. Wade and Rayne sat holding hands while Joe sat with his head held down.

He looked up, suddenly, and asked, "Do you still plan parties up in New York?"

Rayne cut him with a glance, and he fell silent again.

Gerald arrived about ten minutes later with a cousin the size of a linebacker. He and the cousin escorted Joe outside where Gerald demanded, "Give Chuck your car keys. You're riding with me."

"Aw, man, I can drive. I haven't been drinking tonight," Joe lied.

"Breathe," Gerald said. Joe blew his breath in his brother's face. "You've had at least two," Gerald said. "Give the man your keys, now!"

Joe handed over the keys. Gerald took his brother by the arm and shoved him into his black SUV. He looked back at Ben, Wade and Rayne, who were watching from the portico. "Night, folks, sorry about the disturbance."

"The disturbance" looked at them through the car window, a whipped-dog expression on his face. "I'm sorry!" he yelled, but his voice was muffled.

"Good night, Gerald. You take good care of him, now," Ben admonished.

"I plan to," said Gerald. He gave him a curt nod and walked around to the driver's side, got in and was soon off. Cousin Chuck followed in Joe's late-model sports car.

"He's such a cop," Ben said proudly of Gerald.

"Salt of the earth," Wade agreed.

He turned and pulled Rayne into the crook of his arm. "Let's go eat!"

Mrs. Knox was pleased when Ben finally stuck his head in the kitchen and announced, "You're on!"

She tilted her head in the direction of her help for the night, her niece, Jasmine, age sixteen, who was earning extra spending money. Jasmine nervously popped her gum. She'd never served anyone at a fancy house like this before.

"Take that gum out," her aunt Elizabeth said. "Follow my lead, and you won't go wrong. This could turn into a nice little part-time job for you. Mr. Jefferson entertains a lot." Jasmine walked over to the kitchen trash receptacle and tossed the gum in.

Elizabeth led the way to the dining room, carrying a beautifully roasted duck on its silver platter. Jasmine pushed the serving cart that was laden with the rest of the gourmet meal.

Everyone applauded when Elizabeth entered the dining room with the duck. Ben carved the bird and as each plate was passed up, he put several slices on it.

When this was done, Elizabeth motioned for Jasmine to begin serving the six couples. Ben and Mere were at one end of the long table, and Wade and Rayne were at the other, with the other four couples making up the middle of each side.

Once everyone had been served, Ben said, "Thank you, Mrs. Knox, Jasmine. Everyone, this is Mrs. Knox's niece, Jasmine. She was kind enough to come help us out this evening."

Everyone smiled at Jasmine, and she blushed.

She and her aunt then left the room, and the meal was devoured with enthusiasm.

For a while there was no sound except that of silverware clinking against china. Then Mere broke the silence with, "Okay, Benjamin, we've all been in suspense long enough. What held up the festivities?"

Ben smiled at her. "One of the guests, Joe Jakes, suddenly started feeling poorly after he arrived. We had to phone his brother Gerald to come for him."

Mere pursed her lips and looked at him with one brow cocked. "Yeah, and my next book is going to be a best seller."

Everyone laughed because even though Mere was a fine writer, she wrote the sort of literary novels that got raves from highbrow reviewers but few sales. She had often said that if she hadn't been born into a wealthy family and married well, to boot, she wouldn't have a figurative pot to pee in.

When Ben could stop laughing, he said, "Okay, Mere. You're probably going to get it from one of your gossipmongers anyway. Joe was a little intoxicated so we thought it best to send him home. Satisfied?"

"Is that all?" Mere asked, skeptical still. "Everyone who follows sports in Atlanta knows that Joe needs to get help for his problem."

There were nods and a general consensus around the table that her assertion was true.

"I just hope he gets help this time," said Marcus Gaston.

His lovely wife, Anne, put down her fork to say, "You know what the problem is, don't you? His family and his friends were so afraid of his losing everything that they ignored his condition far too long. We, as black people, tend to sweep problems like his under the rug, thinking he'll get help on his own, and we will not have been a catalyst for one more black man becoming a failure. It's the same attitude, sometimes, when we won't call the police on drug dealers in the neighborhood. He's somebody's child. He's Miss Martha's grandson, so we won't drop a dime on him. Sometimes we need to step up and call somebody. Things are not going to get any better while we hide our heads in the sand!"

"Amen!" cried Mere. She frowned when she leveled her eyes on Ben. "He is going to get help this time, isn't he?"

"He is," Ben assured her.

"Good," she said, her face brightening. "Now let me get back to this divine duck. Mrs. Knox certainly did a wonderful job on it." She held up a piece with skin on it. "She even got the skin nice and crispy."

Rayne, sitting beside Wade, couldn't agree more. She'd nearly finished her meal while they had been talking. She did wonder if anyone would ask Ben about her origins. After all, until tonight none of them had known she existed. But they were either too civilized to pose the question, or just didn't care. Either way, she was happy.

Wade spent the meal observing her unnoticed. Or so he thought. Rayne knew he was watching her. She was stealing glances at him, too, thinking that tomorrow night she would be back in American Beach, and it would probably be a long time before they saw one another again.

What neither of them knew was that Ben was watching them both, and he was worried about what he saw.

After the meal, everyone retired to the patio for coffee and, for the gentlemen, cigars. The women sat at a table that was not likely to get the back draft from the men's smokes and talked. Rayne noticed that Wade did not smoke. Being male, he was duty-bound to join the men, though.

"Okay, Rayne, now that we have you alone," said Mere, "tell us all about you. Where are you from? What do you do? Are you involved with anyone? Dish!"

"I was raised in Brooklyn, spent my summers in American

Beach in Florida. I live in New York City now where I have an event-planning business. And no, I'm not seeing anyone special right now."

"How old are you, dear?" asked Dorothy Buchanan. She was an attractive woman in her sixties with solid white hair that she wore in a short, sophisticated style. She wore a black pantsuit and silver jewelry. "Twenty-two, twenty-three?"

"Twenty-six," Rayne replied.

"Well, my Justin could probably benefit from dating an older woman. He's twenty-four."

"Twenty-four going on *fifty-four*," said Mere. "Sorry, Dorothy, but that boy does nothing but fool with those computers. He's as boring as paste."

"He's a computer programmer," Dorothy said, defending her grandson. "And he's not boring, he's an intellectual!"

"The last time I saw him," returned Mere, "I asked him what he thought of the Braves and he admitted he hadn't been to one game this season, or watched one on the tube. The boy lives in Atlanta, Dorothy. That's not normal."

"Not everyone likes sports," Dorothy countered. "Justin has other interests."

"Music?" asked Mere.

"He listens to classical music. He says it's intellectually stimulating."

"I bet jazz or rhythm and blues gives him a headache," Mere said, laughing.

"No, but rap and hip-hop disturb his thought processes," Dorothy admitted.

"I bet you like hip-hop music," Mere said to Rayne.

"I like some artists," Rayne said, trying to be fair.

"What do you think of classical music?" asked Mere.

"The same with hip-hop, I like some classical music," Rayne replied.

"There you go!" Dorothy cried triumphantly. "My Justin isn't strange because he likes classical music."

"No," said Mere. "He's just strange. Period."

The ladies laughed, Dorothy joining in. This wasn't the first time she'd taken a good-natured ribbing from Mere about Justin. She worried that the boy would never marry, herself. He did spend too much time in front of his computer.

"What Rayne needs is someone like her big brother," Anne Gaston put in. She and her husband, Marcus, were the youngest couple at the party. Both in their early thirties, Marcus edited a magazine while Anne was an attorney. She looked longingly at Wade. "He's smart, successful and drop-dead gorgeous!"

"Watch it, Anne," said Dorothy. "You're a married woman now. You've missed your chance with our Wade."

Anne took a sip of her coffee. "I'm married, not dead. I can still look and enjoy."

"Who is Wade seeing nowadays?" asked Bitty Nelson. She and her husband, Dupree, lived just down the street. Both in their forties, Bitty was an operating room nurse, and Dupree had a glass company that specialized in windows built to order. He often did business with Ben and Wade's company.

"Cherie Thompson?" Dorothy asked, not really certain.

"Nah, he and Cherie went their separate ways when she accepted that job in Baltimore. That was months ago," Mere said. "Wade has always been closemouthed about the women he's dated. A good quality for a man to have, I say!"

"You would," Dorothy said with a laugh. "The less your gentlemen friends broadcast about you, the better. You'd have a better chance of sinking your claws into the next victim."

Mere feigned a hurt look. "Dorothy, if I didn't know better I'd think you were jealous of the fact that I still date. Seeing as how you and Randolph have been married since the Jurassic Age."

"Not that long," Dorothy said. "Just since Columbus sailed the ocean blue. Randolph was a sailor on the *Santa Maria*."

"And you were one of the natives that greeted them when they got to the New World. I knew there was a lot of Indian in you, girl."

After the laughter had subsided, Anne asked, "Then no one knows whom Wade is dating, huh?"

"Anne, Wade doesn't have to be dating anyone," Mere said.

Anne shook her head in the negative. "Honey, please, a man like that—he's seeing someone. He has needs, after all."

Rayne felt uncomfortable listening to them discuss Wade's sex life. She really didn't want to hear it. "He told me he's been working too hard lately, and hasn't had time for dating," she said.

"Well, my friend Michelle would be all over that in a hot minute," Anne said. "I've got to phone her and tell her he's available. I'll arrange a 'chance' meeting. Who knows? It might work out."

"Your friend Michelle, the attorney?" Mere asked.

"Yes," Anne replied, her haughty brows raised in a questioning gesture. "What? You don't think Michelle is good enough for your almost stepson?"

"Now, see, you're going too far," Mere told her confidentially. "Alluding to my past relationship with Ben. We were keeping this conversation nice and jaunty until you went there."

Anne looked nonplussed. "Seriously, Mere, I didn't mean anything by it. You and Dorothy joke like that all the time."

Mere looked into the younger woman's light brown eyes and saw nothing but sincerity and a desire to placate her. She didn't know why she'd instantly gotten upset by Anne's remark. Maybe she did still have feelings for Ben. Feelings that had nothing to do with friendship.

She smiled at Anne. "No harm done, Anne. I'm sorry I got touchy all of a sudden. Blame it on my hormones." She fanned with her napkin. "Is anyone else hot?"

Anne eyed Wade. "I am!"

Rayne laughed along with everyone else, but deep down, she didn't find Anne's behavior toward Wade amusing in the least.

She was glad when Anne's husband came over to their table and said, "Anne, honey, I think we ought to be leaving. It's almost time for the babysitter to go home."

The other couples soon said their good-nights, too, and Rayne, Wade and Ben found themselves sitting alone on the patio, talking quietly.

It was a cool night, in the midsixties, and Rayne was beginning to feel as though she needed a sweater. She rubbed her arms. Wade immediately rose, removed his jacket and placed it about her shoulders.

Rayne enjoyed the warmth of the jacket and the lingering smell of his aftershave. It was almost like having his arms around her. "I wish you could stay longer," Ben was saying. "Our long weekend ended too soon for me."

"Me, too," Rayne told him, to his utter delight. "But Dad has his operation in less than a week, and I've got to be there."

"I understand," Ben said, sincerity evident in his tone. "I wish him well."

Rayne believed him. Someday she hoped she would learn why he and her dad seemed to have a grudge against each other. For now, though, she simply wanted to enjoy the rest of her time with him and Wade.

"Thank you," she said softly.

"I do," Ben assured her. "I think it's time your dad and I put the past behind us. Tell him that for me, would you? And tell him I'm going to come see him after he's fully recovered. There are things we should discuss."

Rayne smiled at him. "All right, I will."

Ben sighed and got to his feet. He went to Rayne and kissed her forehead. "I'm going to go to bed and give you and your brother a little alone time. Good night."

"Good night," Rayne said, looking at him with genuine affection.

"Night, Dad," said Wade.

After Ben left them, Wade got up and joined Rayne on the overstuffed rattan sofa.

He put his arm around her and she laid her head on his shoulder. "Who is Cherie Thompson?"

Wade smiled. "The ladies have been running their mouths, I see."

"Answer the question," Rayne said in teasing tones. "I told you about Tony."

"Okay, Cherie and I dated for about a year. She was a great girl, but she didn't want the same things I did. I wanted to settle down, and she wasn't finished seeking the big time."

"The big time?"

"She's a marketing expert with an advertising firm in Baltimore. She had no trouble weighing the benefits of a promotion against our relationship and finding our relationship a less desirable proposition. To me, that's not love."

"Oh, so if she'd asked you to give up your position in favor of following her to Baltimore, you would have done it?"

"She didn't ask," he said.

"Did that hurt your feelings?"

"Yes, it did," he said.

She tilted her face up to his. "I'm sorry."

Wade bent and kissed her forehead. Rayne put her arms around his neck and they snuggled closer. They were cheek to cheek as they talked. "I'm so scared, Wade."

"Your dad's operation?" he guessed.

"Yeah, what if something goes wrong?"

"You can't think that way. You've got to think positively. He's agreed to do it, and now everything else is gravy. He'll come through the surgery with flying colors. Recuperate at home with you at his side and, in a matter of months, he'll be healed. Don't allow room for doubt."

"I wish I could be strong like you," she said.

Her sweet, clean breath was on his cheek, and Wade was thinking that he was anything but strong at that moment. His body was taut with desire for her.

"You are strong," he told her. He kissed her high on her right cheekbone, next to her eye. "And you'll be fine, Rayne. If you need me, call me. I'll come."

"I'll be fine," she said, trying to sound stouthearted.

"I mean it," Wade said, his voice husky. "If you need me, I'll drop everything and get the next plane to Florida."

Rayne planted a gentle kiss on his strong chin. "You're so sweet. I don't know how Cherie could have left you."

They looked into each other's eyes and it occurred to both of them, almost in the same instant, that for the past few minutes they'd been touching as lovers might, not as brother and sister should.

They quickly drew apart, and Rayne slid over on the sofa. "Well, I think I'd better go get some sleep."

She got up, took off his jacket and handed it to him. "Good night, Wade."

Wade didn't rise. If he had she would have undoubtedly noticed the effect she'd had on him. "Good night, Rayne. Safe trip tomorrow."

"Yeah, you take care of yourself," Rayne said, and went into the house.

A few minutes later, Wade went inside, too. Because everyone in the house had retired for the night, he was going to have to let himself out. But as he put his hand on the front doorknob his father cleared his throat behind him. "Wade," he said, "may I have a word with you before you go?"

Chapter 13

Ben paced the floor of the study for a minute or so, trying to think how best to put into words what he had to say to his son. The last thing he wanted to do was alienate him. Or confuse him further. It was obvious the boy was already confused.

Wade stood watching his father. "What is it? Does it concern Rayne?"

Ben saw his entry, and took it. "You care a lot about her, don't you?"

Wade walked over to one of the leather armchairs near the unlit fireplace and sat down. He looked up at his father. "I've come to care for her, yes."

Ben went and stood in front of the fireplace, his hand on the mantelpiece. He did not look Wade in the eyes when he said, "Maybe a little too much?"

Son and father locked eyes across the room. "What are you trying to say?" asked Wade, his tone even.

"Do you want to tell me what happened on that beach, son? The night you two met?"

Wade had not seen fit to tell his father everything that had happened. Even though, the very next day, he'd confessed to Ray Walker that he was indeed attracted to Rayne, he didn't think his father would understand. Or perhaps he was ashamed of his feelings, and until he worked them out for himself, he didn't feel comfortable explaining them to his father. Ray Walker was in essence a stranger. Sometimes it was easier to talk to strangers. Although, after their conversation he'd felt as if he and Ray Walker had somehow bonded.

"Nothing happened. We talked. The next day, as I've told you, I met Mr. Walker at church and we both decided to come clean."

"You meet a beautiful girl on the beach, you ended up being her knight in shining armor and you're telling me that no romantic sparks flew?" Ben asked. "After all, you two had no idea whom you were talking to."

"Of course, I thought she was attractive. I think a lot of women are attractive."

Ben narrowed his eyes at his son and shook his head. "You're lying, Wade. I can always tell when you're lying. Your voice changes. Your whole demeanor changes. Why won't you be honest with me? I'm your father, I'm not going to judge you!"

Ben sighed and calmed himself.

"I love you, son. Nothing's ever going to alter that fact. God knows I'm not a perfect father, but I've always tried my best. If there's something you need to tell me, do it. I wouldn't even ask, but after watching you and Rayne together, the intimate way you speak with each other, how you can't seem to keep your hands off each other, I had to ask."

Wade weighed the consequences of confessing his weakness to his father. It was true, he couldn't be blamed for having feelings for her when he was unaware of who she really was. Nor could he be faulted for a natural human response. But still he didn't think it wise to tell his father Rayne filled him with desire. It was their, his and Rayne's, problem to solve, and it was nobody else's business.

"What can I say? We adore each other already and can't help hugging each other whenever we're in the same room. I've never had a sister before, I didn't realize that hugging them was off-limits."

Ben didn't believe him for a minute but had no choice but to accept him at his word.

"All right, son." He smiled. "No harm, no foul? If there were actually something to it I felt honor-bound to warn you of the pitfalls of being attracted to your own sister. And also to assure you that it's understandable if you're attracted to Rayne. It isn't your fault that you had no idea whom she was. I should have started trying to find out the truth years ago. And I'm sure Ray and Julianne regret not telling Rayne that I'm her father and that she had a brother, years ago, as well.

"What I'm saying, son, is this is a real mess, and it's going to take some time to get it fully straightened out. Ray, Julianne and I need to sit down and talk this through. After that, well, I'm sure that everything will turn out to your satisfaction. In fact, I know it will."

Wade just stared at him, totally confused. "I didn't understand a word you said. At first it sounded like you were trying to warn me not to think of Rayne as more than a sister. Then it appeared as if you'd reversed yourself and were trying to say if we were attracted to each other, we should wait and in the end everything would turn out in our favor. Which is it, Dad?"

"Both, son," Ben told him. "Unfortunately life is never cut-and-dried. And secrets have a way of surfacing whether you want them to or not. Now, on that cryptic note, I'm going to say good night."

Wade pushed himself up out of the armchair. He went and briefly hugged his father. Peering into his eyes, he said, "I'm beginning to wonder if you're getting senile."

"Not yet," Ben said with a laugh. "Come on, I'll walk you to the door."

He was not at all satisfied with the outcome of their conversation. He felt Wade was holding back, and he knew *he* was not as forthcoming as he ought to be. Those secrets he'd mentioned earlier were eating at his soul.

After Ben saw Wade off, he went back upstairs to bed, but he tossed and turned until he finally gave up on sleep, sat up in bed, and reached for the phone on his nightstand.

He dialed Mere's number.

It rang only twice. Mere pounced on it with a snarl. "Benjamin Jefferson, you'd better be glad I knew it was you. I don't let just anybody interrupt my beauty sleep."

"Sorry, Mere," Ben said. "Look, are you going to be home tomorrow, say at around noon? I have to take Rayne to the airport in the morning, but after that I wanted to drop by and talk to you about something. I need an unbiased opinion."

"And you came to *me?*"

"Mere, we've been friends for more than twenty years. We were lovers for only five. I think the friendship supersedes the bedroom. I trust your judgment."

"You sound serious," Mere said softly. After a pause, she continued, "Of course, Benjamin. I'll be expecting you for lunch. Drive yourself. Patty is still upset with Mac for breaking up with her."

Patty was her housekeeper.

"Mac and Patty were a bad combo from the start," said Ben. "He's like a playful puppy and she's more like a lioness taking care of her cubs."

"I know," agreed Mere. "They're both young, but worlds apart in attitudes."

"Thanks, Mere. See you tomorrow."

"Good night," said Mere, and hung up.

Ben's conscience let him sleep after that and soon he was snoring softly.

His son, on the other hand, lay awake for hours wondering what was going on with his father. It was more than apparent that he was sitting on some juicy secret. After Rayne, Wade had figured that all his father's secrets were finally out in the open. But, no, there was something else.

And if his dad could tell him about Rayne, but held back about this new thing, then it must be really major. Huge. Capable of ruining lives or at the very least, changing lives.

He turned over onto his left side and got comfortable. Whatever it was, it concerned both of Rayne's parents. His father had said once he sat down with the two of them their problems would be resolved. The question was, why wasn't his father making an effort to go see Ray Walker now, before his operation? There were only a few days left before he was scheduled for surgery.

Wade didn't like to think that his father was so reluctant to tell Ray Walker what he needed to tell him that he was willing to risk his not surviving the operation. Ray Walker's death would certainly render his need to reveal a deep, dark secret irrelevant. Wade turned back onto his right side. He couldn't get comfortable. Possibly because, like the princess and the pea, something minuscule was bothering him, too. His belief that his father wasn't being honest with him.

He sat up in bed. "Old folks, and their twisted pasts," he grumbled. If not for his father's affair with Julianne, and then Julianne's decision not to tell him when she found herself pregnant, none of this would be happening. He thought all the drama was over. What could his father possibly have to tell Ray and Julianne? Something from their past that involved all of them. He was getting a headache.

He got up and went downstairs to the kitchen where he went to the fridge and got the milk. He poured himself a glass, then went into the cabinet above the refrigerator and pulled out his stash of Chips Ahoy chocolate chip cookies. Leaning against the counter, he ate cookies and drank milk, thinking.

In a perfect world, he and Rayne would not have one drop of blood in common. He would woo her with everything he had in him, give her his heart, and make her his.

He wished he lived in that world.

In the meantime, a chocolate chip cookie would have to soothe his tortured soul.

"Goodbye, sweetheart. Call me when you get there," Ben said as he hugged Rayne tightly. They were standing in the waiting area of the airport for the plane that would take her back home. Passengers were lining up in preparation for boarding.

"Goodbye, Pop," Rayne said with a toothy smile.

"Pop?" said Ben, delighted. "I can work with that." He kissed her cheek.

"It's Pop for now," Rayne told him. "It might be Dad next time, or Father."

"Anything's fine with me," Ben said softly. He released her because the line was moving faster now and he didn't want to delay her any longer. "Thanks for coming to see your old man. I had a wonderful time getting to know you a little."

"So did I," Rayne said softly. She kissed his cheek impulsively, and said, "Go now before I start crying. And you don't want to see me cry—it's really ugly."

"Okay," Ben said, backing away. "But I get to see your ugly cry next time. Deal?"

"Deal!" Rayne told him. Then she turned and got in line. One more person, and she'd be the next passenger to board.

Ben continued slowly backing away, loathe to let her out of his sight.

Rayne was in line about to hand her ticket to the woman behind the counter. She turned and smiled at him one last time, and blew him a kiss.

Ben's heart did a flip-flop, and then he turned and quickly walked away.

He felt foolish when, once he reached his late-model Cadillac, he had to wipe tears from his cheeks with the back of his hand. He sniffed and turned the key in the ignition. Mere was waiting, and it would take him more than an hour to reach her house in Kennesaw, Georgia. Mere had moved out of the city years ago, saying she couldn't sleep with the sounds of traffic and sirens in the background. Kennesaw was a pleasant small town surrounded by magnificent countryside. Ben often enjoyed the drive.

Then there was the mountain. Kennesaw Mountain. Mere had taken him hiking one morning. She'd worn him out. He didn't know where the woman got her energy, but she was like the Energizer bunny, she just kept going and going.

He didn't know what had possessed him to leave her for a younger woman. A woman half her age. He guessed he was going through a midlife crisis. No. He was turning over a new leaf. He needed to start facing the facts about his life: Meredith Huston-Bates had simply not taken any crap. She was honest with herself, honest with others and demanded that the man in her life reciprocated. Being true to herself was more important to Mere than anything else. Ben had not been able to meet her expectations. All he had wanted at the time was a pretty woman on his arm and a good lover in his bed. Mere was both. When he'd asked her to keep their relationship on that level, she was not willing to do so. She needed real intimacy. Not some cheap imitation. And she was willing to give him up to prove her point.

Now, ironically, it was her honesty and her penchant for not pulling any punches that had him driving up to Kennesaw Mountain. She would be his sounding board, and she would tell him just how much crap he was shoveling lately. He was counting on it.

Mere answered the door wearing a pair of well-worn jeans and a white midriff peasant blouse. Ben glanced at her feet. Bare, of course. Nails painted siren red. Her short hair looked like she'd just rolled out of bed. He could tell she'd been writing. Mere was immaculately turned out unless she was writing. Then, she simply didn't care how she looked. Ben smiled. *She really is over me,* he thought. When they were an item she never would have let him see her without makeup, or without her hair in a fetching style.

She laughed. "What? Do you need an invitation? Get in here!"

Ben stepped inside. "I was just admiring your belly button."

"Hey, the old belly button is still sexy, and you know it," said Mere, closing the door and leading him toward the back of the house. Ben thought her bottom wasn't bad either.

Mere was a true Georgian in that she'd had her house on the side of the mountain built of Georgia pine. Big, and airy, it had wonderful flow-through, and she'd furnished it in spare pieces, which made it appear even more spacious.

Ben found himself finding her feline grace quite appealing. Her bare feet made no sound on the hardwood floors, and her movements were so sinuous he was sure she would break into a belly dance any time now. Must have been the midriff top. He was focused on her belly.

He mentally shook himself. He was not here to make a pass at Mere, however enticing the thought was. He had a serious problem he needed help with.

The table had already been set on the deck. The deep backyard was covered in a blanket of healthy grass, and he saw that Mere's flower garden was in full bloom. She often joked that it was a prerequisite for southern women to garden, it was in the bylaws of all southern states. She was keeping up her end of the bargain, because her backyard was a riot of colors: yellow, purple, red, white, deep pink.

Mere walked over to the bar. "I made virgin margaritas since you're driving. We're having that seafood salad you always liked."

Ben went over and took the pitcher of margarita mix from her. "Let me." He adeptly prepared two margaritas and handed her one in a long-stemmed glass. "Thanks for having me, Mere."

Mere held his gaze with a sultry expression in her own. "I haven't had you yet."

Ben smiled. "Does that mean you're interested?"

"Oh, I miss you in bed. You don't miss the water until the well runs dry. But, no, I'm not interested anymore. I'm dating an environmentalist now. I met him when I was hiking one day last month."

Ben was surprised by his feeling of loss. But he recovered with, "I'm happy for you, Mere."

"Thanks," Mere said, turning away to sit at the table. She crossed her long legs then looked up at him. "Shall we talk before lunch, or afterward?"

"After," Ben said. "I don't want you to have any ammunition in case you get the notion to dump something on me."

Mere laughed. "I dump one salad on you, and you never forget!"

"With funky blue cheese dressing," Ben cried.

"Well, you deserved it," Mere insisted. "Taking me to a fine restaurant to break up with me. You thought I wouldn't have hysterics in a place like that. Well, I didn't scream or yell, I simply put my bowl of salad on your head. You should be grateful I wasn't eating chili or soup. At least the salad didn't scald you."

They chatted amiably all through their lunch that was served by a cheerful Patty, who was looking as lovely as ever, Ben was happy to note. He couldn't wait to rub it in to Mac when he got home. Mac thought she was probably letting her looks go since she'd lost him.

After they'd finished eating, Mere took their dishes to the kitchen and returned with steaming cups of coffee. The air was bracing, and she figured Ben might need the caffeine to keep him alert on his drive back to Atlanta.

She set his coffee in front of him and sat down. Regarding him with inquisitive eyes, she said, "All right, I'm ready to hear it. What's up?"

Mere listened intently while Ben talked. She would occasionally take a sip of her coffee and nod, but she didn't interrupt him once. Ben told her everything from the beginning, not leaving anything out. He wanted her to have the entire story so that she'd be better able to judge what his next move should be. When he was done, he felt lighter. Unloading his burden onto someone else's shoulders had freed him. He was no longer the sole living keeper of Deirdre's secret.

Mere didn't open her mouth for a few minutes after he'd stopped talking. She finished her coffee, set the cup on its saucer, then simply looked at him.

Ben's expression changed from relieved to anxious. "Mere,

if you don't have an opinion, then I'm really worse off than I thought."

"Oh, I've got plenty of opinions," Mere said at last. Her eyes narrowed. "My first is that you're an asshole. My next is that you're a coward. My next is that Deirdre was a fool for trusting a selfish person like yourself with such an important mission. What was she thinking, leaving her son's fate in your hands? But then she was sick at the end. Okay, that's her excuse, but what's yours?" She ended on a high note, her voice rising to nearly a screech. She got up and walked to the end of the deck, her back to him. "I don't know why you came to me with this. You know what you have to do. Why don't you go do it?" She spun around suddenly, her eyes fierce. "Wait a minute. You're hoping that Ray Walker dies and you get to keep all the rewards in this twisted game of yours, aren't you?" She didn't wait for his reply. She kept talking as she slowly walked back over to him. "If that wasn't the case, you would have told him once he and Julianne told Rayne about *you*. You bastard!" She came up to him swiftly, catching him off guard, and gave him a slap with all her strength behind it. "The next time you want to clear your conscience, don't come to me, Benjamin." She stepped away, rubbing her hand, which was stinging. Tears sat in her eyes. "I lied about the environmentalist. The fact is, I'm still in love with you. I realized it last night. It's funny, really. It was just a snide remark made by Anne Gaston. But I knew then that my heart still belonged to you. But I'm telling you now, if you still harbor any feelings for me, forget about them. I can never look you in the eyes again, knowing what I know about you."

She turned to go inside, but Ben was on his feet in an instant. He grabbed her by the arm, halting her in her tracks. "Okay, you've had your say. It's my turn now. Sit down."

"No!" Mere said obstinately.

"Sit!"

Mere sat down and looked up at him defiantly. "I don't want to hear this!"

Ignoring her remark, Ben was the one who paced this time. "All right, I concede that I've been selfish. But to be fair, Ray and Julianne kept their secret for years, too. So you think I've done Ray Walker wrong all these years? Well, I think that I was wronged just as much as he was, because he was aware that Rayne was mine. Plus, you've got to factor in my love for Wade. As the years passed, I couldn't bear the thought of doing what you so passionately advocate that I do. And it's still not going to be easy, but I've decided that it's the right thing."

Mere visibly relaxed.

"To complicate matters," Ben continued, "I believe that Wade is falling in love with Rayne. If he isn't already in love with her."

Mere shook her head. "Lord, have mercy."

"He's going to hate me when I tell him," Ben worried.

"Yes, he is," agreed Mere. "At least for a while."

Ben went and knelt in front of her. They peered into each other's eyes. "I'm sorry I hurt you. I'm sorry I've been a disappointment, but I'm trying to act like I have some sense now. I know it's been a long time coming."

Mere gave him a small smile. "It sure has."

Ben rose, bringing her to her feet with him. He pulled her into his arms and hugged her tightly. Releasing her, he asked, "May I call you when I get back from Florida?"

Mere paused longer than he liked, but he was working on being a more patient man, too. "Yes, Benjamin, please do."

Ben smiled, relief written all over his face. He bent his head and planted a soft kiss on her lips, after which he murmured, "Thank you, Mere."

* * *

"Rayne, bring that bowl of homemade barbecue sauce from the refrigerator, too!" called Shirley from the deck as Rayne went through the sliding glass doors carrying a tray that had previously held parboiled pork ribs that would finish cooking on the grill. "Oh, and if Rick and Shannon are in the house playing video games, tell them to get their butts out here and look after the little ones. I'm tired of these rug rats kicking up sand around the grill."

"Yes, ma'am," Rayne said loudly. With the boom box blasting, and the sounds of children's screams of delight, she had to speak loudly to be heard.

She went to the sink, washed the tray and put it in the dish rack to drain. Then she dried her hands on a dish towel and went into the den to see if Rick and Shannon were indeed playing video games in there.

She stuck her head in the room. No Rick and Shannon. Turning away, she called, "Shannon! Are you in the house?" The house, as opposed to the backyard, was silent. Shannon should have heard her.

Rayne paused to lean against the wall, taking a breather. Ever since she'd gotten home from Atlanta it appeared that things were in fast-forward. Her father's operation was going to take place tomorrow. Aunt Shirley had insisted on everybody coming to the house for a Fourth of July get-together. Now there were more than fifty folks in the backyard, including her grandma Vivian, waiting to chow down on Independence Day barbecue. She was pooped. Because she was willing, Aunt Shirley had enlisted her help with everything. She'd washed and seasoned all of the meat, the chicken and the ribs. Made the potato salad and a red, white and blue sheet cake that would feed fifty people. She wished Aunt Shirley would enlist some other willing body to take orders from her.

She was beginning to think her mother had a point about Aunt Shirley being too bossy for her own good.

And as for her mother and father, they were falling in love all over again. Anybody could see the loaded looks passing between them. More than once, Rayne had caught Aunt Shirley looking at them with a frown on her face, and an irritated "hmph!" on her lips. After all, those two were making her worst nightmare come true: they were reconciling. Aunt Shirley put that event right up there with the Apocalypse.

Rayne pushed away from the wall. She'd check the bedrooms before going back outside. She came to her father's bedroom first, turned the doorknob and looked inside. There was no one in there. Next, she tried her mother's room. No one in there, either. She didn't bother looking in her bedroom. But when she approached Shannon's she heard music playing behind the closed door. She knocked. "Shannon, are you in there?"

No reply.

"Shannon?" A little louder in case she couldn't be heard over the music.

"Yeah!" came a nervous reply from the other side of the door. Rayne heard the distinct sound of the door being unlocked. Why would Shannon lock her door? Unless she was changing clothes and didn't want anyone to inadvertently walk in on her while she was in semiundress?

Shannon pulled the door open only a crack. "Hey, Rayne, what's up?"

Her behavior was suspicious to Rayne. On top of that, Rayne suddenly heard the sound of something heavy hitting the hardwood floor. She put her shoulder to the door, pushed Shannon aside, and found a teen boy sitting on the floor below the window, his pants halfway off his hips, in today's style. He'd apparently been trying to get out of the window so fast he'd forgotten to pull up his pants, and his pants had been a hindrance to his climbing through the window. Foiled by a fashion trend!

Rayne looked at Shannon with utter disbelief. Sneaking a boy in her room, and she was only fifteen! She glared down at the boy. "Do I *know* you?"

"He's a friend of Rick's," Shannon cried, talking fast. "I met him when we first got here. Rayne, nothing happened. We were kissing, that's all. Look at me, I'm fully dressed. Honest, Rayne. I just wanted to see, that's all. I wanted to see!"

"What's your name?" Rayne shouted, frightening the poor boy even more than he already was. "And get up from there."

The boy held on to his jeans as he got to his feet, then quickly pulled them up onto his hips. "Pete Jones," he said, his voice low. "I go to school with Rick. Our families are friends."

"How old are you, Pete?"

"Fifteen."

He was short, only as tall as Shannon, who was five-five, but muscular and solidly built. "We weren't going to do anything, honest. We were only kissing. Nothing else. I swear!"

"Yeah, well, you can explain that to Shannon's mom."

"No!" Shannon pleaded. She went and grasped Rayne by the arm. "I'm not lying, Rayne, we weren't going to have sex. I only wanted to kiss him. I've never done it, and all of my friends at school have. I *wanted* to be kissed. Rayne, have a heart. Come on, you were young once."

Rayne wondered when twenty-six got to be old age. "This isn't my call to make, and you know it, Shannon. I'm not your mother. It's up to her to decide what to do about your behavior."

"I promise not to do this ever again, Rayne. Please, don't tell. You're my sister, we're supposed to be able to keep each other's secrets. And no harm's been done. We didn't even get the chance to kiss more than once. Pete was getting ready to kiss me again, and you knocked on the door."

"Okay," said Rayne.

Both Shannon and Pete let out sighs of relief.

"I won't tell Mom about this if *you* do," Rayne finished.

Shannon let out a groan. "God, Rayne, that's not fair. Mom is going to want to start paddling me again like I'm a kid or something."

"You should have thought about that before you invited a boy to your room for kissing lessons," Rayne said.

She walked to the door and held it open. "After you, Pete."

Pete looked back at Shannon. "Sorry, Shannon."

"It's not your fault," Shannon told him. "I asked you, remember?"

"Yeah, but I knew it was a dumb idea. I just like you so much."

The two looked at each other longingly. Rayne rolled her eyes. "Shannon, if you two wanted to date each other, you should have gone to Mom and asked her. Instead of sneaking around like this."

"You know Mom is not going to let me date until I'm sixteen," Shannon said.

"Now it might be later than that," Rayne told her.

The doorbell rang.

Shannon looked at Rayne expectantly. "Want me to get it?"

"No, you've got to talk to Mom. I'll get it," said Rayne.

She let Shannon and Pete precede her down the hallway, and once they were in the living room, Rayne pointed toward the kitchen. "Go on. I'll be out there soon." It was a warning for them to do as she said. The two of them trudged through the living room as if a firing squad were waiting for them once they got outside. As slowly as their legs could carry them. "Move!" cried Rayne. "Don't make me have to go out there with you."

They picked up speed then, and soon were out of her eyesight.

"Coming!" Rayne called as she neared the front door. If it wasn't one thing, it was another. She thought that everyone who was coming to the party was already there.

She peered through the peephole, and her mouth fell open in surprise. Albeit a very good surprise. She couldn't get the door open fast enough, and once it was open, she flung it wide. It was at that moment that she had the presence of mind to realize that she shouldn't appear overly eager, and she tried to contain her excitement, to no avail.

She threw herself into his arms anyway.

Wade laughed, picked her up and hugged her. Rayne noticed Ben standing behind him while she was in his arms. "Pop!" she cried. "You, too? This is going to be one fabulous Fourth of July. Your grandma Geneva's here, Wade."

"Wonderful," Wade said. Rayne peered closely at him. Even though he was smiling, in his eyes was a deep melancholy expression that she'd never seen in them before. She welcomed them inside and closed the door. Both men were in casual wear. Wade in jeans and T-shirt, her pop in slacks and shirt. But she knew instinctively that they hadn't made the trip from Atlanta just to wish her a happy Fourth of July.

In case they *were* here on a social call, she chose to ignore her conviction that the reason for their visit was of a serious nature. She hugged Ben after Wade released her and clasped his hand in hers. "To what do I owe the pleasure of seeing you two again?"

Ben smiled at her. "Sweetheart, I need to speak with your mother and your father. It's important."

Rayne let go of his hand and took a step backward. "Is this that thing you said you needed to tell them?" she asked suspiciously. "Because if it is, I thought you were going to wait until after Dad's operation."

"I think it would be unfair to him to wait until after the operation," Ben told her with sincerity. "I promise you, this is something he's going to want to know. Something that will make him happy. I wouldn't have come here if I thought it would upset him unduly. You could say it's something that will give him more to live for."

Rayne looked at Wade, her brows arched questioningly. She wanted to hear from him that they were not here to upset her father. "He needs to be in the right frame of mind for the surgery," she said. "I will not risk his becoming emotionally distraught, okay? You need to tell me what it is, and if I think he can handle it, then you can talk to him. I'm unmovable on that."

Her pop looked beseechingly at Wade. "Do you want to tell her, son?"

To Rayne, Wade appeared ambivalent. He looked torn, as if part of him wanted to get this out in the open, and the other wanted to sweep it under the rug forever. Rayne willed him to look her in the eyes. Wade's gaze went to hers. "Your life has already been turned upside down, I don't want to add to the upheaval. But, hopefully, this is the last disclosure that my father has to make." He turned sharp eyes on his dad. "It is, isn't it?"

Ben nodded solemnly. "Yes, all of my skeletons will be out of the closet after this."

Wade clasped one of Rayne's hands in his. "Look at me."

Rayne did, she took in his large dark brown eyes with lighter brown striations. She marveled at the way his wide, sensually contoured mouth curved up at the corners. He was smiling at her. And she loved his square, clean-shaven chin.

He led her to a wall that was lined with photographs of her family. Her father, her mother, photos of her, Shannon, the extended family of Walkers, all at various stages in their lives. He stopped in front of a photograph of her father. In it, Ray was wearing khaki slacks and shirt, the sort of boots he'd worn every day when he'd been in the construction business, and holding a hard hat in his right hand.

His smile was warm and full. Dimples showed in both cheeks, and the sunlight made his curly brown hair appear to have red highlights. Rayne studied the photo. It was a picture she'd passed in the hallway for years and years, not really paying much attention to it. Her father was twenty years younger in it.

She peered up at Wade. Then back at the photograph. Wade. The photograph. Wade.

"Oh, my God!"

Chapter 14

"**Y**ou're *not* my brother!" Rayne exclaimed.

"No, I am most definitely not your brother," Wade was happy to report. He watched her with wary eyes, though, wondering what her next reaction would be.

He knew that all of this would take time to process. He was still reeling, and he'd had twenty-four hours to let it sink in. He admired Ray Walker for several reasons, among them his unselfishness in raising Rayne as his own. That took a special kind of man, no matter what his father's opinion of him was. His father, on the other hand, had known he wasn't his son, known his mother wanted him to know his biological father, and still had chosen to sit on the secret for thirty-four years.

He hoped he would one day be able to forgive him, but he didn't know if he ever could. Loving a child was one thing, but keeping him from his family because he hated his biological father was another. It was willfully malicious in Wade's estimation, and he didn't think he was being unfairly judgmental. How hypocritical of his father to cry foul when it was his daughter being kept from him! But when it was the reverse he had decided to play God with people's lives.

Rayne was smiling, but it was impossible to tell what was going on behind her eyes.

"Talk to me," Wade urged her.

Rayne looked at him, then at her second father, who was still hanging back, unsure of his welcome.

"I know some women tend to be attracted to men who remind them of their fathers, but this is ridiculous!" Rayne joked. The expression in her eyes was pained, though. "I feel like I'm going to need a lot of time on a psychiatrist's couch." She was staring at Wade. "You have dimples just like Dad's. Your eye color, your hair color, well, he has some gray now, but identical! Why couldn't I see it?" She shook her head in confusion.

Wade was getting worried. Did she think she was attracted to him only because he reminded her of her father? And if the notion turned her off, did that mean she could conveniently turn off her feelings for him?

He went to her and grasped her by the hand, pulling her with him toward the front door. "Excuse us for a few minutes," he tossed over his shoulder at his dad.

Ben went and sat down in the living room.

Outside on the front stoop, Wade let go of Rayne's hand, preparing to turn her around and make her face him while he argued his case. But the moment he closed the door behind them, Rayne was already walking into his arms and offering him her mouth.

She locked her fingers behind his neck, and Wade pulled her fully into his arms. He bent down and their mouths met, tasting lips, moving further to parting lips and inhaling each other's breath. As liberating as that was when their tongues touched, their hunger increased tenfold. The kiss deepened, their moans of pleasure softly erotic to their ears. When they drew apart, they stood gazing into each other's eyes.

They smiled satisfied smiles. "I think I'm going to enjoy your not being my brother."

"There are certain fringe benefits," Wade told her, and bent to kiss her again.

This time, they didn't stop until they heard someone opening the front door from the inside. They hastily drew apart, embarrassed expressions on their faces.

Ray wore a deep frown. "What in the *hell* is going on? I walk into my living room, and that man is sitting on my couch like he owns the place, then I look out my peephole and catch you two kissing like hot-blooded teens on prom night. Somebody better start explaining something to me, right now!"

Rayne thought a picture was worth a thousand words, so she stepped forward and smiled at her father. "Follow me."

Since Ray wanted to get to the bottom of this mess, he did.

Rayne walked over to the same photograph Wade had used to illustrate the truth.

"Look at him," she said to her dad, referring to Wade.

"I've seen him before," Ray said. "Many times. He's the very spit of his father."

"You've got that right," Rayne said, still smiling.

"What are you smiling so much about?" Ray asked. "Ain't nothin' to smile about when I catch you kissing your own brother like that. Girl, you ought to be hanging your head in shame. You, too!" He gave Wade a sharp look. "Smiling like a damned fool, both of you."

"Look at him," Rayne insisted. "Then look at yourself twenty years ago."

Ray huffed, but he stood closer to the photograph, as he

was nearsighted. And he observed Wade more intently as well. His daughter had taken leave of her senses. What did she expect him to see, looking at an old picture of himself, and this young fool?

Kissing his own sister! Ben Jefferson had raised a heathen, an animal who apparently had no compunction whatsoever about committing incest. He continued to look at the photo, and Wade. He conceded that there was something about the shape of the boy's head and his own, both square heads, big, proud heads. And wasn't that peculiar? Wade smiled in much the same way that he did. Their eyes were shaped the same, too, and the color was similar. Similar? No, damn it, they were exactly the same color of brown and gold. Dark brown with those little flecks of gold in them.

He'd inherited those eyes from *his* daddy, and his daddy had inherited them from *his* daddy. Ray felt weak in the knees.

He frowned at Wade. Wade was nodding his head in the affirmative.

Tears instantly formed in Ray's eyes. "You mean your mother was pregnant by me when she married Ben Jefferson?"

"She didn't tell you because she wanted you to go to art school. She wanted you to have every opportunity to make something of yourself. That's what she told my…dad."

Ben joined them. "Before she died, she asked me to tell you after she was gone. She didn't want to see the regret in your eyes, she said. She'd made her decision, and she always thought it was a good one. But when she learned she was dying, she wanted Wade to know you and she entrusted me with her secret. I'm the one to blame for not telling you before now."

Ray faced him. "I'll deal with you later, but for now I'm going to hug my son."

He and Wade embraced. Rayne stood back enjoying the sight of the two big men, so alike, hugging one another, one of them weeping, the other laughing softly.

When Ray could finally let go of his son, he said to Rayne, "Thank God you two don't have a drop of common blood between you. I thought I was going to have to send you to a convent."

She went and kissed him on the cheek. "No need for that. You want me to go get Mom?"

He nodded. "Yes, and Shirley and the grandmothers, too. Miss Geneva and Momma."

"All right," Rayne replied happily. She left them.

She didn't get past aunt Shirley, who was tending the grill on the back deck. Shirley grabbed her shirttail. "Hey, you! Where is that barbecue sauce I sent you for? And what is going on in the house? Your daddy went in there to get the barbecue sauce, and *he* got lost. It's like the Bermuda Triangle, or something." Rayne's shirttail slipped from her fingers and Rayne ran down the steps into the yard. "Daddy wants to see you inside, Aunt Shirley. Can't you get Uncle Buddy to tend the meat until you get back?"

"Not if we don't want it to burn. He likes everything welldone. Where are you going, child?"

"Daddy wants to see Mom and the grandmas, too," Rayne explained. "Be right back."

"That's what they all say," said Shirley as she turned a slab of ribs over on the grill.

In the house, Ray invited Ben and Wade to sit down. When all three of them were seated, Ray in his favorite recliner, and Ben and Wade sharing the couch, he turned his attention to Ben. "I'm not going to scream and shout at you, Ben. I don't have the inclination, nor the energy. I'm sure the hatred that we had for each other drove us to do things we would normally find reprehensible. I hated you for stealing my girl as soon as my back was turned. Now I learn that it was her decision. She made the decision for all of us. She didn't trust that I would step up to the plate and take care of her and our child."

"That's not it," Ben said. "She thought she was committing a selfless act. Giving you the chance to get the training you needed. She didn't want you to be stuck in American Beach, with no future."

"And yet, here I am," Ray said. "In the place I love best in all the world. Stuck in American Beach, as you say."

"Yes, but you became a world-renowned artist," Ben pointed out. "Where you live is your choice, it's not your only option. Give her that much. That her sacrifice was worth something."

"Okay," Ray said. "I can't vilify Deirdre. Like Julianne, she thought she was doing the right thing at the time. We can argue our points until we're blue in the face, but that doesn't change the fact that we've both missed seeing our children grow up."

"Then we have to move forward from here," Ben suggested. "Two enemies raised each other's children, and both of them turned out pretty well if I do say so myself."

"You don't have to say so by your lonesome," Ray said, looking admiringly at Wade. "You did a good job of raising my son."

"And you and Julianne did a good job of raising my daughter."

A collective gasp was heard from the doorway. Five women stood there: Rayne, Julianne, Shirley, Geneva and Vivian. The younger women allowed the grandmothers to enter the room first.

"I knew it!" cried Vivian. She went straight to Wade and pulled him up for a hug. "My grandbaby!"

"Our grandchild," Geneva said, wanting equal time. Wade bent and kissed her silken cheek.

"Didn't I tell you, Geneva?" Vivian crowed. "The first time I saw that boy in church, I knew he belonged to my Ray! But you said Deirdre would have told you if that was the case. But I remember telling you that there are some things a woman will not even tell her own mother!"

Geneva's eyes were on Ben. Ray might not be angry and was willing to let bygones be bygones, but his mother-in-law was incensed. Her petite body moved swifter than anyone ever thought it could move, and she was on him, pounding him with her fists.

Wade pulled her off his father, and held her firmly about the waist. "Control yourself, Geneva." He never called her Geneva unless he was upset with her. "Today is about forgiveness. Ray, um, Dad, has set the tone. Now, if you want to say something to Dad, go right ahead, but there will be no hitting."

Geneva pouted. "Somebody needs to beat him. He's known all this time, and never said anything. He kept you to himself, and he wasn't even your father."

"He loved me like a father." Wade surprised himself by coming to his father's defense. Even though he felt much the way that Geneva did, he had to give it to his father: like Ray Walker, he'd taken being a father seriously. He had not made him feel as if he were not his flesh and blood. "Maybe after losing Mom, he just didn't want to be alone."

Ben looked up at his son. There were tears in his eyes. Wade had touched on a sore spot. Ben would never admit that he had no one after Deirdre died. But, yes, he had felt alone. He knew that to anyone looking on, they would have thought he was an adulterer who had no love or respect for his wife. But he had truly loved her, and once she was gone, he figured he would never love anyone else as much as he'd love her. He was wrong, though. He'd loved Wade just as much. Wade was a part of Deirdre, and he did not want to give him up.

His voice cracked now as he said, "I know you all don't believe it, but I loved Deirdre. And, yes, it was hard to give up her son. I made all kinds of deals with myself. Every year around his birthday, I would say, this year I'm going to tell him. But I couldn't force myself to do it."

"Sound familiar?" Rayne asked her mother and father.

"Very," Julianne admitted. It was the first time she'd been in the room with Rayne's father in over twenty years. She thought she would want to scratch his eyes out, but instead she found herself feeling sympathy for him. She went and stood next to Ray's recliner.

"All right, so everything's out in the open now. Rayne and Wade are not brother and sister. A fact that I'm sure delights both of them," Ray said. He smiled up at Wade, then at Rayne. "Ben, Julianne and I have all laid down our burdens. Can we go celebrate now?" He looked at Shirley. "Is the meat done yet, baby sister?"

"I left Buddy in charge," Shirley told him. "It's probably as hard as the darned charcoals by now. Y'all come on and eat. Rayne—"

"I know," said Rayne with a grin for her aunt Shirley. *"Get the barbecue sauce."*

Wade was standing beside Rayne, in fact their fingers were entwined, but his new aunt yanked him toward her and planted a kiss on his cheek. "Welcome to the family, baby. Now you go help Rayne get the barbecue sauce, and y'all don't take all day, people are hungry."

"Yes, ma'am, Aunt Shirley," Wade said, a broad smile on his face.

"Wait a sec," Rayne said to everyone present.

All eyes were on her.

"This question is directed to the grandmothers who have lived in this area all their lives—there is no chance that we're distant cousins, is there?"

Geneva and Vivian thought back. After a minute or so, they looked at each other and there seemed to be a common accord between them. Geneva answered for both of them. "No, honey, not that we know of."

"Yes!" Rayne exclaimed, doing a little dance.

Laughing, everybody except Rayne and Wade filed out of the room and headed outside. "That girl's crazy," joked Ray.

"Yeah, she gets it from you," said Shirley.

Alone, finally, Wade pulled Rayne into his arms. "You know what this means?"

Rayne looked up at him coyly as she wrapped her arms around his waist. "No, tell me what it means."

"It means I can lust after you in the open, and not have to do it in secret any longer."

Rayne laughed shortly. "I thought you were going to say we're free to do this." She stood on the balls of her feet, reached up, clasped her hands behind his neck and kissed him. Wade pressed her warm, firm, sexy body closer to his. Her kisses were so sweet to him, he could kiss her all day long and not tire of this crazy juxtaposition of an electric passion, yet a satisfying sense of completeness. That's how he felt when he kissed her, as if this was the most natural thing in the world, yet the most exciting.

As for Rayne, she was not thinking, just feeling. It was such a relief to be able to touch him, she wanted to touch him everywhere. Everything about him was a sensual pleasure from his lips, to his tongue, to his male scent underneath his aftershave. She wanted to breathe him in. She wanted to pull his shirt off and feel his skin against hers.

Wade turned his head, breaking off the kiss. "Sweetie, control yourself."

Rayne's hands were under his shirt, and she nearly had it pulled up to his chin, about to take it off him. She sighed. "I guess my hands have a mind of their own."

"I like them," Wade told her. "But not here." He smiled down at her. "Let's save it for later. Will you sneak off with me after the celebration winds down?"

Rayne gave him a sexy pout. "We can sneak off right now."

"And disappoint my...our dad?"

"You're right. I was being selfish." She took a few steps backward and observed him as if she were seeing him for the first time. In a way, she was. Before, he had been off-limits to her. She couldn't fondle that tall, sleek, muscular body. Nor run her hands through his curly hair, or even dream of sucking on those juicy lips. What was she anyway, a sex maniac? She could wait a few more hours before pouncing on him.

"You're absolutely right," she said as she turned to go to the kitchen. "Dad is scheduled for surgery tomorrow morning at eight. He has to start fasting by six this evening. Let's go so that he can enjoy a meal with his son, and chat awhile before he has to go to bed."

Wade followed her, admiring her just a little bit more. Because, while he had had the fortitude to bring her roaming hands to her attention, he had loved every minute of it. And if not for his desire to talk to his new father for a few hours he would gladly have stolen her away to his condominium for some love in the afternoon.

She was delectable. Even in those old jeans and T-shirt she had on. The jeans had molded themselves to her curves over the years, and what a shape. She had a perfect peach of a behind, long legs that tapered out from her hips. He had to stop himself. If he kept thinking along those lines, he would surely not be fit to go outside and join everyone. At least not until his erection had gone down sufficiently.

In the kitchen, Rayne went to the refrigerator and got a large red Tupperware container. She glanced back at him, a smile on her luscious lips. "If you're done looking at my butt, come on, let's eat."

Wade laughed shortly. "Am I that obvious?"

"Yeah, you are."

He hastily stepped around her to open the door for her. "I'm going to have to get up early to pull a fast one on you, huh?"

"Honey, I was raised by Ray and Julianne, and I have Ben's blood in my veins, too. You *can't* pull a fast one on me!"

Wade looked up as he went through the door. The beach was practically right outside the back door. They were maybe fifty yards from it, and it was packed today. Black folks as far as the eye could see. Some paler folks, too. All either lolling on beach towels, playing in the water, or, as in the case of most of the kids, running here and there. And the day was a gorgeous Florida blue. White sand and blue sky. It was like a postcard scene.

Furthermore, directly in front of his nose were more than fifty people, most of whom were looking at him with interest. His relatives. He felt in the spotlight. All his life, he had not had much to do with his father's family. Ben did not visit home often Even when he'd signed off on the club, he'd left the personal details up to Wade. Ben's brothers and sisters were in their seventies and lived lives much more sedate than their baby brother's. They had little in common. Plus, their children all lived out of state. Wade hadn't seen any of his cousins in years. But now he had a whole yard full of uncles and aunts and cousins.

He followed Rayne down the steps into the yard. He was immediately set upon by a male cousin who looked to be

nearly his age. "Hey, man," the tall brown-skinned cousin said.
"I'm Stephen, oldest son of your aunt Shirley and uncle
William, but everybody calls him Buddy." They firmly shook
hands.

"Good to meet you, Stephen," Wade said sincerely.

And that's how it went for the next few minutes until
everyone had been served their meals of barbecue ribs and
chicken, potato salad, baked beans and garden salad. Then
Ray stood up at his table, cleared his throat and announced,
"I'm going to ask my brother-in-law, Buddy, to bless this food
and welcome our guests this afternoon. Buddy?"

William Stephen Lewis was tall, broad-shouldered, with
an ever-present smile, and an infectious happy-go-lucky
attitude about life. He beamed at everybody. "Thank the Lord
for this day!"

"Amen," said Geneva. She and Vivian, along with Shirley,
with a space saved for Buddy beside her, Julianne, Ray, Ben,
Rayne and Wade were seated at the table closest to the deck. The
other tables were spread out over the lawn of the deep backyard.

Buddy bowed his head. Everyone else followed suit.
"Lord, thank you for blessing us to be able to be here today.
All of us have been beset with problems. No one is exempt.
But we always pull together and make it over, somehow."

"Sho do," Vivian intoned.

"Thank you for the presence of Miss Geneva, who has
been a friend of this family for many, many years. And thank
you for the presence of her son-in-law, Ben Jefferson, who
has brought with him the greatest gift this family has received
in a long time—a newborn son. Well, Lord, he ain't no baby,
but he's new to us!"

Everyone laughed softly, respectfully; after all, they were
in the presence of the Lord.

"We ask that you stay with our brother Ray tomorrow,

Lord, as he undergoes his operation. Take his hand, Lord, and bring him through safely. We ain't tired of him yet! In Your son Jesus' name, amen."

"Amen!" the assemblage chanted.

Immediately afterward, voices commenced to buzz, and it was the last time that silence reigned over the Walker backyard that afternoon.

Rayne looked up and saw Shannon and Pete at a table in the back that was occupied by the teens in the family. She'd forgotten about sending them outside to confess what they'd been doing in Shannon's bedroom earlier.

"Mom?" she said.

Julianne turned, her eyes moderately concerned. "Yes?"

"Did Shannon tell you anything interesting today?" She'd chosen her words carefully because she didn't want to pique her aunt Shirley's curiosity.

Julianne's brows raised questioningly. "No, she just came to me and your dad and asked if some boy named Pete could stay for the meal. We told her he could."

"Okay!" Rayne said brightly. She would have to talk to her mother in private later. She wasn't in the mood to inform on her sister. Not with Wade sitting beside her. Shannon could wait. But not too long. Once Shannon got away with one thing, she would test the boundaries again and again.

Anyway, her father and Wade were deep in conversation, and she was enjoying eavesdropping. "Where'd you go to college, son?" asked her dad.

"I got my undergraduate degree from Morris-Brown," Wade told him. "And my MBA from Howard University."

"Howard?" exclaimed her dad. "Rayne went to Howard. What year did you graduate?"

"Oh, it was before Rayne even arrived at Howard, I'm sure. I received my degree in 1995."

"Yeah, Rayne graduated in 2001. Did you pledge a fraternity while you were in school?"

"No, I'd heard some bad stories about pledges being abused, and it just didn't interest me," Wade said. "Did you?"

"Nah, I never went to college, son. I dropped out of art school less than a year after I started, and started working in construction. Rayne pledged a sorority while she was at Howard. I tried to talk her out of it because I thought her grades would suffer, but it turned out that it was a very good organization. Delta what, honey?"

Rayne smiled. Her dad could never recall her sorority's Greek name. "Delta Gamma, Daddy," she said. To Wade, she said, "Our focus is on service to the community and mentoring young women who might not otherwise have a chance at a college education. Nationally, we award quite a few scholarships on a yearly basis."

"Yeah, I've heard of you all," Wade said, his eyes meeting hers. "You were known for your scholarship at Howard. That, and you ladies put on the best step-shows of any service organization, male or female."

"Now, them's fightin' words," cried Aunt Shirley. "I'm a Zeta."

"And I'm an AKA!" shouted a cousin in her twenties at the next table.

Rayne stood up. "No slight intended, ladies. Wade didn't know we were a 'mixed' family!"

Wade held up his hands as if in surrender. "Sorry, ladies. All of our sororities put on excellent step-shows."

The men laughed. He would learn that Walker women didn't take any guff.

"Moving on," Ray said, changing the subject in a hurry. He smiled at Wade. "Tell me, do you have any artistic talent?"

"I draw a little," he said.

"I want to see some of them. Do you have any with you?"

"I have a few at the condo on Summer Beach. I'll go get them later on if you like."

"That would be nice, son."

Chapter 15

Ben surreptitiously watched Ray and Wade. He wished he could shake these jealous feelings, but they weren't something he had any control over yet. Maybe in time.

He must have been frowning, because Shirley, who was sitting beside him at the table, cleared her throat to get his attention, and laughed once their eyes met. "It's a weird experience, isn't it? Watching your son with his father?"

"Yes, it is," Ben said softly.

"You'll adjust," she told him. "We all will." She eyed him appraisingly. "Did you ever marry again?"

Ben was a little stunned by her question, she'd switched up on him so fast. "Um, no, I didn't. But I'm seeing someone special." He thought a little lie would get her off his trail. If it was one thing he knew, women were always looking for a good man for their friends. He smiled. He liked the fact that she thought he was worthy of one of her girlfriends.

He looked across the table at Geneva. She narrowed her eyes at him. What had he thought, anyway? Geneva had never really liked him, even when Deirdre was alive. She thought he was too materialistic, and too proud. Now she had enough fuel for the "hate Ben" fire in her gut to last her the rest of her life.

Shirley laughed again when she followed his line of sight. "Miss Geneva is a Christian woman. She *has* to forgive you, eventually."

"Is that how it works?" Ben joked.

"They don't get into heaven unless they can love their enemies," Shirley informed him. "It's a tall order, but where's the difficulty in loving your friends? Too easy. Besides, Miss Geneva's too obstinate to let you stand in the way of her heavenly reward."

Ben attempted a smile in Geneva's direction.

She rolled her eyes, pointedly turned away and engaged Vivian in conversation.

"I don't know," Ben said to Shirley. "In *Paradise Lost,* Satan says that it's better to rule in hell than to serve in heaven. Geneva's more of a ruler."

Shirley laughed heartily. Ben laughed with her. He felt comfortable for the first time since he'd stepped foot in the Walkers' house. This making amends thing was hard on a man. But he thought of a certain woman on Kennesaw Mountain and selfishly wondered what sort of earthly reward she would give him for being a good boy. He still needed to work on his motivations for altruistic behavior.

Shirley looked down at his empty plate. "Can I get you anything else?"

"It was delicious, Mrs. Lewis," Ben said. "But, no, thank you. I'm a little tired. I'm going to call a cab, go back to my hotel and get some rest."

Shirley laughed again. "Call a cab? With all of these people here, and all those cars parked out in the yard? I'll get someone to drive you." She looked up and raised her hand high, signaling Rayne.

Rayne immediately called, "Yes, Aunt Shirley?"

Shirley beckoned her. Rayne got up and walked the few feet to the end of the table.

The first thing she did when she got there was to bend down and hug her pop from behind. She touched her cheek to his and whispered, "That was a wonderful thing you did, bringing Wade home."

Ben felt his face grow hot with embarrassment. He was glad she had said it only for his ears, because he had no reply to that. Her thanking him for doing something he should have done a long time ago made him feel about two feet tall.

He knew her sentiments were genuine. He simply didn't know how to accept them.

Rayne gently kissed his cheek, then straightened and regarded her aunt. "Do you need something from the house, Auntie?"

Shirley laughed. "No, honey, I've already worked you enough for one day. Your father says he's tired and would like to go back to his hotel—"

"I didn't want to take Wade's car, so I was going to call a cab," Ben explained.

"No, you're not," said Rayne. "I'll drive you."

"Honey, your dad's car is in the garage and it's blocked, but you can take my car. You know where my purse is inside, just get the keys when you go in the house."

"All right, Auntie, that's sweet of you."

Ben got to his feet, preparing to leave.

Ray had been saying something to Wade, but when he saw Ben getting up, he said, "Hold that thought, son. I'll be right back."

He got up and by the time Ben had thanked Shirley for a pleasant afternoon and said his goodbyes to those at his table, save Geneva, who still would not look at him, Ray was at his side. "I'll walk you out," he offered.

"You two go ahead, I'll catch up," Rayne said. She still had to retrieve her aunt's car keys.

Ray was glad Rayne would be detained, because what he had to say to Ben needed to be said in private. The two men walked through the kitchen to the living room, leaving Rayne in the kitchen.

As he and Ben stood before the front door, Ray extended his hand. Ben took it and they briefly shook. Hands falling to their sides again, the men simply looked each other in the eyes. "It's going to feel strange not hating you," Ray said honestly.

"Likewise," said Ben.

"But this has to be the end of the animosity," Ray said. "For Rayne and Wade's sake. They belong to both of us now. I'm still her father."

"And I'm still Wade's father."

"I know. That won't change. What has to change is how we see each other. You have been my enemy so long, I'll have trouble thinking of you as anything else. But I'll make an effort to regard you as a neutral party from now on. Someone I don't have to interact with on a daily basis, but I do have to tolerate at family functions. I believe I can do that."

"So do I," agreed Ben.

"Good," Ray said, satisfied. "Then, goodbye."

And with a curt nod, he turned and walked away. He passed Rayne on his way back into the kitchen. "Be right back, Daddy," she said.

"Drive carefully, sweetie," Ray told her and continued outside.

He couldn't wait to get back to his conversation with Wade. Wade looked up expectantly when he saw his father coming down the deck's steps. His mind was still getting used to the fact that here was a man who looked like him, who even sounded like him. He remembered how Rayne had mistaken him for her father on the phone a few weeks ago. So many things kept popping up in his mind now. He wavered between feelings of spiritual and emotional fulfillment, and sheer panic. He didn't know if he'd ever learn all these people's names or faces. It was overwhelming.

His father stood next to their table. "Rayne went to take your father back to his hotel. He said he was tired."

"Oh, I could have done that." Wade always felt as if he were responsible for his father. It was so ingrained in him that it was a natural response. Now, he supposed, he would have to divide his attention between two fathers. He had no idea how he and Rayne would cope. They shared fathers. This was so confusing. The only thing that wasn't confusing was his abiding desire for her.

But even that, he knew, would have to be treated more carefully. If something went wrong between them, they would have two families to answer to. It wasn't as if he were involved with a woman who had no ties to the family. They would not deign to get emotionally invested in that sort of relationship. And if they broke up, they broke up. With Rayne, though, he would have his father and his birth father to deal with.

"Want to take a walk with me on the beach, son?" asked Ray.

"Sure," Wade said, rising. He picked up their paper plates and plastic cups and went to drop them into the large trash receptacle someone had placed near the steps. This done, he joined his father, and they began walking toward the beach.

It was around five-thirty and the crowd had begun to thin out. Fewer children were ripping and running through the sand and the surf. Sunbathers were fewer as well.

"I don't see a lifeguard on duty," Wade commented as they descended the slope that led to the beach.

"The county won't pay for one," Ray told him. "It's a public beach, but I guess they don't see a need to."

"Dad says American Beach used to be called the Harlem of the South," Wade said.

"That's because in its heyday, American Beach had night-clubs that attracted the likes of performers like Duke Ellington, my namesake Ray Charles—"

"You were named after Ray Charles?"

Ray laughed. "Yeah, your grandmother saw him perform when he was nothing but a boy himself. She loved herself some Ray Charles. Anyway, the clubs used to be on what was called the chitlin' circuit. The same black performers who played at the Apollo in Harlem would come down here and perform for black folks. You see, American Beach was started by Abraham Lincoln Lewis, who was Florida's first black millionaire, by the way, and founder of the Afro-American Life Insurance Company, because he was tired of being humiliated by the Jim Crow laws. Do you know what those were?"

"They barred black folks from using facilities deemed white-only."

"Yeah, they made you feel like you were less of a person. Certainly less than white folks, and that was the point of them, to keep us in our so-called place. So, Abraham bought 200 acres of land along a 13-mile stretch of beach, and that became American Beach. At first it was to be a place for his employees to vacation without having to deal with racial discrimination. But then he started allowing other black families to buy vacation homes here, and it grew into a wonderful place where upwardly mobile blacks could bring their families for the summer and enjoy all the luxuries they were used to getting at home, including top-notch entertainment. Things were booming for almost thirty years. Then some families started selling their property to developers. Things were never the same. Today, there are only 100 acres left and American Beach has been reduced to a 12-street town. However, many folks still maintain vacation homes here, and we get folks coming to the beach year-round. After all, as you can see, it's a beautiful place."

Ray sighed. "And those of us who are year-round residents try to keep the dream alive by preserving as much of the beach as we possibly can. We keep trying, and keep hitting brick walls, but we keep trying, anyway."

"Is the Beach Lady still here?" Wade asked. "I read about her in the *New York Times* a while back."

"Yes, Ms. Betsch is still here," Ray was happy to report. "She's wonderful. She got Senator Bill Nelson to introduce a bill in Congress that ultimately saved Nana, that was a dune on American Beach until Amelia Island Plantation acquired it in 1991. But in 2004, due to the bill in Congress, it became part of the National Park Service Timucuan Ecological and Historic Preserve. You didn't hear about that?"

"No, sir," said Wade, enjoying his history lesson. "What was so significant about saving a dune?"

"You have to take into account that we've lost so much already. Nana is the tallest dune on Amelia Island and lots of folks have climbed it over the years. It has sentimental value. Ms. Betsch has even said that when she dies she wants her ashes mixed with the sand of the dune. American Beach is just that magical a place to some of us. It's hard to explain if you haven't frequented the beach over the years. Plus, it's the fact of not just preserving a place but an ideal—that we owned something beautiful where no one could tell us we had no right to be."

They had walked about fifty yards from the house. Ray paused. "I don't have the energy I used to. As for American Beach's natural value, it's a habitat for the threatened logger-head turtle and is important calving grounds for the North Atlantic Right Whale. It's worth preserving."

Wade nodded, understanding. "I realize now that Dad's sending me to try to get you to sell to us was only a ruse. He knew you would never sell."

Ray smiled at him, and started walking again. "Maybe he subconsciously wanted us to get to know each other or, at the very least, recognize that we had some similarities."

"I think it worked," said Wade. "I admired you from the beginning. Your strength of will, even your stubbornness. I had no idea of the dynamics going on under the surface, but I did think you were an okay guy."

"Thank you, Wade." He stopped again to look at the ocean. "Now I have to get serious on you and ask you for a favor, even though we've just learned we're father and son."

"Anything," Wade said at once.

Ray turned to look him in the eyes. "If something should happen to me tomorrow—"

"Nothing's going to happen to you, sir," Wade assured him. He'd been thinking the same thing, though. Wouldn't fate be cruel to give him his biological dad one day only to take him away the next?

"*If* something should happen to me," Ray reiterated more forcefully, "I want you to promise me you'll take care of Rayne. I know how you feel about her. The passion between you is unmistakable. But passion of that kind doesn't last, Wade. If you truly love a woman it comes and goes. One minute you're merely friends, the next you're obsessed with her. That's how it is with me and Julianne. I love her. I'll always love her. But she is a dear friend most of the time. And a passionate lover sometimes. I think if I live we may finally be able to live together. This experience, Rayne finding her biological father, and you finding yours, has affected us all positively. I refuse to think otherwise. That's why I'm asking you, if I should die I hope you'll always be there for Rayne. Even if something should happen to break you two up. In that case she won't want your help because she's stubborn, just like her mother. But continue to be her friend anyway. I believe you two will have that kind of relationship."

Wade listened without interrupting. Then he said, "I gladly accept the responsibility for caring for Rayne. I can't explain it, but I've known from the beginning that we were meant to be together. I suppose that's why I could not get her out of my system when we thought we were brother and sister. No matter what the facts were supposed to be, my heart felt something more profound."

"I'm happy to hear it," said Ray. He placed a reassuring hand on Wade's shoulder and met his eyes. "And I thank you."

Wade nodded solemnly. He meant everything he'd said. He would cherish Rayne, even if she began having panic attacks like she'd experienced after getting engaged to her former boyfriend, Tony. He smiled at the thought. She could be kooky sometimes, but he even loved that about her.

"Well, let's turn back," Ray suggested. "The party's winding down and I should be there to tell everybody goodbye. They're superstitious that way, especially Momma. She's going to have a rough day tomorrow, worrying about me. I should humor her tonight. I haven't forgotten about those drawings of yours, either. I'd still like to see them tonight."

"I'll go get them as soon as we get back to the house," Wade promised.

"Not until Rayne gets back from taking your dad to his hotel. She's going to want some time alone with you," Ray said knowingly.

And I with her, Wade thought. He just smiled at his dad.

Chapter 16

Rayne was in one of the bathrooms in Wade's condo on Summer Beach. She'd gone in there presumably to use it, but actually she'd gone in there to calm down. Or, rather, cool down. She looked at her reflection in the mirror. Her long, wavy hair was in slight disarray. She peered at her nails. After cleaning and seasoning forty pounds of chicken and ribs, she could use a manicure. She sniffed her fingers. Was that the smell of raw chicken on her fingertips? *Oh, my God....* Okay, she was officially in panic mode.

She and Wade had kissed in the car coming over here. They'd kissed once they got through the door. Her lips were a size larger due to all that kissing, and she wanted more than kisses. Wasn't she the same girl who'd been lusting after him for weeks now? Yes. Wasn't she the girl who had teased him shamelessly for being turned on by his sister? Yes. Well then, where the heck was that girl now? Body-snatched, that's where. Miss Insecure had taken her place, like some alien pod person. They looked the same, but they certainly didn't behave the same. The other girl would be out there right now making Wade do a striptease for her, and enjoying it! Miss Insecure was worried about her funky fingertips. She sniffed them again, then picked up the soap, turned on the water and vigorously washed her hands.

Admit it, girl, she thought, *you're not really worried about where your lust for Wade has gone, because it hasn't gone anywhere. What you're obsessing about is the fact that you may lose your dad tomorrow and you don't want the last memory of him to be your feeling uncomfortable in his presence because you'd just made love to his son.*

She nodded at her reflection. That was it, exactly. She would have to tell Wade how she felt. Plain and simple. She finished washing her hands, dried them on a towel and went back to the living room where she'd left Wade sitting on the couch going through his drawings, which were spread out on the coffee table in front of him.

He looked up and smiled when she reentered the room. "I thought I'd have to come looking for you."

She sat on the chair next to the couch. She'd removed her sandals when they'd come into the living room, and now she wore only jeans and a T-shirt. She stretched out her long legs.

"What are you doing over there?" Wade protested. "I want you close."

She got up and sat beside him. Wade pulled her against his side. "What's going on, darlin'? You worried about your dad?"

Rayne's body betrayed her. *Resist, resist,* she told herself. But her body was ripening still. Her nipples grew hard and tender. Her female center throbbed annoyingly, drawing attention to itself. She imagined it as a flower. Its petals were slowly, agonizingly blossoming. Opening with anticipatory delight.

She decided to be perfectly honest with Wade. "I can't make love to you tonight. I couldn't go back and spend time with Dad knowing what we'd been up to. I know it's silly, but making love, engaging in the ultimate pleasure, just before he goes under the knife would feel like the most selfish thing in the world."

"If not now, when?" Wade asked. He was looking at her with such love and understanding that she knew his question hadn't been asked out of self-interest. "What I mean is, making love is one of the most life-affirming things you can do. When two people care for one another, it lifts, it comforts. It confirms your emotions. I naturally want to be as close to you as I possibly can be. Being inside you is as close as I can get."

Be fearless! The thought suddenly came to Rayne. *Tell fate to take a hike! Dad is not going to die tomorrow and there will be nothing to feel guilty about.*

Wasn't that what faith was? The belief in something yet unseen? Tomorrow wasn't here yet, but she was going to invest in it, and make love to the man she wanted more than she'd ever wanted anyone else in her entire life.

She glanced at her watch. It was nearly seven. They'd promised her dad they'd be back by eight. It only took about seven minutes to drive over to American Beach. Wade was still looking at her, waiting for a reply to his speech about seizing the day. She didn't say anything. Instead, she pulled off her T-shirt.

Wade pushed the coffee table aside with his foot, pulled her toward him and buried his face in her cleavage. Her beautiful brown skin smelled like honeysuckle. He kissed the tops of her breasts. Those full, gorgeous breasts. He reached behind her and undid the clasps. Rayne pulled down the straps and removed the bra. Wade's penis received the message his eyes had sent to his brain almost instantly. Her breasts dipped as heavy breasts should, but they were firm and mouthwateringly sensuous. He cupped them gently, then bent his head to tongue her left nipple. The feel of that warm, hard bud on his tongue was such an erotic sensation that he moaned softly and grew even harder. He glanced up at Rayne and saw that she was having much the same reaction. With her eyes closed, her long, thick lashes were nearly touching her cheeks as she languidly sighed. Her kiss-swollen mouth was slightly open.

His hands moved to her waist, he pulled her to him and kissed her. Kissed her with all the pent-up longing he'd saved for this moment. He felt like moaning out loud, she felt so good to him, but he didn't want to scare her.

Rayne gave as good as she got. She could not get close enough to him. She knew this tension was only because she'd wanted him for so long, and had been denied him. Still, she could not turn it off.

As their lower bodies pressed together, she felt his erection. It frightened her and delighted her simultaneously. She could hardly catch her breath as their kiss deepened. She broke it off and inhaled, exhaled and rasped, "At the risk of sounding like a loose woman, make love to me now!"

Wade picked her up and carried her down the hall to his bedroom. The door was slightly open. He nudged it open the rest of the way with his foot. He placed her on the comforter of the king-size bed, her head on a stack of pillows. "Don't move," he ordered as he opened a drawer in the nightstand next to the side of the bed he slept on and chose a foil-wrapped condom from a new box. He closed the drawer and put the condom on the nightstand.

"Now," he said, returning his attention to Rayne, "let's see what treasure these jeans are hiding, shall we?"

He bent and slowly undid every button on her button-fly jeans. Then he ran both hands inside them, on either side of her waist, beginning at her flat belly, moving around to work his way to her firm buttocks, all the while pulling the jeans down.

Rayne squirmed her hips, helping him ease off her jeans. In reality his hands simply felt so good on her that she felt compelled to facilitate the use of them on her. After he'd gotten the jeans down to her knees, he went to the foot of the bed, grabbed each leg of the jeans by the hem and pulled them off her. He tossed them onto a nearby chair.

Next, he sat on the bed close to her feet. Rayne was obliged to move over to make room for him. He drew both feet onto his muscular thighs and massaged them. He wanted to touch her from the bottom of her feet to her graceful neck. When he was satisfied with the soft, pliant feel of her feet, he got up and ran both hands all over her shapely legs and thighs. He coaxed her legs opened, and slowly ran his hands up and down the inside of her thighs, too. He sat on the bed again. One of her legs was on his thighs, while the other was behind him. He splayed his hand over her bikini-panty-sheathed sex. He gently rubbed her. She was warm, so warm. Their eyes met, and Rayne licked her lips. He felt the folds of her vagina contract against his palm. He had wanted to postpone the actual sex act with her, but feeling her move like that against him filled him with an urgency he could not deny. He reached for both sides of her panties and pulled. Rayne raised her hips from the bed, and her panties were off, and tossed onto the chair with her jeans in under five seconds. Wade quickly removed the rest of his clothing and his athletic shoes, not caring where they landed when he tossed them behind him in his rush. He then went and straddled her, holding his body suspended above hers with just the strength of his arms. He looked like he was in the middle of doing a push-up. "I knew you would be beautiful naked." His lips curved in a wicked smile. "If I were a stronger man I could make this anticipation last longer, but I'm weak for you."

Rayne's response was to pull him down for a kiss that left no doubt in his mind that she was impatient for things to progress faster, not slower. He let go, and covered her with his body.

Rayne's hands moved over him, caressing the muscles in the backs of his powerful arms, back and butt. She writhed beneath him, enjoying the feel of his body. When he'd straddled her he had been only semierect, but now she felt his erection on her thigh, and he was hard and throbbing. She pushed against him. He moaned and broke off the kiss. "Not yet," he said hoarsely. He pushed up on his arms and balanced on his knees. Leaning over, he got the condom from the nightstand, ripped it open and turned it over, preparing to roll it on.

Rayne sat up. "Let me," she said.

Wade handed her the condom and their eyes met. She grasped him, and in response to her touch, his penis pulsed. Rayne smiled as she put the condom on him. Done, she lay back on the bed. Wade bent his head and kissed her belly, then nuzzled her between her breasts. He took the time to lave both nipples until she was moaning with want of release. Finally, he allowed his heavy penis to slap her belly, and then he was at the entrance. Rayne eagerly thrust upward and he moaned with pleasure because she was so tight and he would require patience, which sent currents of anticipatory delight throughout his taut body. "I don't want to hurt you."

"You won't hurt me."

He looked down at her. Her hair was spread out over the pillow, and her deep brown eyes were smoldering. He pushed a little farther inside her. Rayne arched her back. Her nipples seemed to become even more distended, and there was a modicum of sweet pain in them, and in her vagina. She wanted him so much it hurt.

She smiled up at him. "Do you know how many times I lay in my bed imagining us in this very position? With you between my thighs?"

"About as many times as I had wet dreams about you," Wade told her. He pushed and he was inside her. The walls of her vagina contracted around him. "Oh, God," he said in a breath. He was in anguish, trying to hold on when all he wanted to do was thrust until she cried out in ecstasy. Control was the man's province, though. If he didn't have control, there was no life in the bedroom. Just a lot of starts and un-fulfilled endings. No satisfaction in that for the woman, and very little for the man because he measured his worth in bed by his ability to please his mate.

And he wanted to please Rayne.

"You're so beautiful," Rayne told him.

He laughed shortly. "I've been called worse."

Rayne laughed along with him. "No, seriously, you're a beautiful man, Wade, and not just physically. Your spirit is beautiful, too."

He thrust deeply. Deeper than any of his previous thrusts. Rayne moaned loudly with pure, bone-turning-to-jelly pleasure.

"Is that spiritual enough for you?" Wade said softly.

"Yes, oh, yes!"

Every time he thrust and pulled nearly out of her, it left her with rivulets of ecstasy fanning out from her feminine center to every pleasure point in her body. Wade would not be happy, though, until he felt her body rock with an orgasm that was sure to make her glimpse heaven.

Rayne's legs were wrapped around his waist, and she met him thrust for thrust. Wade enjoyed the sight of her, her breasts moving with each thrust, their nipples still erect and so delectable looking that he wanted to bend and taste them again. But he knew if he did it would send him over the precipice and he wasn't ready to go yet.

He reached up and placed her legs higher. Upon his shoulders instead of around his waist. Her bottom was completely off the bed. He was so hard now, and in want of release, that he could barely hold on.

Rayne couldn't believe it. He'd found her sweet spot the first time out. He'd found it and was working it like a master. If he placed his hands on her buttocks and squeezed, she was going to scream. She felt his hands moving up her thighs. He grabbed handfuls of her ample backside. Grabbed it and squeezed. He was so deeply inside her at that point that their groins were rubbing. Rayne let out a loud moan. Wade followed that with a low growl deep in his throat. Several more thrusts, and both of them collapsed back onto the pillows, smiling and deliciously spent.

Neither of them spoke for several minutes. They simply breathed, and looked into each other's eyes, smiling the whole time.

Wade was the first to speak. He sat up and looked down at her. "I'll have to run you a bath so you won't get your hair wet."

Still a little dazed from their lovemaking, Rayne had to think about what he was saying. Oh, yeah, she couldn't go back to her father's house smelling like sex. She sat bolt upright. "You're right, and we'd better get a move on."

Wade got up, reached back for her, and pulled her to her feet.

He admired her in her nakedness again before turning away, discreetly removing the condom and holding it in his hand until he could dispose of it. "Come on," he said.

Rayne followed him into the bathroom and pretended not to notice his dropping the used condom in the trash next to the sink. Rayne twisted the ends of her long hair, rolled it into a ball at the base of her neck, then tucked it in. That should keep it out of the water as she sat in the tub.

She looked at the big, deep tub. "It's big enough for both of us."

"Not a good idea," Wade said with a regretful smile. "I'd only end up wanting to make love to you again if we bathed together. I'm going to shower in the other bathroom."

Rayne pouted, and he leaned over and kissed her. "Don't be like that. It's seven-thirty now. We don't have time. I promise you, we will bathe together soon. Just not tonight."

With that, he put the plug in the tub and turned on the water. He pointed out the clean towels, washcloths and soap before he left her to go take his shower.

Ten minutes later, he walked back in with a towel around his waist. Rayne was still in the tub. He immediately hardened upon seeing her glistening breasts rising above the suds.

He grabbed a large bath towel and went to give it to her. "Come out of there, sweetness. We've got to be going."

Rayne got to her feet, took the towel from him and removed the stopper with her toes. Wade could not draw his eyes from her lovely form. Brown skin, unmarred and glowing. Her body so full and luscious. No skin and bones for her. His gaze lowered to her vagina. Dark hair sparkling with water droplets.

His mouth watered.

Rayne saw where he was looking. She smiled. "We haven't got time, remember?"

"Listen," Wade said urgently. "If we take sponge baths, we can still be out of here in twenty minutes. It only takes seven minutes to get there. That leaves us three minutes to spare."

"You're suddenly an efficiency expert?" Rayne asked, amused. But she was hastily drying off because she wanted to make love to him again. She ached with the desire to feel him inside her.

They didn't waste time getting back out to the bedroom. Wade got another condom from the drawer and placed it on the nightstand. Towels flew toward the chair, missed, hit the floor instead. And they were on the bed, naked, kissing, suckling and laughing through it all. "Girl, you look so good naked. All beaches ought to be clothing optional," he joked.

She wrapped her hand around his erect penis. "Get real. You and I wouldn't be able to go together, you'd get thrown out because you wouldn't be able to control this."

Wade bent and kissed her slowly and deliberately. "Then we'd have to go to a very private beach. Just for the two of us."

They didn't waste time with words after that. Wade quickly put on another condom and by the time he'd done that, Rayne was ready for him.

Twenty-five minutes later, they were pulling into Ray's driveway and jumping out of the car to run up the sidewalk to the front door. They paused to catch their breaths at the front door. Rayne smoothed her hair and looked up at him. "How do I look?"

"Like you've been thoroughly made love to," Wade told her, and bent to kiss her mouth.

"That's not what I wanted to hear," Rayne told him, smiling at him.

His eyes raked over her. "You look like a woman in love."

"Am I that obvious?"

"Only to the man who loves you back," he told her.

Rayne felt like tearing up, she was so happy. But this wasn't the time nor the place for this conversation. More than likely, her dad was going to fling the door wide and ask them to come inside and stop scandalizing the neighbors. She gave him a quick kiss on the lips. "Listen, Ray Walker has already caught us kissing once on his doorstep. I don't want a repeat of that. Just tell me that I look virtuous. Lie if you have to."

Wade eyed her appraisingly. "Okay, you look extremely virtuous."

Rayne breathed a sigh of relief.

"And sexy as all get-out," he added.

Rayne frowned at him as she rang the doorbell. Leave it to her to forget to bring a key with her. All she was thinking about was finally being alone with Wade.

Shannon answered the door. "If it isn't the only daughter in this family who's allowed to be alone with a male."

Rayne stepped into the house, followed by Wade. "I guess that means you and Mom had a little talk while we were gone."

"Yes, and I've been grounded until school starts in the fall. I can't go anywhere by myself. Not even to the beach!" Shannon complained loudly.

"If I hear another word out of you, you're going to be grounded until you graduate from *high school*," came Julianne's strident voice from the living room.

Chapter 17

There was standing room only in the waiting room of the surgery unit at the hospital the next morning. Twenty-seven relatives showed up at eight o'clock. Some of them came to stay only long enough to let Rayne and Julianne know that they were praying for Ray. Some only stuck around until eight forty-five because they had to be at work by nine. Others stayed the full two and a half hours, the duration of the procedure.

Dr. Kimble had told Ray that it could last anywhere from one and a half to four hours. There were nineteen people waiting to hear how it had gone when Dr. Irving Kimble strode into the room. Rayne, Wade, Julianne and Shirley all got to their feet to meet him in the middle of the room. The others respectfully remained seated.

A tall, hefty fellow in his early forties with curly brown hair and brown eyes, Dr. Kimble smiled warmly at them, which immediately put them at ease. He wouldn't be smiling if Ray had died on the operating table, would he?

Because Shirley was the only one of them he'd previously been introduced to, he directed his comments to her: "It couldn't have gone smoother. The anesthesiologist put him under in less than two seconds. His vitals remained stable throughout. When we got in there, we saw that the cancer was contained in one area. We were able to get it all, and identify the nerves on either side so that they were left alone, which is something Ray was concerned about. He should make a complete recovery. If there is no incidence of staph infection he should only have to stay in the hospital for about three days. Followed by three to five weeks of recuperation at home."

"Thank you, Doctor!" Julianne cried, so relieved that there were tears in her eyes.

Every one of them wanted to shake his hand. Shirley gave him a hug.

"You're the man!" she said enthusiastically.

He beamed his pleasure. "Thank you, Mrs. Lewis. Now, Ray will be in recovery for about an hour, after which he'll go to the intensive care unit. You can get further instructions about his room number from the desk in ICU. You all can breathe a sigh of relief now and, hopefully, the rest of your day will be stress-free." Still smiling, he nodded genially in their direction and left the waiting room.

Jubilation broke out, quietly, in the room. They'd all been listening intently as he was talking, so they knew Ray's prognosis was good. They hugged and laughed and generally commented on the goodness of God.

Wade pulled Rayne aside and kissed her forehead. "There, you see, you didn't have to worry. He's going to be as good as new in a few weeks."

Several of Rayne's relatives said goodbye to her as they walked past her and Wade on their way out of the waiting room. She thanked them for coming. Thanked them for their prayers. Some gave walk-by hugs. She squeezed them back, accepted their kisses on the cheek.

After everyone else had gone, there was just her and Wade, her mother, Shannon, whom her mother wasn't letting out of her sight any time soon, and Shirley.

"Mom," Rayne said, "why don't you take Shannon home and get some rest? Wade and I will stay until Dad is moved to ICU."

"No, honey, I'm staying until Ray wakes up. I want my face to be the first thing he sees when he opens his eyes."

"That's ridiculous," Shirley put in. "What if he doesn't wake up for hours? You need to go get some rest. You're exhausted." She spoke as if her word was law.

Julianne openly stared at Shirley. Five-five to Shirley's five-ten, she looked like a child next to her, but she was not going to back down this time. She was tired of Shirley always telling people what to do. Maybe it was the stressfulness of the situation. Maybe it was years of pent-up frustration from having to bite her tongue whenever Shirley said something insulting to her in passing. But she looked up into Shirley's eyes now and said, "You and me. Coffee machine. Now!"

Shirley rolled her neck as if she were getting the kinks out of it in preparation for a fight. She narrowed her eyes at Julianne. "Be happy to."

"Mom, wait. Come on, this is no time for arguing. Aunt Shirley didn't mean anything by that. She was just looking out for you," Rayne said, trying to reason with her.

"Honey, stay out of this. This has been a long time coming," Julianne said, turning to leave the waiting area.

"*Long* time," Shirley agreed wholeheartedly.

The coffee machine was located in an alcove on the same floor. It would afford them some privacy, however, because it was enclosed on three sides and because of that the sound of voices was buffered better than in the open design of the waiting room.

Rayne started to follow them, but Wade grasped her arm. "This seems like it's important to your mother, sweetheart. Let her handle it."

But Shannon was even more worried than Rayne was. Even though she was angry at her mother for grounding her, she didn't want her to get a beat-down from aunt Shirley! Aunt Shirley must outweigh her mom by sixty pounds, at least.

She ran after them. Rayne wrenched her arm free of Wade's hold and ran after her sister. She grabbed her around the shoulders and held on to her. "Wade's right. Mom's been taking crap from Aunt Shirley for years. Maybe it *is* time for her to have her say." When Shannon stopped struggling, she eased up on her grip somewhat. "Listen, we'll go stand around the corner from where the coffee machine is and if it sounds like they're about to trade blows, we'll rush in and save Mom. Deal?"

Shannon nodded.

Wade calmly walked up to them, a smile on his face. "I'll never lack for drama in this family."

Rayne smiled at him. "No, brother dear. You certainly won't."

They all walked slowly around the corner where they would stay out of sight while the two nemeses had it out.

In the alcove, Julianne and Shirley circled one another, eyes sizing up their opponents and finding them wanting. "I've had it with you, Shirley Walker-Lewis," Julianne said quietly but fiercely. "This is the last time you will interfere in my life, do you understand me? I don't care if you like me or not—you *will* respect me. Especially in front of my daughters. You are not to treat me as if I'm a little girl who can't make her own decisions. If I want your opinion on anything, I will ask for it!"

Julianne took a deep breath and continued. "What's more, I love your brother and if I want to stay here in this hospital until he comes out of the anesthesia, I'll do it. In fact, I might even spend the night, and there's nothing you can do about it. We're back together. I know that means you'll have to think up new insults for me, so get busy doing it because I'm going to be around from now on. While I'm at it, I have to tell you, I know you must have been doing back flips when you found out that Rayne isn't Ray's biological daughter. I know you suspected it all along, and it turned out to be true so, in your opinion, I'm the no-good woman you always said I was. But you know what? If I'd been stronger eighteen years ago, I never would have left Ray. I should have stayed and worked on the relationship instead of running away because I didn't think I was good enough for him. He loved me, and that should have been all that mattered. Instead, I let comments from you and my own insecurities get the best of me."

Julianne had let all the vitriol spill out in a rush. She hadn't even noticed that Shirley hadn't said a word once they'd gotten to the alcove. In fact, Shirley was smiling at her. And in her eyes was a genuine look of respect. Admiration, even.

"What are you smiling at?" Julianne asked sharply.

Shirley laughed shortly. "Girl, it's about damn time you told me off and stopped acting as if you have no backbone. You should have told me to go to hell eighteen years ago, then we wouldn't be going through this now. You don't let someone deride you without fighting back. If I'd done that, my mother-in-law, God rest her evil soul, would have suc-

ceeded in breaking me and Buddy up years ago. She wanted
him to marry someone else. But that's another story." She
shook her head. "I never hated you, Julianne. I just wanted
you to fight for your man. Oh, yes, I've been saying some
pretty rotten things about you since you left Ray. That's
because nobody hurts my brother without getting a tongue-
lashing from me! I thought you should have stayed and
worked things out instead of leaving. That's why I was so hard
on you. Hell, I've been saying that for years, but people tend
to tune me out after a while. I know it. But I could no more
stop saying what's on my mind than stop breathing. So, if
you're going to stick around, please do, but if you mess with
my brother expect to hear from me. Fair enough?"

Julianne eyed her warily. After several seconds she finally
said, "Fair enough."

They turned to leave the alcove.

"Now, you need to go home and get some rest," said Shirley.

"Shirley, go to hell!"

Shirley laughed. "At the rate I'm going, I just might one
day. But not today, dear Julianne. Not today."

Julianne laughed.

They turned the corner and ran smack into Rayne,
Shannon and Wade.

"Just watching your back, Mom," said Shannon, going to
put her arm around her mother's waist.

"I had yours, Aunt Shirley," Rayne lied, going to hug her aunt.

"Yeah, right," said Shirley. She kissed her cheek. "I'm
outta here, y'all. I'm going home to take a nap. I'll come back
later on."

"Shirley," Julianne called. "Would you take Shannon with
you? I'm going to be here awhile and, at least with you, I'll
know she's being well taken care of."

"Mom, I don't need a babysitter," Shannon protested.

Shirley ignored Shannon's comment. "Sure, no problem."

"Put her to work, too," Julianne told her. "She's on punishment."

"Great," said Shirley. "I was going to hire someone to pull weeds in my garden, but she'll do just fine."

When they were out of earshot of Julianne, Rayne and Wade, Shirley told Shannon confidentially, "Don't worry, I wouldn't put you to work in the hot sun."

Shannon was visibly relieved. She smiled at her dear, sweet aunt Shirley.

"Why don't we stop by the Dairy Queen and get a burger and a milkshake?" suggested Shirley. "I'm famished. Worrying always makes me hungry."

"Sounds good to me," Shannon was quick to agree.

Julianne's face was indeed the first thing Ray saw when he opened his eyes and came to himself. He smiled. "I'm still here, huh?"

Julianne smiled broadly. "Disappointed?"

"Not unless I'm a eunich now."

"Not a chance," Julianne reassured him. "Dr. Kimble says you're going to make a complete recovery. They were able to leave those vital nerves alone."

"Well, hallelujah," said Ray. His eyes began closing. Soon he was asleep.

Julianne stood there looking at his dear face a few minutes longer, then went in search of Rayne and Wade, who'd gone to the hospital cafeteria to get a bite to eat while she waited for Ray to awaken.

She was concerned for Rayne. No one could miss the fact that she and Wade were in love. Julianne was afraid that their relationship was moving too swiftly. She knew what passion felt like. It had gotten her in more trouble than she liked to admit.

She hoped that the two of them would stop and take a look at the big picture. They were interconnected now in ways that a mere broken love affair could never sever. If something happened between them, they would still have to see each other and, perhaps, get their hearts broken all over again due to the encounter.

Standing in front of the elevator, she sighed tiredly. Rayne might be a grown woman, but she would always worry about her as though she were still a two-year-old.

"Everything went really well," Rayne told her pop. She was outdoors sitting at an umbrella-topped table on the grounds of the hospital. It was an area reserved for those who wished to eat alfresco, or grab a smoke. The hospital asked visitors not to smoke nor use their cell phones in the building.

"Good, I'm glad to hear it," Ben said. "I'm heading back to Atlanta now, honey. Please call me if you need anything, and even if you don't."

"I will," she promised. "You take care of yourself."

They rang off and Rayne put her phone back in the inside pocket of her shoulder bag.

Wade had been sitting and listening to her conversation with his father. He still found it hard to have any sympathy for him, but was pleased that Rayne seemed to have an easy rapport with him.

"When I drove him back to his hotel yesterday he asked me to let him know how Dad's surgery went," Rayne told him.

"That was big of him," Wade said dryly.

"You won't believe this, but one day you're going to forget what he did, and you'll even count yourself lucky for the way your life has gone so far."

Wade looked skeptical. "People always say that. That if not for everything they've experienced in life, the good and the bad, they would not be the person they are today. I say, what if your life could have been even better than it is right now? If given the chance, Ray Walker could have been a better father to me than Ben Jefferson."

"Who knows?" Rayne asked. "However, I say don't dwell on it. It'll only give you an ulcer. What's done is done. You can't go back in time and change it. You've got to live with it."

"Like we lived with being brother and sister before we found out the truth?" Wade asked. He knew he had her. Neither of them had been able to simply accept that.

"All right," Rayne conceded. "But your situation with your father is different. In your heart, he's your dad, no matter what he did. And the heart always wins over the head. You can disagree all you want to, but you still love him like a son loves a father. You're just angry right now. Believe me, I was angry at Mom and Dad for lying to me all my life, too. But as for Ray Walker no longer being my father, the father of my heart, that's a load of bull. He's the real thing as far as I'm concerned. Right now, *Pop* feels more like a father who abandoned me at birth and now he's come back into my life, trying to make up for lost time. I know it wasn't his fault that I didn't grow up knowing him. But now my love for him is going to take time to develop. I didn't look at him and instantly love him simply by virtue of the fact that we have the same blood flowing through our veins. That's my point. *What is a father?* It's someone who has been there for you all your life, who has loved you, cherished you and seen that you were protected when you couldn't protect yourself. That's a father. And if Ben Jefferson did all of those things for you to the best of his abilities, he's the father of your heart."

Wade leaned over and kissed her. He smiled at her. "Sometimes that's the only way to silence you."

"You're having too good a time hating him right now, huh?" she guessed.

"Something like that," he admitted. "I'm kind of in my righteous outrage stage. I feel justified in detesting what he did even if I truly don't detest *him*. Do you understand?"

Rayne nodded. "Of course. I went through the same thing. I wanted to punish my parents for lying to me."

"Yes," said Wade. "Although I haven't yet come up with a suitable punishment for my father."

"Move to New York," Rayne playfully suggested.

Wade saw the hopeful expression in her eyes and smiled slowly. "*You* move to Atlanta. Dad would gladly give you a suite of offices for your business. He's hoping to marry you off to an eligible Atlanta bachelor, anyway."

Rayne laughed. "Is he really? If his choices run to guys like Joe Jakes, he's bound to fail as a matchmaker."

Wade moved closer to her on the shared bench. "Speaking of Joe Jakes, his family forced him to go to a drug treatment center. He'll be there for three months."

"Wow, I thought those places only kept you for about a month or so."

"He needed intensive treatment. His team's owner is threatening to tear up his contract if he doesn't come back clean and sober, and stay that way. One infraction after he comes out, and he's gone."

Rayne sighed. "Well, maybe that's what it'll take for him to turn his life around."

Taking advantage of their being alone, Wade bent low, put his big hand behind her head and pulled her close for a slow, deep kiss. When they came up for air, he said, close to her ear, "I've got to go back to work, sweetness. I hate to leave you."

"When?" Her beautiful sable-colored eyes met his.

"I'll have to drive back tomorrow morning."

"Then we can spend the night together."

"No, we can't. You're staying in your father's house with

your mother and your sister. That wouldn't look right. But I *can* take you out to dinner tonight, and then take you to my place for some intense loving before driving you home and walking you to your door."

"I can live with that."

"Hey, you two!" Julianne called as she approached their table. "I looked all over the cafeteria for you, and then someone told me about this area." Her gaze settled on Rayne. But then she regarded Wade, as well. "Your father woke up for a couple of minutes, joked with me and went back to sleep. I'm going to go home now, get a little shut-eye and then come back tonight. Maybe he'll be more alert by then."

Rayne got up. "I have your car keys. Do you want me to drive you?"

"No, honey, you stay if you like. Wade can drive you home later."

Rayne retrieved the keys from her shoulder bag and handed them to her mother. "All right, I did want to take a look at him before leaving."

Julianne took the keys, smiled at them both and left.

Rayne watched her go. "Sometimes I look at her and wonder how I got so lucky."

"Yes," Wade said. "You have wonderful parents."

Rayne smiled at him. "Yes, they are wonderful. Imperfect, just like all humans are. But wonderful, nonetheless."

"You're still on the subject of my father," Wade observed.

"Only because my parents' example illustrates the fact that everybody makes mistakes."

"Their mistakes were of a different nature than his," Wade insisted. "He willfully lied. Your mother decided not to tell him she was pregnant with you because she didn't have any reason to believe he'd want you. He was a married man passing himself off as a single man, after all. Your dad went along with her because he loved her, and he also came to love you. Those were selfless reasons. My dad, on the other hand, committed a totally selfish act. Letting your father know I was his son would have benefited not only your father, but his entire family. Keeping the secret to himself benefited only him. And I rest my case," Wade said with a quick kiss to the tip of her nose.

"I still say you're going to forgive him one day."

"Probably," Wade said. "Like my biological father, I am, in essence, a forgiving sort of guy. But not for a while, my love."

Rayne's heartbeat sped up at the mention of his endearment. "My love." It had been a long time since she'd been anybody's love.

They sat and talked awhile longer and then got up to go back upstairs to check on their father. When they entered the room, all was silent except for the various beeps and hums of the life-support monitors he was hooked up to.

They walked over to the bed and peered down at him. Except for his pallor, Ray looked much the same. His big right hand lay on his flat stomach, an IV tube stuck in it providing sustenance.

"I've never seen him look so helpless," Rayne whispered, a catch in her voice.

"Now, don't start crying," Wade said softly. "You don't want him to hear you."

"He's asleep," Rayne said, sniffing.

"He's not," said Ray. He opened his eyes and looked at his daughter and his son. "Why don't you people go home and let a body get some rest?" he asked. He smiled at Rayne. "Dry those tears, honey, your trick worked. The old man had that nasty cancer removed. Now go somewhere and celebrate for me."

"You and your celebrations," Rayne sassed him. "You and Aunt Shirley will throw a party at the drop of a hat."

"Our ancestors come from the islands, don't you know?" said her father. "We understand that *everything* is a cause for celebration. Now get out of here. I don't want to see you until tomorrow."

"I'll have to go back to Atlanta tomorrow, sir," Wade told him.

"I understand, son. Go, I'm in good hands. I'll probably want to get away from all these women before it's over with."

Rayne bent and kissed his warm, dry forehead. "We're going. Love you, Dad."

"Love you, too, baby girl."

"Sir," said Wade, conveying his respect and admiration with a word.

"Until next time, son," Ray said.

Her father had admonished them to go celebrate on his behalf, and Rayne could think of no better way than to go to the beach. And she told Wade so once they reached his car. "Your beach or mine?" he asked.

"My beach, of course," she said as if there was no other beach in the world. "Your beach *was* my beach before it was *your* beach."

Wade started the SUV and backed out of the parking space. "Am I going to get another American Beach lesson? I think I can already pass the written test," he joked.

"I almost forgot you were the enemy," Rayne joked back. "I'm in love with a developer!"

Wade laughed. "There's no accounting for love."

He swung by his condo to change into swimming trunks and get a change of clothing for afterward. Then he drove Rayne home. The house was quiet when they entered.

Rayne went to her mother's bedroom and, sure enough, she was sprawled on the bed, sound asleep. She carefully closed the door. Shannon wasn't there, so she guessed she was still in Fernandina Beach with Aunt Shirley.

She went outside to the back deck where Wade had said he'd be when she was done checking on her mother. She paused in the middle of the kitchen to watch him, unobserved. He was standing on the deck, looking out to sea, wearing only his bathing trunks, which were the baggy kind that came midthigh. They were navy blue. He'd taken off his T-shirt. He looked magnificent standing there, his chest bare and his golden brown skin so vibrant and glowing with health. He had a broad, muscular chest, a long torso, a narrow waist, a washboard stomach and long, muscular legs.

Rayne admired him a moment longer and then opened the door. "She's asleep. I'll leave her a note on the fridge and then change into my suit."

"Need help?" he asked mischievously.

"Thanks, no," Rayne said. Her eyes raked over him. "You look so good, we'd never make it out of my bedroom."

She turned and left.

Wade sat in one of the chairs at the table on the deck. The deck was covered so he wasn't in direct sunlight, but it was a warm day. Easily in the eighties. He would welcome a dip in the ocean. And he anticipated seeing Rayne in a swimsuit. He'd never seen her in one. Okay, he'd seen her naked. But there was something about a woman in a swimsuit that was nearly as sensual as seeing her naked. He'd pegged her as a bikini type. Yes, her sexy belly button was definitely worth showing off.

A few minutes later, he heard Rayne coming through the door. "I'm ready," she announced. Wade turned around and his heart stood still. Rayne was wearing an Asian-inspired tank suit in black, trimmed in white piping around the plunging neckline that revealed a devastating glimpse of cleavage. It was split where her full breasts met and there were two white embroidered clasps holding the darned thing together. It was cut high on the thigh, and made her legs look even longer. Entirely feminine, it displayed her enticing body so vividly that Wade thought the bikini might have been more modest.

Rayne laughed at his reaction. "Too tame?" she asked.

"What? You don't have a thong?" Wade asked.

"Have you ever tried to wear one of those things? I don't want to be sexy that badly," Rayne told him. She put on her big, floppy hat and her sunglasses, then picked up her beach bag, which had her swim cap, sunscreen, towels and bottled water in it.

She moistened her lips and looked at him expectantly. Wade swallowed hard. He wanted to grab her and throw her across his shoulder, fireman style, and take her back to the condo and ravish her. Forget about the swim.

A man had to have patience, though.

"After you," he said, bowing and gesturing toward the steps in a courtly manner.

Rayne smiled and regally took the steps down into the yard.

A few minutes later he was racing her toward the ocean. They dove in and swam, although not too far out, their intention was only to expend a little energy while cooling off in the ocean, not to train for a marathon. Momentarily, they began floating on their backs side by side. Wade reached out and grasped Rayne's hand. They floated, their arms and legs spread wide, their hands entwined. While she drifted, Rayne sent up a prayer of thanks for her father's successful surgery. She sent up thanks, also, for the man at her side. Life was good.

Chapter 18

"I know you'll never show Dad this one," Rayne said of the drawing Wade was doing of her. She was reclining on her left side on the bed, her torso turned so that her heavy fall of hair cascaded across her right shoulder. She was completely nude, except for her favorite ruby stud earrings. It was a demure pose. But she still felt naughty doing it.

"No," said Wade. "This will go on the wall of our bedroom."

"You mean on the wall in your bedroom in Atlanta?" Rayne assumed.

"I live in an apartment in Atlanta," Wade told her. "No, I mean in the master bedroom of the house I'm going to build for us."

Now she knew what he was doing, he was painting scenarios that might never come true. Well, she could do that as well as he could. "In our house in New York City?"

"Perhaps our second house will be in New York City, but our primary home will be in a suburb of Atlanta." He looked at her over his sketch pad. "My business is there. I might not look it, but I'm a traditional male. I like the thought of providing for my wife and kids."

Rayne's brows rose in surprise. "We have kids in this daydream?"

"At least four."

"Really? Are you going to carry two of them?"

"If I could…"

Rayne laughed. "But you can't."

Wade went back to sketching. "I've always thought that a woman is at her most beautiful when she's carrying a child."

"You would," Rayne joked. "Like most artists, you have a madonna complex. Dad painted Mom when she was expecting me. Thank God she was fully clothed."

"I'd like to draw you again when you're expecting, only I want you nude," Wade told her, looking at her with his passion for her mirrored in his eyes.

Rayne's first reaction was to adamantly refuse to even speculate on such a thing occurring in their future. His eyes pierced her, though, and her body instantly reacted to the promise of passion. Her nipples hardened.

Wade smiled when he saw what had happened. "Don't move," he reminded her.

"I didn't move."

"Your nipples are more prominent than they were when we started."

"You ought not to turn me on while I'm naked," she said, refusing to take the blame for the natural results of the stimuli he was providing. "It's not fair. I'm naked and vulnerable while you're clothed and capable of hiding your state of arousal. Especially with that sketch pad in front of you."

Wade got up, set the sketch pad and pencil on the bed and

began removing his clothing. "You're right. I was taking unfair advantage of you."

Rayne watched as he peeled off everything except his boxers. Then he stood before her with his arms raised at his sides and his palms turned up. "Satisfied?"

"I feel better," Rayne said truthfully. Of course, now she was also throbbing between her legs.

"Okay," Wade said. "I aim to please." He picked up the sketch pad and pencil, then returned to his armchair. He once again focused on her body as he continued to draw. He smiled when he saw that her breath was coming in shorter and shorter intervals.

"Darlin', you're moving again."

"I am not!"

"You're practically panting."

It came as a surprise to Rayne that she was, indeed, breathing rather raggedly. She took a deep breath, exhaled and made a concerted effort to breathe more normally.

"Better?" she asked.

"Much," he replied. "Thank you."

"Your wish is my command, my king," she said sultrily. Her eyes caressed his face and then her gaze slowly traveled the length of his body. She moistened her lips.

"Don't do that," Wade said irritably.

"Do what?"

"Lick your lips like that. It doesn't lend itself to the mood I'm trying to achieve in the drawing."

"Which mood is that?"

"A sense of innocence. When you lick your lips, all I can think about is making love to you. I don't want you to appear as a sexual being in this drawing. I want it to appear as if you're just reclining on the bed with nothing as carnal as making love on your mind."

"I'm nude, on a bed. What else do nude people do in beds besides make love? Contemplate the meaning of life?"

Wade sighed. "Let's not talk for the next few minutes. I'm almost done."

Rayne didn't respond. She had a great deal more respect for models. She hadn't realized how tedious sitting still could be. She didn't look at him. Instead she stared into space. Touchy artists!

Wade drew for a while without speaking. Then he said, "You're angry with me." It wasn't an accusation, just an observation.

"You don't say?"

"I do. Why?"

"You're leaving tomorrow morning. After we returned from having dinner, all you wanted to do was draw me. I only agreed because I thought it was some kind of kinky foreplay. As it turns out, you really wanted to *draw* me."

He laughed softly as he quickly put the finishing touches on the drawing. "Can't it be both?" He rose. "It's done."

Rayne smiled. "Really?"

He walked over to her and handed her the sketch pad.

She took it and peered closely at the drawing. He'd captured her so explicitly that it appeared as if her skin, while only in sepia tones, glowed with vibrancy. The lines of her body were so graceful, she could not believe that was her. Yet, it looked exactly like her. She recalled all the times her father had told her that the true nature of portraiture was to capture both the real person and nuance of their personality than mere visage could convey. An artist captured the spirit of the person on canvas. And Wade had done that, even with her pestering him the whole while.

She looked up at him with genuine admiration and awe. "That's not me. That's a woman with true spiritual beauty."

Wade took off his boxers, then went to her. Taking the

sketch pad, he looked at the drawing, then at her. "That's you as I see you." He placed the sketch pad on the nearby night-stand. "That drawing will go back to Atlanta with me. I'll hang it over my bed and, like I said, when we build our dream house it'll go in our bedroom."

He leaned in and gently kissed her lips. His big hands moved along her sides until they rested on her waist, after which he pulled her more fully into his embrace.

Rayne fairly melted. She wrapped her legs around him as she lay back on the bed and sighed contentedly. He slipped right inside her. He had been right, while he had been drawing her, he had been seducing her at the same time. She was so ready for him. But…she suddenly wondered if he'd remembered the condom.

She reluctantly turned her head, breaking off the kiss. "We forgot the condom."

Wade kissed her forehead and the tip of her nose. "I put one on when I went to get my sketch pad. We're covered."

Rayne closed her eyes and surrendered herself. She realized she'd always be safe in Wade's arms.

Ray came home from the hospital on July 8th. Several of his female relatives volunteered to come nurse him back to health, but he was adamant about hiring a professional nurse to care for him the first few days he was recovering at home. "None of you are going to see me naked," he told them. "Now, if you want to come *visit,* I'd be glad to see you. But you're not giving me a sponge bath!"

Rayne, Julianne and Shirley were all used to his tirades, but he hurt some of the others' feelings and wound up having to apologize for his plainspoken manner later.

With ruffled feathers smoothed, his recovery also went smoothly.

By the time Julianne had to catch a plane to Canada on the 16th in order to report on the 17th for her ten-day acting job in an independent film, Ray was feeling more himself and no longer required the daily visits from the nurse. He said his farewells to Julianne and sadly watched her go.

He was still surrounded by females, but the number had dwindled to two, Rayne and Shannon. He was greatly anticipating Wade's weekend visit starting on the 22nd. And Julianne had promised to be back home before Rayne's birthday on the 31st.

Rayne, also, was looking forward to Wade's returning. She hadn't seen him in fifteen days, although they'd spoken many times since he'd left on July 6th.

On Saturday morning, she made breakfast as was her usual routine, and took a tray to her father in his studio where he was sitting on a donut, a strange pillowlike thing that was supposed to make sitting less painful for him, while he painted. He only spent an hour or so working in the morning, then another hour in the afternoon. But working seemed to calm him, and Rayne would not try to discourage him from doing it. He was healing quickly, and for that she was grateful.

When she brought his tray this morning, he put his paintbrush down and regarded her. "Thank you, sweetie," he said.

"My pleasure," she returned with a smile. She tried to catch a glimpse of what he was painting before he flung the drop cloth over it, but wasn't fast enough. She pouted.

"You are so superstitious."

Ray laughed shortly. "If it ain't broke, don't fix it. And my method has served me well over the years."

"It's just an affectation," Rayne accused lightly.

"Sure, but I like it," her father replied.

She'd placed the tray on a high worktable next to him. He

swiveled on his donut and picked up his orange-pineapple juice. After sampling it, he said, "What time will Wade arrive today?"

"Around eleven, he said," she answered, trying to keep the excitement out of her voice. She missed him so much she felt a nearly constant ache of longing in the pit of her stomach. Why was it she'd never associated lovesickness with physical manifestations before now? She hadn't felt this way when she'd broken up with Tony. Perhaps her pop had been right, and she'd never really loved Tony. Perhaps that's what those panic attacks had been trying to tell her: don't marry him, you're not in love with him.

She couldn't imagine panicking should Wade ask her to marry him. She might joke about preferring to live in New York City should they marry, but the truth was, she would happily relocate to Atlanta. Her business was such that she could start up in another city with very little effort. She would have to rebuild her client list, but that task didn't seem excessively daunting to her. She didn't have any qualms about actively seeking to represent her pop's friends in order to get her business going.

She mentally shook herself. No use thinking along those lines when Wade might not ever propose to her. Sure, he was the first to bring up the subject of marriage but that didn't mean he would be ready to settle down any time soon.

And what of her resolve not to seriously consider marriage until she turned thirty? Well, it was a woman's prerogative to change her mind. She would be twenty-seven soon. That was old enough for a serious consideration of holy matrimony.

She was smiling at her father as he ate his breakfast of oat cereal, fruit juice and black coffee. Dr. Kimble had suggested a change of diet in order to best help prevent a recurrence of the cancer. No more sausages, eggs and grits. Too much fat and cholesterol. And he was to resume physical exercise after four weeks at home. She knew her father was looking forward to his daily walks on the beach.

He looked up at her and caught her smiling at him. "You know you look just like your mother when you smile like that."

"You miss her a lot, don't you?"

"About as much as you miss Wade."

"That's a lot."

"I love her, and as soon as I'm back to normal, I'm going to get on my knees and beg her to marry me."

"No begging needed," Rayne assured him. "Mom is no longer unsure about you and her. She's ready. You're ready. Heck, we're all ready for this to happen. Even Aunt Shirley."

"What about Shannon?" worried her father. "She would have to go to a new school, make new friends. Living down here all year long would be much different than simply spending the summers here."

"I love it here," Shannon said from the doorway.

She walked farther into the room. Still in the sweatpants and tank top she slept in, she yawned and rubbed the corners of her eyes. She went to Ray and hugged him good morning. "I know who my father is, and I still wish you and Mom had made me together," she told him.

"Honey, your dad loves you," Ray told her, trying to coax that hurt expression out of her eyes.

"I know he loves me," Shannon said. "But I'm not a priority with him. Acting is. He's always making excuses. This job, or that job. It's not like Mom does it. She tries her best to book jobs around my schedule. She's rarely missed a school event that I participated in. Most of the time it's just us girls. But down here, well, it's nice to have a man around who actually listens to me when I talk, and who cares about me."

"Honey," Ray said softly, "I would never try to take your father's place, but I'd be the best stepfather I possibly can be. And I promise to always listen to you when you come to me."

Shannon smiled at him, briefly hugged him again and turned to leave. She faced them again just before she left the room. "That's good enough for me. Ask Mom to marry you. She needs a good man in her life."

She left then.

Rayne laughed shortly. "There you have it." She impulsively kissed his cheek and turned to leave as well. "I'll be back for the tray."

"Thanks, baby," Ray said.

He watched her go. She had his heart in the palm of her hand. Had it since she was a tiny baby. Would have it until the day he died.

Rayne's cell phone was ringing when she walked back into the kitchen. She picked it up from the countertop and peered at the display: it was Dottie. With a twinge of guilt, Rayne answered the phone. She hadn't spoken with Dottie in at least two weeks. And all Dottie had talked about then was how Steven had begun delivering various delicious entrees to her at work. Steven was a chef and apparently knew the way to her best friend's heart, because the last time Rayne had spoken with her, Dottie was warming to him.

"Hello," Rayne said, delight at hearing from Dottie evident in her tone.

"Rayne!" Dottie said excitedly. "Steven proposed last night and I said yes! I don't know what happened. I finally agreed to go out with him again after weeks of being estranged from him, and after our meal, he pulled out this beautiful ring and asked me right there at the table. Oh, Rayne, I missed him so much, I would have said yes to anything. But when he asked, I automatically said yes. Now I'm afraid I might have acted too quickly. I'm scared! I'm so scared that Steven and I aren't suited for each other. I mean except for the money thing we are completely compatible, but is he going to be happy married to someone who earns more than he does? If I could be sure of that, I wouldn't have any issues. But I'm so afraid that he's going to begin harping on the subject again once we get married, and then it'll be too late. You know my parents divorced when I was a kid. I always said that I would try my best to honor my marriage if I ever got brave enough to take that step. But what if Steven's insecurities come back?"

"Dottie," Rayne said, "first of all, sit down. I can tell you're pacing. Sit down and take a deep breath."

She waited until Dottie said, "Okay, I'm sitting."

"Now, you need to talk to Steven and tell him exactly how you feel. Don't leave anything out. Tell him that if he hasn't truly changed, that's a deal breaker. You have to be honest about your feelings. And he has to be honest about his. Tell him that. I'll be praying that his answer is yes, he's worked through his issues. But if the subject is driving you this crazy right now, you have to get it resolved before the wedding. Promise me you'll do that, Dottie."

"I don't want to hurt his feelings," Dottie said softly.

"Better to hurt his feelings now than to get engaged to him and hurt them later. I ought to know," Rayne said. "I still feel guilty for breaking my engagement to Tony even though I know it was the right thing to do."

"Okay," said Dottie. She laughed suddenly. "Girl, he was so nervous when he proposed, sweat broke out on his forehead, his hands were shaking. He'll probably pass out if we make it down the aisle."

"Do you love him, Dottie?"

"God, yes, I love him."

"Then get this straightened out and marry him. But don't

marry him until I get back to New York. I'm still your maid of honor, aren't I?"

"You know it," said Dottie with sister-friend enthusiasm.

"I couldn't be happier for you and Steven," Rayne told her. "You're a great couple. And you belong together."

"Thank you, Rayne. You always did believe in us."

"A love like yours is easy to believe in."

"Speaking of love," Dottie said, "how are you and Wade doing?"

"He's coming for a visit this weekend," Rayne told her. "And I can't wait to see him."

"All right," Dottie cried. "Another Delta Gamma woman gets her man!"

Chapter 19

Wade left Atlanta at five in the morning. He was usually an early riser anyway, and he was looking forward to the six-hour drive to American Beach. He listened to the radio, drank coffee and, using his headset, made phone calls while he drove. His first was to his father, who was also an early riser, although not as early as five-thirty on a Saturday morning, which was when Wade phoned him.

"Wade?" He actually sounded surprised to hear from him. Wade supposed that was his fault. Except for business, he hadn't been speaking to his father. He thought that best since he hadn't gotten everything off his chest yet. It was small of him, but he somehow felt better hanging on to the hurt instead of getting it out in the open. He knew Rayne's opinion on the subject: it would give him an ulcer.

"I'm on the way to American Beach," he told his father. "Just wanted you to know in case something came up and you needed to reach me in the event of an emergency. I won't be only a few minutes away this weekend."

"Don't worry, son. I was taking care of emergencies by myself long before you were born."

"I wasn't worried about you," Wade denied.

"Yes, you were," Ben said. "You're worried that I'm depressed over this whole mess. You might not have spoken to me in the past two weeks aside from during the course of our workday, but I know you. You may hate me now, but some part of you still thinks of me as your father, and you were always a good son."

"I'm going to hang up now," Wade warned.

"Not yet, son," Ben implored. "You shared your news with me, I want to share mine with you. I'm seeing a therapist."

Wade couldn't help it, he was concerned about his father. "Because?"

"I need to get to the source of my reason for doing what I did. I feel like I can't go forward unless I do."

This was so unlike his father that Wade wondered what else he hadn't told him. He was seeing a therapist. Was he also on medication? "Is that all you're doing, talking to someone? Are you on anything?"

"Just a little Zoloft," Ben told him.

"Zoloft? That's for depression, isn't it?"

"I learned that I've been depressed for years. This isn't a recent development, in case that's what you're wondering. You didn't do anything to cause it."

"I didn't think I did," Wade said evenly.

"I brought this on myself," Ben continued to explain. "Apparently, deep down, I thought my keeping you from Ray was a bad thing, and I turned it inward. I continued to hide the secret, but I paid for it by becoming clinically depressed. It was only after I'd broken the silence that everything came crashing down on me. I cried for two days straight."

"That's why you took those days off?"

"Yes," Ben replied. He sighed. "But the fact is, I wouldn't have gotten this far if not for Mere. She told me I needed to talk to someone besides her. She's been my sounding board over the years. But she refused to talk to me about the aftermath of giving you up, saying she wasn't a professional, and I needed to see someone who was trained to cope with that kind of trauma."

"Trauma?" Wade asked skeptically.

"That's what it's referred to when you experience an emotional upheaval that changes your life."

Wade laughed against his will. "*You've* been traumatized? What about me?"

"That's what I want to talk to you about, son. I think you need to see a therapist, too."

"I don't need to see a therapist. I just need to quit working for you, and never see you again. That'll solve all of my problems," Wade said, angry now.

"That's good, son, get it out," Ben said patiently. "But seriously, you can't quit. The business belongs to you and Rayne. If it goes down, so does your future. And hers."

"What do you mean by that?"

"I talked to my lawyer when Rayne was here. When I die, everything will be divided between the two of you."

"I can't believe you did that. I'm not your son any longer."

"You will always be my son. Ray and I were in agreement on that. Rayne will always be his daughter and you will always be my son. I'm sure he's probably changed his will by now, as well. How is he doing, by the way?"

"He's recovering nicely, thank you," Wade answered tersely.

Ben laughed. "Of course he is. He was always tough."

"Listen, I'm not going to have a conversation with you about my...father."

"Still having trouble with that, huh?" Ben deduced. "Do what Rayne does and just call him whatever pops into your head when you're talking to him. The awkwardness will pass. I spoke with her last night. She must have called me dad, pop, father *and* daddy before we hung up." He paused. "Okay, I'm going. Just tell me one thing, son."

"What's that?"

"What are your intentions where Rayne is concerned?"

Wade laughed. His father had some nerve. "That's—"

"Don't say it's none of my business, because it most certainly *is* my business. I don't want either of you to get hurt. Just take things slowly, know where you're going and what you're feeling before making any decisions. That's all I ask."

"What? You're afraid we're going to sneak off to Vegas and get married, or something equally irresponsible? Rayne and I are both too grounded for that."

"Good," Ben said, sounding pleased. "Bye, son, have a good weekend. Hug her for me."

In his anger, Wade hung up without saying goodbye. Here he was, getting relationship advice from a man who stole another man's girl, married her, cheated on her, was entrusted by her with an important duty on her deathbed, then promptly went about failing to comply with her wishes. He could have eaten nails, he was so mad.

Before his conversation with his father, he had begun to think perhaps he was being too hard on him, and maybe he was being unnecessarily judgmental. Now he was sure it would take him twice as long to forgive him. Sympathy be damned. He couldn't believe he'd allowed him to play on his emotions with that therapy bit. Ben Jefferson needed therapy like a chinchilla needed a fur coat. All he required to get over his trauma was another willing victim whose life he could destroy. And, come to think of it, his father was probably seeing a therapist only because Mere had told him she would not allow him back in her life unless he got help first. A reward. His father usually required one in order to motivate him to do anything remotely selfless.

A therapist! His father had often joked in the past that therapists were charlatans. All they did was listen while you talked, and nod and collect astronomical fees.

He was so upset he dialed Rayne's cell phone number before he noticed that it was only 5:47 a.m. She would still be asleep. He hoped she had her phone right next to her.

She did. She answered after the second ring. "Hullo?"

"I'm sorry, baby. It's too early. I'll call you back later."

"Don't you dare hang up. What's the matter?"

"I just had a weird conversation with Dad, that's all, and I wanted to run it by you."

"Pop?"

"Yeah."

"I talked with him last night."

"I know, he told me."

"Well, what did you talk about?"

"He's getting therapy—"

"He told me," Rayne said, cutting him off. "I think it's great. He needs to unburden himself to someone who can tell him how to forgive himself."

"Forgive himself?" Wade asked, incredulous. "He needs to punish himself, not forgive himself."

"Don't you think losing you is punishment enough?" Rayne asked reasonably. "I mean how much punishment does a man have to take? And how long are we to withhold forgiveness?"

Wade sighed. "I know. You were able to forgive your parents almost instantly. But I'm going to need a little more time."

"Your problem is, you don't believe a person can change. Or just one person, your father. You think he's incapable of letting go of his former bad habits and embracing some new, more positive, ones." She paused. "Oh, my God, Wade. I'm such a hypocrite!"

"You? Never!"

"I am," she insisted. "I forgot all about Grandma Layla's letter." She went on to tell him how she'd carried her grandmother's letter around with her for five years before confronting her mother. "I had five years to get used to the idea," she said now. "But you, you're still stunned, sweetie. No wonder you can't just forgive and forget."

Wade thought for a moment. "You mean I could be traumatized? I can't believe that maniac could be right. I'm thirty-four years old, not a child. I can handle this without therapy."

"But if you find it's still weighing heavily on your mind for much longer, promise me you'll get help."

Wade paused a long time before saying, "All right, darlin'. If I'm still nuts in say, two months' time, I'll make an appointment. Now go back to sleep. I should see you in about five hours. I love you."

"I love you so much," Rayne told him, her voice deep and sexy.

"Want to go to the club tonight and work off some steam?" he asked. "We haven't gone dancing yet. And you haven't seen the club."

"All right, sounds exciting," Rayne said.

"Good. I'm going, then. The sound of your voice is turning me on. Bye, darlin'."

"Bye," Rayne said softly, and hung up.

Rayne felt like a player in an English drama about manners. When Wade had arrived, she'd wanted to throw her arms around his neck and kiss him until she passed out, but she couldn't because both her dad and Shannon were equally excited to see him again, and had accompanied her to answer the door; her father a little slower than she and Shannon were, and bringing up the rear. So she and Wade had ended up looking at each other with longing, and having to be satisfied with that.

She felt his eyes on her throughout lunch on the back deck. Intensely aware of him, her body tingled all over and even her palms grew itchy. But they did not so much as touch each other's hands as they sat at the table and enjoyed the crab salad she had made.

"So, son, tell me more about your work. Do you like it?" Ray asked just after they sat down.

"I love it," said Wade.

Rayne noticed how his eyes lit up when he talked about his job.

"There's nothing like watching a building go up, from the blueprints to the final detailing that will make it distinctive from any other building. It's very satisfying. You worked in construction, sir. You must know what I mean."

"There is some satisfaction in doing something meaning-ful with your hands," Ray agreed. "Plus, to tell the truth, I enjoyed the thrill of kissing the sky."

"You like heights?"

"Yes, always have. Never had one twinge of fear. Crazy, I know. It must have been something I was born with, because I felt that way the first time I went up. It didn't have to grow on me."

Wade grinned. "It's genetic. Has to be. I'm the same way!"

"You don't say!" Ray was very pleased to find out he and his son had something else in common.

Rayne and Shannon looked at each other across the table and burst out laughing.

"What?" Ray asked, puzzled.

"You two have some of the same mannerisms," Rayne explained. "When Wade said the word "way" he looked just like you, Dad. And, Dad, when you said, "You don't say!" you were wearing the exact expression. It's spooky."

"Yeah," Shannon agreed. "It's like looking at you, Ray, and knowing how Wade is going to look in twenty years, and looking at Wade and knowing what you looked like twenty years ago, before I was born. It's very cool!"

After the meal, Rayne got up. "I'll do the dishes."

"I'll help," Wade volunteered.

"No, you're a guest," Shannon protested to everyone's surprise. "I'll help Rayne with the dishes."

"Honey," said Ray, "let Wade help her."

Shannon looked at Ray and he winked at her. She smiled. "Oh, all right."

"Beat you at a game of checkers?" Ray asked her.

"Beat me? Aren't you being optimistic?" Shannon said as she got up to walk across the deck to a cabinet where she knew all sorts of board games and sports equipment such as softballs, baseball bats and volleyballs were stored. She knew why he'd challenged her to a game, though. To give Rayne and Wade some smooching time alone.

Ray even got up and moved to the umbrella-topped table that was nearer to the storage cabinet, where they wouldn't have a view of the kitchen through the French doors.

That spoiled her fun, because she'd been looking forward to sneaking a peek at Rayne and Wade in the "throes of passion." She'd begun reading her mother's stash of romance novels and was familiar with the phrase.

Wade followed Rayne through the doors, enjoying her hip action in her snug-fitting jeans. As soon as they were inside, Rayne went and put the dishes she was carrying in the sink.

Wade followed suit and then she doubled back, closed the door, quickly spun back around, grabbed him by his shirttail and pulled him into the laundry room adjacent to the kitchen. Even if Shannon came into the kitchen, which she knew was a possibility with her nosy sister, she would not see them in there.

They fell into each other's arms and kissed desperately, as if they would die if their lips didn't touch at that very moment and not a millisecond later. A they turned their heads this way and that, each position seemed sweeter than the last.

"God, you taste good," Wade said between kisses. His hands were on her waist, her buttocks, her back. He wanted to touch her all over.

He backed her against the washing machine, and wound up lifting her and sitting her atop it so that he wouldn't have to bend to kiss her. Rayne moaned deep in her throat, and opened her legs so that Wade could get closer to her. They kissed that way for several minutes, with her sitting on the washing machine and Wade holding her close, nuzzling her neck, kissing her mouth, her eyes, her throat, between her breasts.

Both Rayne's hands were in his curly hair as she held on to him. She could have cried with the physical and emotional relief she felt at once again being able to touch him.

At last, they drew apart and looked into each other's eyes.

Wade smiled at her. "The real you is always better than the dream you."

Rayne knew exactly what he meant. "Ditto." She reached up and ran her finger along the scar that slashed through his right eyebrow. It must have been quite bad when he first got it, but now it was very faint. She leaned in and kissed it. Wade loved the feel of her mouth on his forehead. He, in turn, kissed her in the spot just below her lower lip. Her skin smelled sweet, like her breath. And it was soft against his lips. "If we were together a hundred years, I would never tire of discovering sweet spots on your body."

"I'll always have my cell phone," Rayne told her father when Wade came to pick her up for their date that night. Ray was lying in bed channel-surfing, and not really paying attention to her. He was getting to the point where he was tired of being babied by her, Shirley and Shannon. Independent by nature, he found that this recuperating wasn't all it was cracked up to be, but he would follow the doctor's orders to the letter if it meant he would be a fit and healthy husband for Julianne. "Yes, sweetie," he said to Rayne, which usually meant he'd agree with anything. And he'd learned that usually pleased the women in his life.

Rayne smiled at him and bent to kiss his cheek. "Okay, we're not going far, just to Fernandina Beach to check out their club."

This, he heard. "A club on a Saturday night? Honey, be careful. And if they start shooting, fall to the floor and cover your head."

Rayne laughed. "Dad, it's a nice club, it's not a hole-in-the-wall."

"Nice club, bad club, some fool always gets too much booze in him and wants to shoot somebody over his woman. You be careful."

"Okay," Rayne promised. It was easier than staying to argue the point with him.

Wade was waiting for her in the living room.

She passed Shannon in the hallway. "Have a good time, sis. And don't worry about anything. I know what to do in case of an emergency."

"What?" Rayne asked, testing her.

"Scream my head off?"

Rayne grabbed her around the neck with both hands and pretended to choke her. "One of these days!"

She hugged her, and turned to leave. "See you later."

Wade rose when she entered the room. Shannon had answered the door, and this was the first time he'd seen her this evening. Rayne was wearing one of the dresses her pop had bought her in Atlanta: the white Tashia of London tank dress with matching cardigan. It was a warm July night, and the dress would be cool enough. If it got cooler due to a weather front, she would have the cardigan to drape across her shoulders.

His eyes took all of her in from her shapely form in the dress whose hem fell just above her knees. Long, gorgeous legs, and pretty feet in strappy white leather sandals.

Rayne walked up to him. He looked very handsome in a white silk pleated long-sleeve shirt and black slacks and black oxfords. All expensive, and all fitting his body to a tee. She tiptoed and kissed his clean-shaven chin. "Mute tonight, handsome?"

"You take my breath away."

She tossed her long, curly hair across her right shoulder. "Wait until you see what I'm wearing underneath." She said this in a very low voice, and close to his ear.

Wade smiled slowly as he put a hand under her elbow, and they walked to the door. "I can't wait." He opened the door for her, and before closing it behind them, made sure that the lock was properly engaged. He checked it again once they were on the other side. Rayne noticed all of this and was charmed by it. He cared about the safety of her father, and her sister. It was little things like that that endeared him to her.

Wade opened her door for her, and handed her in. As he jogged around to the driver's side, he glanced up at the night sky and counted himself blessed for having Rayne in his life. Tonight, he wanted to forget about the drama with his dad and totally focus on her.

The first thing he did when he got behind the wheel of the car was to lean over and kiss his woman. Rayne, so soft and fragrant tonight, kissed him with as much pleasure as she'd demonstrated the first time she'd kissed him. That's what amazed him about her. Every kiss was as wonderful as that first one, and he hoped he would always feel that way. He peered down into her eyes after they parted. She was looking at him as if he'd hung the moon. He didn't care what anybody said about relationships never lasting. When your woman looked at you like that, you *believed* in forever after.

Before he had time to run his thoughts through his feverish brain, he blurted out, "Rayne, if I asked you to marry me, do you think you would start having panic attacks again and run the other way?"

He saw her eyes stretch in surprise. She opened her mouth to say something, thought better of it, and just shook her head in the negative instead. "Does that mean, no, you wouldn't freak out and start having panic attacks and leave me at the altar?" he asked.

"Yes," she said, her voice hoarse. She cleared her throat. "Yes!"

He pulled her into his arms. "Yes, you'll marry me?"

"Yes, I'll marry you, tonight if you want to!"

He kissed her forehead and touched his forehead to hers. "Oh, baby, you've made me so happy."

They were both grinning broadly.

"But, no, not tonight," he said, babbling in his excitement. "Too many relatives would be outraged if we didn't invite them. How about at the end of August? Can we pull things together by then? You're the event planner."

Rayne's mind was racing. Her vacation ended in late August. She was booked up from September to October. New Yorkers found so much to celebrate in the fall months. Marriages, anniversaries, birthdays, retirement parties. It was one of her busiest seasons. How was she going to manage being a newlywed and working her butt off in New York City while her new husband would be hundreds of miles away in Atlanta?

She hated it when reality intruded on her dreams.

"We can get married in late August," she said. "But then I'm going to be busy working from the first of September to late October. When would we have time to go on a honey- moon?"

Wade, who by virtue of an accident of birth was a male, thought of the perfect solution. "Sweetie, you don't need to work. I can support both of us."

Rayne, who by virtue of an accident of birth was a female, swiftly shot down that suggestion with, "I know you can, baby, but I like being able to support myself."

Wade gently smoothed her brow and placed a kiss on her right cheekbone, close to her eye. "I didn't mean to suggest that you won't still be able to support yourself, sweetness. I only meant that you *would* be supporting yourself by supporting me. After all, you stand to inherit half of the company. You have an investment in it."

The expression on Rayne's face told him that his father had not informed her of his generosity. "He did that without consulting me?" she asked in total disbelief.

"He was looking out for your future," Wade said.

"He was trying to control my future, that's what he was doing," Rayne vehemently disagreed. She moved over as far as she could without getting out of the car. She regarded him as if he were a coconspirator with his father. Her hand was on the door's handle. "And now you ask me to marry you and give up my business as if I could so easily do as you say. As if I haven't struggled to build my business from the ground up and it means absolutely nothing to me. After all, I'll be the little wife who stays home to prettify the house, plan dinners and be barefoot and pregnant year-round!"

"Then how do you suggest we solve this problem?" Wade asked tightly.

"Problem? My business isn't a *problem*." She took a deep breath and tried to relax. Earlier that day she had wondered how she would react if Wade actually wanted to marry her. She had decided that she could easily move her business to Atlanta. But to totally give it up? That hadn't crossed her mind. But here he was suggesting that she should be a stay-at-home wife and, eventually, mother. That didn't sit well with her. "What I suggest," she said slowly so that he would get every word without her having to repeat herself, "is that you get used to the idea that I'm not going to stop working once we get married. That is, if you still want to get married. And if I truly share the business fifty-fifty, get used to my learning more about how it operates because, as you've pointed out, I have a vested interest in it."

She wrenched the door open.

Wade reached over and closed it again. He grasped her by the shoulders and made her face him. "Okay, so my thoughts on a man's duties as a husband are far off base. I'm some throwback to the fifties or something. But I love you, Rayne and, damn it, I will adjust to the idea of your having a career. Blame me for wanting you to be a woman of leisure. I thought that was the goal of all working women, to finally get to the place where they don't have to work if they don't want to. But, apparently, you haven't gotten to that place yet. Okay, my mistake. And maybe I was thinking of Cherie in this instance. She preferred a career over me and, God knows, I didn't want to think that you could be anything like her, so I projected my feelings onto you. I should have asked how you felt before jumping in, feet first."

Rayne couldn't believe her ears. Okay, he was indeed a throwback to another era. But he was definitely a man who could evolve with the times if he made an effort.

She'd been rigid while he held her captive between his powerful hands, but now she relaxed and let out a sigh. "I know someone who would gladly buy my clientele list," she told him. "Which means she would take over the business in New York. But I plan to be up and running in Atlanta within three months of our wedding. Deal?"

Wade released her, and she offered him her hand to shake.

"I prefer a kiss," he said. He took the proffered hand, drew her close and possessively kissed her, leaving no doubt in her mind that their first argument had ended on a positive note.

"Do you still want to go to the club?" he asked once they'd come up for air.

His vulnerability was showing. He thought she might still be angry with him, and Rayne found that facet of his personality to be very touching. "I just want to make love to you," she told him. "No going out to dinner, no dancing."

Chapter 20

Wade took out his cell phone and began dialing a number. Rayne stared at him. She'd just told him she wanted to make love to him, and he was making a phone call? What was wrong with the man?

He smiled at her. "Since you don't want to go out to dinner, I thought we'd pick up something on the way to the condo. Sorry, but there is nothing there to eat except a few frozen dinners, and I'm not going to feed my baby a frozen dinner."

Someone must have answered. "Yes, what's your special tonight? Lasagna?"

He raised his brows questioningly at Rayne.

"Yes, I like lasagna," she told him.

"Great," he said into the receiver. "Two lasagna dinners, garden salads, garlic bread and for dessert, do you have any of that cherry cheesecake you make so well? Yes? Good. That, too. That'll be all."

He waited. "Fifteen minutes? All right, that's Jefferson. Thank you."

He hung up and turned the key in the ignition. "We're set."

"You just phoned Gourmet, Gourmet, didn't you?" Rayne asked.

"How'd you know?"

"You said it was nearby, and that's the only restaurant that's nearby."

"Maybe Dad's supper club isn't such a bad idea," Wade said. "Except he needs to choose another location."

"That's an understatement," said Rayne with a laugh. She fastened her seat belt and got comfortable. "I still can't believe Pop was serious about wanting Dad's property for a supper club."

"Who knows what motivated him?" Wade said as he pointed the SUV toward A1A. "Your father thinks it was my dad's way of putting the two of us, your dad and me, together. He thinks he did it subconsciously. And this morning, my dad told me that he'd felt guilty all these years for not telling Ray about me. So maybe that was his reason. I don't know. I don't want to think about it anymore."

"It's all too deep," Rayne agreed. She laughed suddenly. "You know, I just thought of something. When we do get married, I can't complain about your father because your father is *my* father, and you can't complain about my father because of the same reason. And if Mom should have another child by Dad, he or she will be both *my* brother or sister and *your* brother or sister. It gives me a headache just thinking about it."

"I know," Wade said with a sigh. He reached for her hand and squeezed it reassuringly. "What counts is that you and I aren't related."

"Amen!" said Rayne, laughing shortly.

About thirty minutes later they were walking through the

door of the condo. She carried the packages with the food in them to the kitchen while Wade took care of the alarm system, and adjusted the thermostat so that the warm air inside could be replaced with fresh, cool air. He joined her in the kitchen when he was done. His golden brown eyes roamed over her shapely body in that formfitting dress. She was standing at the counter, removing the food cartons, preparing to set them in the microwave oven for easy warming later on. He came up behind her, lifted her hair off her neck and kissed her on the nape.

She continued putting the food containers in the microwave except for the one that had the cheesecake in it. That one she picked up and carried to the refrigerator across the room. Wade followed and when she turned around from putting the cheesecake in the fridge, he picked her up. Rayne wrapped her arms around his neck. "I should pass on that cheesecake since you just *love* picking me up so much."

"Don't start dieting, I like your body just as it is," Wade told her as he hurried to the bedroom. Rayne saw that he'd gone in there and turned on the lamps on each nightstand and turned back the covers on the bed.

He set her on the bed, and she immediately rose and began unbuttoning his shirt. He let her, looking intently into her eyes the whole time. She finished, and pulled the shirt down, off his shoulders. He shrugged out of it and it fell to the floor. But he was wearing a sleeveless T-shirt as well. Rayne pulled that up and over his head. It went the way of the shirt. Now she could run her hands over his chest. He wasn't especially hairy, which she liked. His chest muscles were well defined, as were his arm and stomach muscles. She bent and kissed him in the center of his chest.

Wade reached up and tilted her chin with a finger, then bent his head and kissed her mouth slowly, and with great intensity. With purpose. Rayne had enjoyed every kiss he'd ever given her, but this one, somehow, seemed different, more meaningful. And she knew it could be her imagination, because he'd just asked her to marry him, but she didn't think so. She opened herself to him, and simply rode the wave of emotions that they were creating together. And when he raised his head, and she looked into his eyes, breathless, intrigued and wobbly in the legs, she felt as if she'd filled the void that had been in her since her foolish episode with Tony. Tony, a man she thought she loved. She'd been a child then. A mere girl. She hadn't even touched the surface of true love. This was love. A burning in your soul that could not be extinguished. No, it would forever burn brightly because you shared real passion that did not depend on aesthetics. Or perfection. She felt safe with Wade. Knew that even if they argued, it wouldn't break them up, it would only strengthen them.

She silently raised her arms. He pulled the dress off her and tossed it on the chair next to the bed. The material was opaque, so she hadn't needed a slip underneath to hide her light-colored lingerie, and oh what lingerie. He took a step back, the better to admire her in the lacy bra and barely-there bikini panties. No thongs for her. She'd been serious about that. But her voluptuous body was so delectable that he certainly didn't miss the offending item.

The bra closed in the front. He dispensed with it in no time. Her breasts spilled into his big hands, warm and heavy, their tips hardening the moment he touched them. "Oh, baby," he breathed and dipped his head to taste the sweet nectar. Rayne nearly swooned standing there only in her bikini panties and high heels. Wade didn't stop until he'd lovingly given the other breast equal time. Then, a little dazed himself, he placed her hand on his erection, and Rayne, taking the hint, loosened his belt buckle, removed his belt, tossed it atop her dress on the chair and began working on the clasp on his slacks. She carefully undid the zipper and pushed his slacks down. He took the time to kick off his shoes first and then he stepped out of the slacks. Not bothering to pick them up, he just stepped forward and kind of danced her backward to the bed where, when the backs of her legs touched the edge of it, she sat down.

He reached down and smoothed her hair back behind her ears and observed that she was wearing her favorite ruby stud earrings again. Good. His mind back on the matter at hand, he bent and kissed her ripe mouth and she fell back on the bed with him on top. She scooted backward on the bed until her entire body was prone, and he moved with her. It wasn't graceful, but it certainly did feel good. His mouth was doing crazy things to her equilibrium. He would kiss her, then tongue her nipples, then lick her in the most unusual places, places where a tongue had never been, like, *dear God,* her navel. She never thought a tongue on her navel could drive her so crazy with lust.

Wade paused long enough to remove her panties. Then he was once again on a mission to drive her mad with passion. His hands cupped her buttocks, forcing her to writhe sensuously on the bed, thrusting her hips forward, which only enticed him to taste of the sweetness that her movements made all the more irresistible. He bent his head and once his tongue parted the folds of her feminine center, she went perfectly still as though his actions had shocked her. He felt her rebel against what he was about to do. She grew rigid. She sat up and looked at him, her eyes dreamy with desire. "I've never tried that before," she said her voice low and full of wonder.

He just smiled, placed his big hand on her stomach and coaxed her to lie back down.

To relax her, he decided it would be best if he started at the top, so to speak, once more. So he stood, removed his boxers, got a condom while he was at it, opened it and put it on, then went to her and kissed her mouth. "Listen, if you're really uncomfortable about this, we don't have to do it, but I want to experience every part of you, and I think you'll enjoy it, too, once you relax a little. I promise, it won't hurt a bit." He smiled. "Don't look at me as if I'm a freak in the bedroom."

She laughed, and turned on her side, her legs, he noticed, closed. "I know it's a common practice between lovers. It's just that I've never had it done to me."

"So, you have the book learning, but not the experience," he said, smiling. "This is going to be fun. Did you know that most women don't even experience orgasms with just the man's penis inside them? They need clitoral stimulation. Sweetie, this is the ultimate clitoral stimulation. Just don't box my ears with your thighs once you reach climax, okay? So, should we try this?"

"Okay."

"Spoken like a good little girl being tempted by the devil," Wade joked. "Come here."

He fell on top of her, kissing her mouth gently and thoroughly until Rayne felt as if her bones were turning to water. He had her cooing his name as he kissed her body from that dimple in her chin, downward to her navel, past her navel to the spot just above her sex. When his tongue parted the folds of her vagina this time, she did not tense up, she opened her legs farther and his tongue plunged into her warm, fragrant softness. Rayne moaned softly and grabbed his head.

Wade smiled, and continued. He took his time, his tongue slipping and sliding in a rhythm that created just enough delicious friction to whip her into a frenzy, yet not send her over the precipice just yet. He slowed down, and she kind of sighed and let go. When he felt her surrender to him, that was when his tongue touched her clitoris, and he changed up a little and instead of licking her, he sucked gently. Rayne cried, "Oh my, my…"

Wade felt her thighs tremble. He stopped sucking and licked her again. Rayne screamed in release. Wade knew to get up. Her thighs closed, and she squeezed her vaginal muscles tightly, convulsions rocking her, blossoming outward from her center to encompass her entire body. Wade climbed back on top and while she was coming down, he penetrated her. Rayne experienced a pleasure she had never known before. His penis rubbed her clitoris as he slipped inside her, and she came again. She'd never done that before. She didn't even know it was possible to have two orgasms nearly on top of one another.

Wade felt her vaginal muscles contract around him, and it felt so good to him that his thrusts became more urgent, deeper, more satisfying. He peered into her beloved face and she suddenly opened her eyes and looked at him. He exploded inside her.

Rayne clung to him, her legs wrapped tightly around him, and finally, they fell to their sides onto the bed. They gazed into each other's eyes, secure in the knowledge that to eat, to sleep, to go to work, all the things that people take as mundane day-to-day tasks would all seem that much more bearable as long as they had each other.

At last, they also knew that a combustible passion was not something that existed only in romance novels. They'd created it themselves, here, tonight.

"Are you hungry *now?*" Wade asked mischievously.

"Famished."

"Race you to the bathroom. We can eat in our robes after our showers."

Rayne's feet were the first to hit the floor, but Wade picked her up and dropped her butt-first back onto the bed. "You big bully," cried Rayne, laughing.

She clambered up again and followed him into the bathroom.

They behaved themselves as they showered together, Rayne with her hair covered by a shower cap. Wade dried her off afterward, and thoroughly enjoyed it.

Then he was the one to get the plates and glasses from the cabinet, fill her plate with food and pour her a glass of red wine. As they sat across from one another, eating their lasagna, he, as always, watched her intently. He did not think he would ever tire of simply observing her movements. He didn't know what had possessed him to assume anything about her, especially that she would be content to be a stay-at-home wife and mother, when each time he saw her, it was a revelation.

When it was time for dessert, he got up to get the cheesecake from the refrigerator and put the slices on dessert plates. He returned to the table and placed her plate in front of her. Rayne looked down at the rich, luscious dessert, all red and creamy-looking. At first, she didn't notice the ruby and diamond ring sitting atop one of the plump cherries.

Wade calmly sat down, and trained his eyes on her face.

He smiled when he saw her eyes stretch in surprise, and her mouth fly open in astonishment. She picked up the ring, and wasted no time putting it on her finger.

She also didn't waste any time getting out of her chair, which she toppled, and jumping into Wade's arms. He didn't topple. "It's beautiful." She kissed both of his cheeks. Tears formed, and spilled onto her cheeks. Wade kissed them away.

"How did you know my favorite stone is the ruby?"

He smiled. "I took a wild guess," he joked. "You always wear your ruby earrings when you want to look special, and the ruby is your birthstone. I wanted to get you a diamond, but I compromised. You have a diamond on either side of the ruby, so we're both happy."

"Was it expensive?" she ventured, suddenly worried about the cost.

"It broke me," Wade said with a grin. "But you're worth it."

It seemed to Rayne that time sped up after she and Wade got engaged. The next day, they went together to her dad and told him and Shannon they intended to marry.

To her relief, her father hugged both of them, and wished them well. She had expected him to tell them they hadn't known each other long enough.

Shannon didn't appear surprised by the news at all. All she wanted to know was, "Will I get to be a bridesmaid?" Rayne told her, yes, she would.

When she phoned her mom and told her, she said, "I'm so happy for you two, honey. I can't wait to get back home so that we can start planning the wedding."

Only her aunt Shirley offered any opposition. "Child, please," she said. "Y'all ain't through the lust phase yet. Wait until his habits start irritating you, then consider whether or not you can live with them the rest of your life."

Of course, neither of them listened to her warnings.

Her mother came home on July 28th. They threw a birthday party for Rayne on Monday, July 31st. Wade couldn't make it, but he phoned her and sent flowers.

August blew in with winds and rain. The days were gray, and the nights on the chilly side since they got the breezes off the Atlantic Ocean. Rayne and Wade had set the wedding date for Saturday, August 26th. The invitations were sent the first week in August. The church was booked soon afterward. The reception was to be held in the ballroom of a luxury hotel.

In mid-August, Rayne sold her business to a competitor in New York City. Around the same time, Dottie and Steven went crazy and eloped. Dottie sent her photos of their wedding in a chapel in Vegas via e-mail with a note: Sorry, but Steven and I couldn't wait any longer. My mother was driving me crazy with all the plans she had for our wedding, anyway. It was like she was living vicariously through us, so we decided to just do it, like the Nike ad says.

Dottie moved in with Steven, and since the apartment was in Rayne's name, it was Rayne's responsibility to either sublet it or give it up. She decided on the latter, and took a weekend trip to New York City to pack up her things. It rented in a heartbeat.

After that she felt adrift. Her business was sold. Her apartment rented.

Her mother told her that she would always have a home in Brooklyn if she needed it. She wasn't giving up the family home. She and Ray had decided that they could be a two-city couple. She would continue to work as an actress, although she would not work as often. Her choice. He had not asked her to do that.

Julianne lifted Shannon's sentence, and she went off punishment after a month. And Pete was allowed to visit her again, although he wasn't allowed within fifty feet of her bedroom. If Shannon toed the line, she would be able to date starting in December, her birth month. Only at supervised functions, like school dances, though. She had to be supervised on any other dates, such as going to the movies or to school sporting events.

The day before Rayne and Wade were to be married, Ben came to the house. By that time, Ray had been home from the hospital for seven weeks. He was pretty much healed, having a stitch in his side from time to time, but nothing worth mentioning. His energy level was good. All other bodily functions, especially the one he'd been afraid wouldn't ever be the same, were working well. He hadn't yet made love to Julianne, but he knew when the doctor gave him the go-ahead he would, well, be able to "go ahead."

So it was with vigor in his steps that he went and answered the door. When he saw Ben standing there, he stepped aside and said, "Come on in. I think I know why you're here."

Rayne had told them that she wanted both of them to walk her down the aisle. Ray would begin the trek down the aisle with her, and midway, Ben would take over. It was meaningful to her because that's how they'd come into her life. Ray was with her from the beginning, and Ben had come along later. When she'd told Ray about it, he had smiled and said, "That sounds beautiful, sweetheart."

When she'd told Ben about it, he'd said, "I'd be honored, sugar."

Ray looked into Ben's face now and wondered if he'd come there to make trouble the day before their children linked them all together as a family forever. He hoped not, but if he had come to make trouble, Ray felt fit enough to punch him in the nose and send him on his way.

He must have been frowning, because Ben smiled and said, "Don't worry, I'm just here to make sure what Rayne is planning is okay with you, Ray. Because if it isn't and you would prefer to walk her down the aisle on your own, I'd gladly step aside."

Ray narrowed his eyes at him. "No need for that," he told him. "Rayne knows what she wants, and if the way she wants it done is significant for her, then that's all that matters. It's her wedding day, after all."

"Spoken like a true father," Ben said. He offered him his hand. "Thank you, Ray."

Ray shook his hand. "No problem."

"I hope that one day Wade and I will be as close again as you and Rayne are now," Ben told him. "But he still doesn't trust me."

"It takes time to rebuild trust," Ray said. "He'll come around."

Ben shook his head sadly as he turned to head back to the door. "I don't think so, Ray. I really don't." He forced a smile. "Well, I'll see you at the church tomorrow."

Rayne wore a nontraditional wedding dress. No lace, no train, no veil. It was a sophisticated dress whose hem fell just above her knees and showed off her best assets, her legs. Sleeveless and with a scoop neck, it was off-white, in a matte fabric with clean, crisp lines. Her dark curly hair was up in an intricate lattice style in the back. On her feet were three-inch-heeled leather strappy sandals in the same shade as the dress, and the only jewelry she wore was her ruby stud earrings and her engagement ring.

The time was two in the afternoon. It was summer's end. And the sky was Florida blue: pale blue with not a cloud to be seen. The palm trees swayed in the breeze. The guests wore their summer finery, the ladies in dresses and hats in various pastel shades. The gentlemen in lightweight suits. Though the sun was not blazing hot, the temperature was in the low eighties.

The church, the same community church that the Walkers had been attending for fifty years, was packed to the rafters. The choir was humming *Amazing Grace* when Rayne walked in on Ray's arm. The guests rose and turned to look at the bride and her father. They smiled warmly at her. Some ladies waved their perfumed handkerchiefs. Halfway down the aisle, Ben stepped up and offered her his arm. Rayne took it and smiled at him. He walked proudly the rest of the way to the stage where he placed her hand in Wade's. He and Wade looked right into each other's eyes, and Wade said, "Dad."

Ben nearly collapsed in tears because it had been the manner in which Wade had said it that had gotten to him. He'd

said it as if he loved and respected him. There had been no
rancor in his voice. None of the sarcasm that had accompanied practically everything he'd said to him lately. Ben was
lucky to make it to his seat beside Mere without falling.

Rayne and Wade wanted a traditional service. The minister
recited the vows. They repeated them, and at the end, the
church said, "Amen!"

Whereupon, Wade scooped his bride up into his arms and
carried her down the aisle to the accompaniment of Miss
Sadie Sawyer singing, *How I Got Over.*

As he and Rayne exited the church, she looked back in
wonder at the sight of all of her family and friends smiling at
them. Her heart was full. Her soul was glad. And as she put
her arms around her husband's strong neck, she didn't have
to wonder about how she'd gotten to this point in her life. She
knew. *She'd fallen in love.*

Dear Reader,

I hope you enjoyed *That Summer at American Beach*. I tried to capture the beauty of American Beach as vividly as I could, giving you a little history and atmosphere in hopes that you would feel as if you were a part of the story.

Ms. MaVynee Betsch, whom I mentioned in the book, and who was affectionately known as the Beach Lady, passed away in September 2005. She was a warrior for American Beach and she will be missed!

I think I mentioned the name Sadie about five times in this book. That's a little nod to a certain Sadie who told me I've never mentioned her name before.

If you would like to write me, please feel free to do so at P.O. Box 811, Mascotte, Florida 34753-0811. Or you can visit my Web site at www.janicesims.com.

Look for my next book entitled *Constant Craving*, Franklyn and Elise's story in the Bryant Winery trilogy, later on this year.

Warm blessings,

Janice Sims